A FRIEND AT THE HIGHLAND COURT

CELESTE BARCLAY

Copyright © by Celeste Barclay.

0 9 8 7 6 5 4 3 2 1

Published by Oliver Heber Books

 Created with Vellum

"Friends show their love in times of trouble, not in happiness."
~Euripides

At times we treat those who we love most the worst. It's through adversity that we often find the deepest and longest lasting connections.

Happy reading, y'all,
Celeste

THE HIGHLAND LADIES

ONE

Alexander Armstrong woke to a throbbing pain in his left arm that threatened to steal his breath. Sweat dripped from his brow and coursed down between his shoulder blades. He glanced at the pillow and sheet, already certain they were soaked, much like they were most nights. He lifted his limp arm into his lap and rubbed the pain in his upper arm. He struggled to calm his breathing after the terrifying nightmare. It was the same night after night: the memory of his last battle flashing before his eyes. The scent of death filled his nostrils, and the cacophony of metal on metal and screams of death blended into the most horrifying melody he'd ever heard. As the pain dulled to its regular constant, Alex wiped the sweat from his brow and laid down once more. He prayed that would be the only nightmare he suffered that night, almost unwilling to return to sleep.

Ever since the Armstrongs' battle with Clan Scott, he'd felt unmanned. He knew his cock still worked, but he faced a problem far worse than that. He'd lost his ability to fight, to be a warrior. To be the heir to a powerful border clan. As he rested on his damp bed, he recalled the most gruesome fight he'd ever endured. The carnage was greater than normal, and he'd come the closest to losing his life that he had since he first rode into battle at six-and-ten. This most recent battle, ten years later, was the first time he'd been that scared.

The injury to his arm wasn't his first serious battle wound either, but it was the only one that remained. Even the jagged scar that ran along the right side of his face had healed, marring his once-handsome visage. He recalled the laceration he'd taken to his left thigh three years earlier. He—along with his family and the healer—feared he would lose his leg. But with time and effort, it healed, and Alexander returned to the lists, horseback, and fighting. His right hand brushed the raised scar on his left ribs, remembering the pain from that puncture and the broken ribs that had accompanied it. That had healed, despite spending six moons feeling like he would never again take a deep breath. But his arm. That would never heal.

Alone in his chamber, his maudlin thoughts consumed him. There were still elements of self-pity that he was no longer the attractive and fierce warrior he'd once been. But what crushed him daily was guilt. Battling alongside Clan Elliot, Clan Armstrong defeated the Scotts that day, so it wasn't the victory that haunted him. It was knowing he could never lead his clan as they deserved. For the past six months, he'd argued almost every day with his father and brother that Brice should replace him as heir and tánaiste. Neither considered it, both growing red in the face. Now they both walked away rather than hearing or indulging Alex's protestations that he remain next in line to the Armstrong lairdship. He lived with the constant feeling of failure, and no one understood.

With dawn approaching, Alex accepted that his

opportunity to sleep had passed. In his previous life, the one before he became worthless, saddling his horse and an hour's ride resolved his inner turmoil. Now he couldn't even saddle his own horse without help. Once mounted, which was a trial in and of itself, he could still maneuver his mount. He'd had the destrier since he was a colt and had trained him to the sensitive signals from his thighs and how he held the reins. He could ride one-handed with ease——because he once wielded a sword in the other.

It took Alex several weeks and countless attempts, along with curses that painted a blue streak in his chamber, but he'd learned how to tie the laces of his breeks and button his waist-length doublet. He refused to allow his mother or servants to dress him like he was a child. He kept what dignity he could muster. As the earliest morning rays inched above the horizon, Alex donned his clothes and opted for a walk.

"I heard you moving around," Brice said as he fell into step with his older brother, who wore a perpetual frown at odds to Brice's perpetual smile. They'd fought back-to-back against the Scotts. It was when Brice took a blow to the head that knocked him away from Alex that their opponent struck, nearly severing Alex's arm from his body. He still couldn't explain how he maintained the strength to slice through his opponent and drag Brice out of the melee. He supposed it was the vow he'd made to his mother six years earlier, that the brothers would always fight together and protect one another, that gave him the strength. He couldn't allow his baby brother, three years his junior, to perish. But in the end, it was Brice who'd bound his shoulder and applied pressure to the bleeding. His younger brother kept him alive. And Alex wasn't certain he was grateful.

"Woke up early," Alex muttered.

"You know I'm coming with you." Brice spoke as though it were obvious.

"And you know I don't need a nursemaid."

Brice pulled on Alex's right arm, making him stop as Brice stepped in front of Alex. "Stop being an arse to me. I'm not bluidy well minding you. Once upon a time, we enjoyed each other's company. You may be different now, but I still want my brother."

Alex blinked several times before he nodded. He was different, and it wasn't just his appearance. It was the guilt, the memories that haunted him, his obvious inadequacies. That was what changed him. His mind was still as sharp as it had always been, and his father still counted on his advice on clan matters, particularly those dealing with diplomacy and strategy. With time on his hands since he no longer went to the lists, he managed the clan accounts and ledgers with their seneschal. He also continued to read and write most of his father's correspondence. He accepted that he was still useful to an extent, but he knew he only had those additional duties because he was incapable of performing the ones expected of him.

"I'm sorry," Alex mumbled. "You're too easily and too often the scapegoat to my foul temper. It's not right."

The two men slipped through the postern gate, acknowledging the guard who stood watch beside the portal. They remained quiet until they were certain the men on the battlements couldn't hear their conversation.

"I didn't sleep well last night," Alex admitted. When did he ever? Between resting on his injured arm or the nightmares, he hadn't slept through the night since he was unconscious with fever.

"Neither did I," Brice whispered. When Alex furrowed his brow, Brice swallowed. He'd said nothing about his own nightmares because he'd feared only making Alex's worse. But perhaps he did his brother a disservice to allow him to think he suffered alone. "I see it over and over, every night. It never leaves me."

"You dream of it too?"

"I'd hardly call them dreams. There's nothing pleasant aboot them. They're nightmares far worse than any child's who's afraid of the dark. They're so vivid that I'm certain it's really happening until something jolts me awake. Everything was just so much worse."

The brothers fell back into silence, both recalling the sheets of rain that fell, creating bogs that made horses go lame or sucked men's boots in like drying mortar. The wind had nearly blown even the most enormous warriors to the ground. The midmorning sky had darkened to what appeared like early night. The Armstrongs' and Elliots' combined forces outnumbered the Scotts, but their enemy had elevation to their advantage. The Armstrongs and Elliots fought not only their enemy but also the slope of the hilly terrain. Had the weather not sabotaged them, it would have been inconvenient and impractical, but it wouldn't have been so lethal. The Scotts swarmed and overpowered their rival partners. Alex was certain it was an act of God that granted victory to the Armstrongs and Elliots.

"I didn't realize," Alex said as they reached the Liddel Water's bank. The river flowed before them as they stood staring toward the Hermitage. Neither could glimpse it, but they knew where it lay. It was near there that they met the Scotts. "Why didn't you ever tell me?"

"And make you feel worse?" Brice glanced at Alex, who stared at him. "I didn't want you to think you're to blame, and I know you would have. You already swear it's your fault that the ogre struck me down. The enemy was in front of me, not behind or to the side. You couldn't have known. You fought your own opponent, but you still blame yourself. Alex, I'm no more a child than you are. You may have three years more experience, but that was hardly my first battle. Would you blame someone else the way you blame yourself if I'd partnered with, say, Angus? Or Brant? Or Peter? Would you never forgive them?"

"You never should have been there."

"Are you blaming Mother now?" Brice said, aghast, but Alex realized his brother was mocking him. "It was she who made us swear to always fight alongside each other. So it's her fault?"

"Who's being the arse now?" Alex demanded.

"It's a fair question if I follow your reasoning."

"You should have remained here. It's foolish that we ride out together. What if we both died? Who would be heir then?"

"Now you really are treating me like a child."

"I'm bluidy well thinking aboot our clan. What if you'd died, and I was left like this? What then?" Alex fumed.

"You'd be laird when Father dies, like we've always known."

"I can't lead the men out of a bucket," Alex snarled.

"Because you won't even try. The only person who's given up is you, Alex. The only person who thinks you're useless is you. No one else. You. And unless you broke your cock too, then you'll likely have an heir soon enough. I know you want—"

"Say it, and we will both discover whether I can still fight. I will not sentence her to life with half a mon."

"Sentence her? You've been in love with one another since you were children."

"She's never been in love with me," Alex argued. "Fond, maybe infatuated and enamored once, but not in love."

"You really might not be capable of leading this clan. You're fucking stupid." Brice spun away from Alex, leaving him along the riverbank.

Alex didn't watch his brother walk away. He was certain Brice wasn't returning to the keep. He was merely finding his own spot farther along the waterway. Once they were old enough to understand arguing in front of their clan members was unwise, they'd brought their disagreements to the riverside. They also confided in one another here, knowing the walls had ears in Mangerton Tower, just like any keep. Alex sighed as he turned toward Brice and made his way to his brother's new spot.

"I don't want to talk aboot her, but would it make you feel any better to talk aboot your nightmares?" Alex asked as he eased himself to the ground. Much like he had that morning as he sat in bed, he lifted his limp arm into his lap. Brice frowned and sighed but sat beside his brother.

"It's always the same," Brice began. "I watch the mon rushing toward me, and I take my eyes off the mon I'm fighting for just a moment. I catch sight of the blade sweeping toward me as I duck and feel the hilt strike me. Except this time when I fall, I'm not unconscious. I watch as he slices into you. I watch you fall beside me as I struggle to stand, to grab my sword, to defend you. You land with your head turned toward me. All I see are sightless eyes staring back at me. I let you die because I didn't pay enough attention."

Brice turned his head away, unable to meet Alex's gaze as he swallowed the lump in his throat and

7

fought to keep his tears from falling for the millionth time. He failed and moved his shoulder to wipe away the moisture inconspicuously.

"You think it's your fault," Alex stated. "I never ever have, Bri. Never. Not even once."

Brice glanced back at Alex, tears still misting his eyes. "But it is. Your injuries, the way you are now, how you feel. All of it. If I hadn't glanced away, I would have remained on my feet. I was winning. Instead, I left your back open to attack. If anyone is to blame for *supposedly* losing father's heir, it's me."

Brice's revelation stunned Alex. He stared at the ground, unable to meet his brother's gaze for a moment. "I've made you feel that way. I've taken out my guilt and bitterness on you and everyone else. And you've accepted it, let me vent my spleen. All the while, I've undoubtedly only made you feel worse. I know you didn't want to tell me this."

"I didn't. But it's crushing me to watch you shoulder all the responsibility for that day, for thinking you're ruining the clan. I can't keep letting you think that."

"Letting me? Brice, this doesn't change aught. I'm glad I learned how you feel, and I swear I will no longer make you endure my foul moods. But I'm still not fit to lead. I can't ride into battle anymore. People will mock our clan and assume us weak when half a mon takes over the lairdship. I can be your seneschal when the time comes, and you can pick your own second-in-command."

"You will not be my servant," Brice hissed, and Alex recognized the tone. It took much to make his jovial brother angry, but Alex had just unwittingly unleashed Brice's temper. "I can't believe you degrade yourself and our family to think you should be a servant to me. Neakail is likely the best seneschal we've had in generations, but he isn't a member of

8

the laird's family. He serves our father, not the other way around. You will never serve me."

Brice's eyes narrowed to slits as he glowered at Alex. Each word sounded more outraged than the last. Alex suspected that if he didn't have a lame arm, Brice would have launched himself at Alex, and they would roll around in a brawl. Alex could feel the waves of anger rolling off Brice; he was tempted to raise his good hand to see if he could touch them.

"You are Father's tánaiste and ride out on his behalf often. He trusts you, but he knows he needs to stay alive—and don't say it's because of how you are now, because we can both count how many times you rode out before this happened. Do you not trust me as Father trusts you? When you become laird, if you don't have a son auld enough, I become tánaiste until your son can be. I could ride out in your stead just as you do for Father. It would be no different."

"Of course it's different!" Alex bellowed, his own temper flaring. "Everyone along either side of the border all the way to Stirling knows Father still *can* ride out to fight. He's not useless and weak."

"Useless and weak?" Brice grabbed the front of Alex's doublet and yanked him to his feet as Brice rose. Without warning, he pitched forward toward Alex, his entire bodyweight moving toward his older brother. Instinct drove Alex to push back against Brice, keeping him on his feet. "Weak, huh?"

"That is not the same."

"Mayhap not, but you are hardly weak. You have more strength in one arm that hasn't trained in months than most men do in both. I'm not exactly light." At well over six feet, Brice stood as tall as his brother. But where Alex was broad-shouldered and naturally lean through the chest and waist, Brice was barrel-chested and thick. None of it was fat, but he weighed at least a stone more than Alex, who was

9

close to sixteen stone himself. Brice hadn't restrained himself and had launched his full, dead weight at Alex. Alex hadn't even taken a step back.

Brice raised his fist and swung toward Alex's face. Once more instinct took hold. Alex's forearm blocked the punch before he twisted and wrapped his hand around Brice's wrist. Ever since they'd grown to be the same height and strength, they'd never used their full force on one another when they wrestled or tussled. Alex knew Brice hadn't restrained his punch. He was certain because his right forearm now throbbed as badly as his left arm always felt.

"Weak?" Brice mocked. He backed away from Alex, placing several yards between them before he drew his sword. He raced toward Alex, who no longer carried his sword but still wore several dirks. He thrust his sword forward with all his strength, trusting Alex's instinct to prevail, making him draw his dirk and fight as the senior warriors had always taught them when their opponent had a sword, and they did not.

Alex's body was still agile, moving away from Brice while drawing a dirk in one fluid motion. He sliced toward Brice, careful not to cut his brother but engaging in the mock fight they'd practiced for years. He blocked Brice over and over until he found his opening, stepping forward and pressing his blade to Brice's throat.

"Weak?" Brice croaked. Alex swiftly twirled his blade and sheathed it at his waist. He shoved Brice's gloating mien away from him.

"That's still not the same as riding into battle."

"But are you weak?" Brice persisted. "You haven't trained in six months, and you still fight as though you were in the lists yesterday."

"You want me to show up to a battle with just knives?" Alex sneered.

"I want you to at least come back to the lists. I —" Brice clamped his mouth shut.

"You what?" Alex demanded.

"I miss you," Brice snapped. The men stood staring at one another. Alex's shoulders slumped.

"I miss you, too," Alex admitted. "I miss training with you."

"Then come back. Train with dirks, with a battle axe, with whatever you can wield. But come back," Brice begged.

"A battle axe? You'd turn me into a Highlander? And what aboot when the men watch me fight like half a mon?"

"Why do you persist in saying that? It's not half. You have two arms and two legs. Only one of those four isn't working. And you still swear your cock does, even if you won't go near a woman. As long as that's still attached, you're more mon than most I know."

Alex sighed and cast his eyes toward the sky. It was still dawn, but he was aware the men were only now arriving at the lists. His lips flattened before turning down, but he nodded. "I'll come today."

"And tomorrow, and the next day, the day after that, and on and on," Brice insisted. "Today won't be easy. You may feel like a failure, but you didn't walk back into the lists as you had before battle either of the previous times your injuries were severe. You had to train to regain your speed and your strength. Don't let hard days defeat you, brother."

Brice clapped Alex on his good shoulder and squeezed before pulling Alex in for an embrace. Alex hesitated, then wrapped one arm around Brice as they leaned against one another. When they pulled away, they grinned and playfully punched each other in the shoulder before turning back to the keep.

TWO

"Alex, Brice," Laird Tavin Armstrong called as he approached the brothers while they walked toward the lists. The men switched direction and met their father halfway across the bailey. "Alex, I need you to go to court. You leave in two days."

"What's happened?" Alex asked, preparing for the argument he was about to begin.

"The king is fed up with hearing the Scotts complain. He's not so thrilled aboot hearing from us either. He demands a representative from the Armstrongs, Scotts, and Elliots appear before him."

"And you think that should be me? Stand before the entire court to represent our clan with my arm dangling useless at my side while I stand beside a mon from the very clan that made me useless?"

"Back to that," Brice muttered.

"You're my tánaiste. Until I die and you become laird, you're my representative in clan matters like this," Tavin stated. As a child, and even as a young man, his father's expression normally made Alex cease the conversation with agreement and a nod. But he was no longer a child, and he refused to shame his clan.

"And I've told you I shouldn't be any of those. You want to humiliate our entire clan? Then send me. If you want to prove to the Scotts that they can't have our land, our cattle, or our keep, then send someone who represents our clan's strength."

"Strength is not only muscle, and well you understand it, Alexander," Tavin stated as he crossed his arms. "This is not a time for muscle. This is a time for diplomacy and strategy. There is no one better suited than you." Tavin spun on his heels and marched back to the keep's steps. He glanced over his shoulder at his sons, a hard edge to his stare before he disappeared into the castle.

"Let's go," Brice said as he nudged Alex and turned toward the lists.

"I can't go to court looking like I came out on the losing end of a fight." Alex shook his head.

"Then don't lose." Brice cocked a brow, his expression taunting Alex as it had since childhood.

"Very well, little brother. I hope you didn't exhaust yourself already."

Men noticed Alex enter the lists, drawing one of his longer dirks. He sensed many wanted to stare, learn what he could do, discover why he'd finally come back. But they all had the sense not to be too conspicuous. Alex weighed the feel of the blade in his hand and remembered his third-and-ten saint's day, when his father gifted him with the dirk that had once been his. Alex recalled how he'd polished the hilt every day until his father teased he would wear it away. It felt natural in his hand, as though he'd never put it down. He turned toward Brice, who once again had his sword drawn. Alex froze.

"You cannot expect me to always best you, or even match you, if you have a sword and I have a dirk," Alex whispered as he leaned toward Brice.

"You've never 'always' bested or matched me," Brice scoffed. "Your memory is what's gone, big brother. I will knock you on your arse if I can, but I'm confident I'll end up on mine just as often." Brice inched forward, causing Alex to move away as they began circling one another, leaning forward, light on their feet. They waited, neither one intending to strike first.

"Aren't you going to swing that gigantic sword? You claim it's always hard," Alex taunted, hearing men around them laugh.

"Aren't you going to thrust with that tiny knife of yours?" Brice replied, causing several snickers. He raised his arm, adjusting his stance, and it was the opening Alex needed. He barreled forward, his good shoulder slamming into Brice's chest as he swept Brice's feet out from under him.

"I don't need a tiny knife when you have my size," Alex boasted as he reached down to help Brice up. Brice attempted to pull Alex off-balance, and Alex pretended to stumble, only to place his boot on Brice's shoulder. It was Alex's turn to cock an eyebrow. He stepped back, allowing his brother space to get up on his own. They repositioned themselves as Brice grasped his sword; Alex twisted the wrist that held his dirk, readjusting it in his palm. Once more, they circled.

Brice raised his arm as if to strike overhand, but at the last minute slashed toward Alex's legs. Dancing away, Alex used his slightly longer reach to press the tip of his knife against Brice's throat, as the latter's sword swished through the air, striking nothing. Brice knocked Alex's arm away and shoved him backward, their taunting over and their competition fully heated. Brice sliced an arc through the air as he brought his sword down toward Alex's right ribcage. Alex lurched backwards, allowing Brice's momentum

14

to unbalance him. He pressed his blade against Brice's sternum.

They separated and repositioned themselves. This time, Alex went on the offensive. He feinted left, then right, as he tried to maneuver himself to where Brice couldn't defend his ribs with his enormous broadsword. But Brice spun at the last minute and slammed his shoulder under Alex's chin, making his head snap back. Brice's sword hilt landed in Alex's gut and knocked him to the ground. Brice stepped back as Alex sprang back to his feet and launched himself into Brice's abdomen, knocking them both to the ground. With his forearm against Brice's throat, he shifted to get a knee on top of each arm, pinning them to the ground.

"Yield," Alex demanded. Brice tapped his hand on the ground. Alex removed his weight immediately. Brice stood, bent forward slightly from the pain that still radiated through his middle.

"Weak, huh? You tricked me," Brice accused with a grin before leaning forward to dry heave at his feet.

Alex wiped the sweat from his brow, more shocked than anyone that he'd defeated his brother not once, but thrice. It stunned him that Brice only knocked him down once, and not during their first round. He perceived the men staring at them, bewildered by Alex's unexpected return. They no longer attempted to be polite. He turned when his childhood friend, Adam, stepped forward.

"Aboot bluidy time. Your brother is bossier than a ten-year-auld lass," Adam teased as he smirked at Brice. "And he knows half as much."

Alex stared at Adam for a moment, surprised but appreciative that his friend welcomed him back to the training ground and eased his self-consciousness.

"I thought to let him play pretend for a while.

He's always wanted to grow up to be me," Alex replied. He looked back at Brice, who grinned.

"Aye, but thank God I'm better looking." Brice could have bitten his tongue off, having forgotten about Alex's scar and how his face was now striking, but not because of his good looks.

"You are mighty bonnie," Alex jested, choosing to ignore the tightening in his chest. He was aware he'd once been handsome, but it wasn't the loss of his handsome appearance that made him uncomfortable. It was the stares and whispers about his face that made him uneasy. Brice opened his mouth, then closed it again, regretting his mocking comment. "Don't worry, little brother. One day you'll get the face of a mon. You might even grow some whiskers."

Alex ran his hand over his jaw. He'd grown out his beard to hide half his scar, but Brice had never grown facial hair as quickly or fully as Alex. He wrapped his arm around Brice's shoulders and pulled his brother to his side.

"Shall we discover if cook has any tarts to go along with your milk and honey?" Alex teased.

"Shall I help you up the steps, auld mon?" Brice replied, his grin back in place. They left the lists, Alex's hand resting on the back of Brice's shoulder. When they were out of earshot, Brice said, "That was thoughtless. I'm sorry aboot my comment."

"Bah. I'm grateful you convinced me to go in. That's the first time I've enjoyed myself since before we rode out. Thank you." Alex's appreciation was heartfelt, and they could both hear it in his voice. They made their way inside, truly intending to stop in the kitchens to see if they could filch any tarts like they had since they were children, when they spotted their mother hurrying toward them.

"Alex?" Lady Coira Armstrong rushed forward,

looking over Alex's dirty face and disheveled clothes. "What happened? You didn't try to train, did you?"

Alex stiffened at his mother's question. He understood her worry, but it rankled to hear her speak to him as though he were a child or the incapable man he'd felt like for months. The excitement and accomplishment he'd felt only minutes ago withered.

"What aboot me, Mother? I look worse than him," Brice intervened, pretending to be petulant. "He knocked me over almost every time. He's claimed he's weak. He tricked me, Mother. It's not fair." Brice grinned, looking back and forth between his parent and his sibling, hoping his humor eased Coira's concern. It was as though she didn't hear him speak.

"Alex, what were you thinking?" Coira reached for Alex's cheek. He didn't pull away as she cupped it, but he flinched. "Are you hurt?" she demanded.

"No, Mother. But neither do I need any more coddling. I'm glad I sparred with Brice. It's the most I've felt like my auld self in months."

"But—" Coira tried to argue.

"Mother, Alex was incredible," Brice interrupted. He cast his eyes at Alex, locking gazes with him. "To be honest, it worried me. I feared humiliating him and regretted asking him to come in. But I'm serious, Mother. Either he's been telling half-truths aboot his strength, or he really didn't realize that he's as strong as he ever was. I didn't give in. He knocked me down because he was better and stronger."

Tavin joined them as Brice spoke. He observed his older son before turning his attention to Brice. "Were you arrogant, assuming you could beat Alex?"

"No. I mean, no more than any mon is when he taunts his opponent." Brice shook his head and smiled at Tavin. "Father, he beat me because I underestimated him, and he was better. I think I know my brother better than just aboot anyone else, but I didn't know he could do that."

"Alex?" Coira asked, worry still lacing her voice.

Alex shrugged, wincing as he forgot the unavoidable pain that shot through his arm with the gesture. While they stood talking, stiffness and soreness settled in. He regretted being so forceful, assuming he was fitter than he was. His sparring at the riverside built his confidence, but now he wanted nothing more than to retire to his chamber where he could vomit from the pain in private.

"Alex," Coira cried as she stepped forward. "No. I won't stand for it."

"Coira," Tavin shook his head. He watched Alex intently, understanding the young man both appreciated and was annoyed by his mother's clinging. He shared his wife's fears but never expressed them freely like Coira. But he admired Alex's decision to return to the lists. He'd feared his son might never recognize his value again. He'd gone up to his chamber to peer through the window. It had a view out to the lists, and he'd watched Alex. It surprised him at how strong and agile Alex remained. He could only imagine the full force his son once possessed. He doubted anyone realized how strong Alex must have been before his injuries.

"Tavin, no," Coira argued. "I—"

"Mother, I got dirty. I'll have some bruises and may find some scratches. But I got worse when I was a wean playing in the bailey. I'm fine," Alex stated. He'd tried to gentle his words at first, but by the end they were more forceful than he intended. His mother pulled away, but he caught her hand and kissed the back of it. He whispered, "Thank you for worrying, Mama."

Coira nodded, mollified. She shifted her gaze to

Brice and smiled. "Was your brother horrid to you?" It was the same question she'd asked time and again when Brice cried as a child because Alex was bigger and faster, leaving Brice behind.

"Positively wretched," Brice chortled.

"Perhaps baths for both of you are in order. You're not very—fresh," Coira said as her nose wrinkled. They all recognized she exaggerated, but they all understood steaming baths were one of the few things that eased Alex's constant pain.

"Don't confuse the soap this time, Mother." Alex grinned. "I didn't care for smelling like lavender last time."

"Aye, well…" Coira never admitted she gave Alex the lavender soap, hoping it soothed him enough to sleep that night. "I will sniff it myself. Hie yourselves off to your chambers while I send maids up with the tubs and buckets."

Alex and Brice leaned forward to kiss their mother on her cheeks, just as they had since they were young and trying to avoid punishments. They made their way up the stairs together as Tavin and Coira watched.

"Coira, I understand it scares you. You're not alone in that. I thought to have you join me as I watched Alex from my chamber but I feared upsetting you if Alex got hurt. But he's impressive. Nay, he can't use both arms. He made it clear he didn't need to. Do I plan to send him off to battle again? No. But am I more reassured that he can defend himself? Yes. Was it the boost of confidence he needed? Absolutely. Brice did what no one else could. He gave Alex back some self-respect."

Tavin smiled at the woman he'd married nearly three decades earlier. They weren't in love and never had been. But he loved his wife with a warmth that had grown over the years, and they respected one another. In a rare moment of affection, he wrapped his arm around Coira's shoulders and kissed her forehead. She leaned against Tavin and nodded. Together, they watched their sons until they disappeared abovestairs.

THREE

A lex gritted his teeth as each step his horse took
jarred his left arm, even while trotting. He'd
repositioned his limp arm several times when it
slipped from his lap. They'd been on the road for six
days, and Alex grew more miserable by the day. He
couldn't imagine how his father thought he'd be
diplomatic with anyone, let alone a king, after riding
for six days and spending five nights sleeping on the
ground. While he'd been able to keep up with the
other men when they pushed their horses faster, he'd
been in agony with each movement. It humiliated
him that he couldn't stand his turn at watch, every
man there knowing he couldn't protect them if attacked. The cold from the earth seeped into his
bones and made his injury ache besides throb. He
hadn't known it was possible.

The little self-confidence Alex built from
spending two days in the lists shattered as he realized
how much of a strain it was for him to make this
same journey he'd done countless times before. He
wanted nothing more than to slip into his chambers,
unnoticed by anyone but the servants who brought
him a bath. But he knew King Robert the Bruce
would learn of his arrival and expect him to wait

among the other petitioners outside the Privy Council chamber. Even if the chamberlain didn't grant him entry, King Robert expected the Armstrongs to respond to his summons immediately. He also accepted that the one person he both longed to and loathed to see resided at court. Encountering Caitlyn Kennedy was more inevitable than meeting with the king.

As they entered Stirling Castle's bailey, Alex glanced around to determine if Queen Elizabeth de Burgh's ladies-in-waiting were anywhere near the stables. He breathed easier when he saw no woman he recognized. He relieved his men of duty and sent them to find food and cots in the barracks. Opting to risk King Robert's ire, he slipped into the castle and made his way to the bachelor men's floor. It wasn't long before he had a chamber assigned to him and a bath on the way. While he waited for the servants to arrive, he kicked off his boots and peeled off his stockings. He bade them enter when he heard the knock, turning to watch as two men carried the narrow tub, fearing he might lodge himself in it and never get out. Women smiled at him as they poured bucket after bucket of water into the tub. But each struggled to stifle their gasps when he turned his face fully toward them. He watched as the coquettish behavior turned to revulsion, as it had the few times he'd thought to approach a woman.

Alex had sought the company of tavern wenches in the village outside Mangerton, women he'd known since the first time he'd stumbled in. They were women he'd bedded before who no longer drew near, put off by his marred appearance, uncomfortable near his deformed arm. He hadn't even been that interested in tupping any of them so much as confirming his suspicions: he now repulsed women.

Settling himself in the tub with his knees up to

22

his nose, Alex sank his aching arm and shoulder beneath water that was uncomfortably hot to the rest of him. Sitting curled was moderately more comfortable than the lip of the tub biting into his legs. He would never understand why carpenters built the tubs to accommodate women. He could only imagine what his Highland acquaintances did. He was a large man, but they were mammoth. He soaked until the water no longer eased the pain, then he scrubbed himself. Glancing at the bed, it tempted him to retire until morning, ignoring the king's expectations, but he knew such a decision would do him—or Clan Armstrong—no good.

Alex heaved himself out of the bath, struggling to get his feet under him with only one arm to help lever his body. He took several calming breaths before he attempted to get dressed, willing himself not to get impatient and frustrated. He stared at the empty scabbard propped against the foot of the bed. He'd worn his sword while he traveled on the off chance that he needed to go to such lengths to defend himself. It was a relief when he had to relinquish it at the gate. He didn't feel so ridiculous wearing it when everyone recognized he was no longer a warrior. He was now, at best, a courtier. He grimaced at the thought. He summoned servants to remove his bath while he fought to pull on his stockings and boots. This time, none of the women glanced in his direction. He supposed it was better than having to witness their unease and dislike.

Alex was nearly to the last turn before entering the passageway leading to the Privy Council chamber when he heard women's voices. One particular voice had him ducking out of sight until they passed.

Coward. You've known Caitlyn since you were seven, and she was five. You're hiding like a naughty wean.

23

Despite reproaching himself, he didn't step out of his hiding place until he no longer heard any women. He made his way toward the doors leading into the Privy Council chamber and announced himself to the chamberlain. It shocked him that the doors opened to him as soon as the chamberlain returned. Alex entered the meeting room and swept his gaze over the occupants. He stifled a growl when he noticed not one, but three, representatives from Clan Scott. He recognized Angus Elliot, heir to Clan Elliot, standing across the room from the Scott men. He'd never cared for Angus or his younger brother, Graeme, especially not after rumors circulated about how their family treated their youngest sister, Allyson. Fortunately for Allyson, she married the reformed rogue Ewan Gordon and lived far from her clan of birth. But much as he disliked Angus, he respected his prowess as a warrior and a leader. He moved to stand with Angus.

"Armstrong," Angus acknowledged. His eyes widened when he realized Alex's injury hadn't healed as everyone hoped. He forced himself not to stare at Alex's scar either, shifting to only peer at Alex's left side.

"Elliot, how long have you been here?" Alex inquired.

"I arrived yesterday, but this is the first time they've admitted me. Not that it's mattered since I've been waiting in here for two hours. The king hasn't glanced in my direction. But then, he hasn't looked at those bluidy Scott arseholes either."

"Do you think we'll gain an audience now that I'm here?" Alex suspected they might, but for no reason other than King Robert's morbid interest in Alex's condition. If it allowed him to leave court sooner, he wasn't beyond dragging his arm on the floor and picking at his scar. He watched alongside

Angus as the Bruce finally turned his attention in their direction. He narrowed his eyes at them before turning to glower at the Scotts. His scowl etched into his face, he waved the men to the table that sat in the middle of the chamber. He pushed aside the parchments strewn before him as he sat. The five Lowlanders waited for the minor nod that indicated they could sit as well.

"How do you have time to fight one another when you're still reiving and being reived by the English?" King Robert demanded with no salutations offered. None of the men offered an answer, and none shifted their stares. They all gazed at spots over the king's shoulders. Alex refused to volunteer any information for which the king didn't directly ask. The lines seemed to sink deeper into the king's face as he waited. "Very well. What the bluidy hell in August were you thinking?" King Robert turned his ire toward the Scotts.

The Scott men sat silently, none of the three wanting to speak first. Finally, the one in the middle answered. "*They* claimed land that isn't theirs. We aimed to get it back."

"And what land would that be? They aren't neighbors to one another." King Robert swung his gaze toward Alex and Angus. "What reason do they have to fight over a single strip of land?"

"Both the Armstrongs and Elliots sent crofters onto our land, saying it was theirs," the Scott delegate explained.

"And one clan thought it prudent to take on two of the most powerful border clans," the Bruce scoffed. "Mighty big bollocks your laird has."

"I'd say we didn't fare too badly all things considered." The Scott representative who sat closest to Alex smirked. Alex kept a rein on his temper, expecting the taunts and attempts to humiliate him.

25

"You lost," King Robert stated, deadpan.

"For now," the same Scott spoke. "They both sustained significant losses." This time the man had the audacity to grin. But it faded when Alex didn't react.

"And every mon who rode or marched onto that battlefield lived to return to your land," the Bruce quipped. The three Scott delegates shifted in their seats. "I may not spend as much time near the border as I once did, but I know the land well. The Hermitage lies closer to the Armstrongs and Elliots than it does the Scotts. You met to fight there because it was land near there that you claimed the Armstrongs and Elliots stole. Tell me: How does one steal their own land? That land has been no one's but the Armstrongs' and the Elliots'. My son oversees the Hermitage."

While King Robert had two legitimate children, Marjorie by his first wife and David by his current wife, he had a number of bastards who shared the king's distinct russet hair. His oldest illegitimate son, aptly named Robert, fought alongside his father during the Wars. For that, he was gifted oversight of Hermitage Castle. The Bruce was hardly unaware of what happened there.

Alex, watching from the corner of his eye, was certain he noticed the Scotts squirm in their seats. To anyone else, it appeared he watched the king. He would never be blind to where any Scott was ever again. He maintained his posture with his back straight, chest broad, and head held high. He was aware some called it arrogance, and once it had been. Now it was more bravado, but he mustered all that he could, so he never appeared cowed before another clan. As he sat, he'd inconspicuously lifted his left arm into his lap and now clasped hands. He did so to keep his arm from sliding from his lap, but it gave him the air of looking at ease. His right hand had to hold tightly against the weight of his left arm, but he still had enough strength and dexterity in his left hand to curl his fingers over the back of his right hand, making the position appear natural.

"Armstrong, what say you?" King Robert demanded.

"What is there to say, Your Majesty? They encroached upon our land, and we showed them the way off," Alex answered.

"Save your glib comments for the taverns, Alexander," King Robert warned. "How did you and the Elliots wind up at the same fight?"

"It's no secret that neither of us care for them," Alex said. It was clear to whom he referenced while naming no one or even looking in the Scotts' direction. "We are not on bad terms with the Elliots. It seemed efficient to work together."

"'Not on bad terms,'" King Robert scoffed. "Everyone knows you're allies. But that doesn't explain how you ended up fighting together in that battle."

"My father sent a missive to Laird Elliot, mentioning the inconveniences we've faced. Laird Elliot commiserated and offered to help us be less inconvenienced," Alex said with a shrug. This time he expected the pain that came with the gesture. It didn't diminish it, but his face didn't reflect the burst of agony.

"Since you are being dodgy, Alexander, I shall ask Angus." King Robert focused his sights on Angus, whose expression gave away none of his thoughts. Alex's respect extended to Angus as a fellow strategist. "Why did the Elliots ride out with the Armstrongs?"

"We're allies." Angus offered nothing more. Ire flashed across the Bruce's face before it settled back to a scowl.

"Recalcitrance will win you no favors," King Robert warned.

"Your Majesty," Alex spoke up. "We have the deeds to our land, just as the Elliots have the deeds to theirs. I expect the Scotts are the same. Any number of maps show the boundaries to the various territories. The land is not up for dispute. They refused to move, so we moved them."

"And you're satisfied with how you came to win?" King Robert cocked an eyebrow as his gaze locked on Alex's arm.

"My clan lives to see another day, so I'm satisfied," Alex answered. What did the Bruce expect him to do? Complain about being maimed. Whine that he could no longer defend his people? Ask the king to avenge him? None of those options were worth considering. He wasn't there out of self-interest; he was there to represent his clan.

"Angus, are you satisfied with the outcome?" King Robert asked, his tone daring Angus to answer when it was so obvious that Alex's injury would never heal.

"My clan members along the border are safe. I am satisfied with that." Angus's face appeared set in stone, recognizing the king's test and not appreciating being backed into a corner that would have easily made him appear like an arse. King Robert nodded.

"I will consider what I've heard. I will give you my decision when I am ready," King Robert declared. Alex wanted to ask what there was to decide. As far as it concerned him, the matter had been decided, first when the Scotts encroached on other clans' land and then when the Armstrongs and Elliots defeated the Scotts. He understood King Robert procrastinated to give himself an air of control. All three clans had been loyal to the Bruce's crusade.

The monarch couldn't afford to alienate any of them, particularly not the Armstrongs and Elliots, whose lands lay at the Scottish-English border.

Without looking at one another, the delegates from the three clans rose, prepared to leave. There was hesitation over who should leave first. Alex jutted his chin toward the door as he smirked at the Scotts. The gesture was condescending, as though he granted them permission to go before him. His emerald-green eyes mocked them. Rather than argue before the king, the Scotts accepted the offer and filed out. Angus and Alex moved away from the chairs, but Alex froze when the king ordered him to remain behind.

"Alex, sit," King Robert issued the command, but his tone had softened. Alex didn't want anyone's pity. The king studied Alex for a long moment, considering what to say first. "Would you visit my physician?"

"There is naught anyone can do," Alex answered.

"Naught that a healer can do. Mayhap my mon can do something a village woman can't." King Robert waited, but Alex said nothing. "Do you fear another person telling you it will remain as it is?"

"I don't fear it because I've accepted it," Alex countered. He'd accepted it all. The pain, losing his former life, the discomfort his presence caused others. He'd accepted his anger and his bitterness, even if he wished he could move past them. The only thing he hadn't accepted was other's insistence that he remain his father's heir.

"Not everyone knows aboot your injuries," King Robert said pointedly.

"It matters not who knows. Naught will change from now on." Alex set his jaw, hoping the king understood his subtle meaning as Alex had understood the Bruce's. He rejected trapping any woman into a marriage with him.

"Do you believe that's fair to her? To decide without her?"

"And how fair is it to shame her into marrying a mon who can't defend her? To marry a mon who will embarrass her and make her appear a fool? I wouldn't do that to any woman, particularly not her."

"But Ca—"

"No, Your Majesty. It's not an option," Alex said resolutely. He perceived his resistance took the king aback, but he didn't need the monarch to play matchmaker for him. The king's other arrangements had worked out for the couples, but he wasn't interested in being the one that didn't.

"You will hurt her if you avoid her."

"I will hurt her far more if I humiliate her." Alex wished he could cross his arms.

"Very well. Do as you must," the Bruce said with resignation. He dismissed Alex, who heard the evening meal's bells toll. It felt like a death knell.

FOUR

Alex entered the Great Hall with his men. They followed the Elliots toward tables that kept them away from the Scotts or anyone else they wished to avoid. However, their path took them past the table he most wanted to avoid. He caught sight of the dark hair and olive skin he knew so well. He could glimpse Caitlyn's profile, the smile that graced her face as she laughed at what the woman who sat beside her said. He watched as her eyes widened, and she twisted on her bench to find him. Her smile radiated warmth and excitement, and Alex's heart stuttered before he forced the wall back around it.

Caitlyn stepped over the bench and straightened her skirts before making her way toward Alex. He fought, and barely succeeded, to keep his eyes from feasting on Caitlyn's petite stature. His relationship with Caitlyn had been a constant for nearly his entire life, but once again the dynamic had shifted. He watched her weave through people until she came to stand before him. He watched her eyes widen for a moment and prepared for the pity or disgust that inevitably came when people caught sight of his scar for the first time. He was unprepared for her smile to brighten as she took another step closer.

"Alex." Caitlyn's melodic voice filled his ears. He'd listened to her sing alongside her mother and sister, Cairren, countless times over his years fostering with her clan. Even her speaking voice reminded him of a songbird's trill. He was aware she expected as warm a greeting, but he kept his gaze fixed beyond her. She turned to glance behind her, but she appeared confused when she faced him again. Alex knew she couldn't figure out at what he stared. He intended to stare at anything or anyone but her. Unable to ignore her, he continued to gaze past her.

"Caitlyn."

"Caitlyn? When have I ever been aught but Caity?" Caitlyn asked, and Alex heard the surprise and hurt in her voice.

"It is a pleasure to see you," Alex said instead of answering. He made to step around her, but Caitlyn shifted with him.

"You make it seem like seeing me is the most unpleasant chore you've ever had. In fact, I'm uncertain you have seen me since you refuse to look at me," Caitlyn accused. Alex wanted to say that he'd seen everything about her that he loved. He'd seen her twinkling gray eyes with the green flecks, the sun-kissed light brown skin, the figure he'd spent years fantasizing about. But his adolescent dreams died on the battlefield six months ago.

"Then you will have to excuse me." Alex tried once more to move away, but she grasped his left arm. He was unprepared and couldn't keep from flinching. Caitlyn's eyes opened to saucers, but there was still none of the pity he expected. She released his arm, clasping her hands before her instead.

"What happened?" Caitlyn whispered.

"Battle. Good eve."

"Arse," Caitlyn mumbled. Alex glanced down at Caitlyn and regretted it at once. He'd seen the pain in her eyes before, but this was the first time that he was the cause.

"Caity," Alex murmured. He made to reach for her, but his left arm refused to cooperate. It was a blinding reminder of why he needed to keep his distance.

"Mayhap this isn't the right place. Will you talk to me later?" Caitlyn asked, hoping discretion was all that he needed.

"No."

This time Caitlyn moved aside when Alex attempted to walk past her. She swallowed before turning away. She didn't understand what had transpired, but she was certain it was Alex's injuries and nothing else. The Armstrongs and Kennedys were still allies, and Alex and Caitlyn hadn't said a cross word to one another in years. She returned to her seat, her eyes on her trencher rather than following Alex.

"He was once so attractive," Caitlyn heard Lady Sarah Anne Hay announce. "But now? That heathenous beard does naught to hide that hideous scar. He should have the good graces not to scare ladies by showing his face."

Caitlyn turned a contemptuous glare at Sarah Anne, but before she could say anything, Lady Catherine MacFarlane spoke up. "You should take pity on the mon. With his limp arm, he'll never be a warrior. He was once so desirable."

"I wonder if his arm is the only thing limp," Lady Margaret, Sarah Anne's older sister, snickered. "I wonder what other battle scars he suffered. I might have let him toss my skirts, but what's the point if he's been unmanned. Besides, I don't want that hand touching me, even if naught else has gone lame."

"He's not a leper," Caitlyn seethed. "You know him to be my friend. Cease."

"He didn't appear to be your friend when you had to hold him in place to talk to you," Sarah Anne mused.

"I think Lady Caitlyn has finally found a suitable mon," Margaret chimed in again. "Between his deformed arm and face and her deformed skin color, they suit one another."

Caitlyn had heard many prejudiced comments about her skin tone since she arrived. The ones she'd heard about Cairren were far worse, but no one had ever called her older sister "deformed," at least not to her face. But as much as the snide comment about her olive hue bothered her, she was livid at Margaret calling Alex deformed. Without thinking, she stood and tossed her brimming chaliceful of wine at Margaret and let the empty vessel roll across the table and into Margaret's lap.

"If I had a sword, I would run you through," Caitlyn declared, uncaring that everyone at the surrounding tables and halfway across the Great Hall watched and heard her. "Speak like that again, and it will be your blood, not my wine, that stains your gowns."

Caitlyn left the table a second time, but this time she stormed past stunned faces. She spared Alex a glance as she approached, but her only acknowledgment was a narrowing of her eyes. The guards at the doors barely opened them and moved aside in time. Caitlyn was too angry to think straight. She was uncertain where she wanted to go. She only recognized she needed to escape before she jabbed her eating knife into Margaret's eye.

Anger at the women and hurt from Alex's coldness coursed through her until she wanted to both scream and cry. She stopped at an arrow slit and gazed out over the gardens. The stars and moonlight were bright, and she could glimpse the rose bushes she walked past while she accompanied the queen on her daily constitutional. She sighed as she leaned against the cool bricks, her cheeks feeling on fire in comparison. The heightened emotion seemed to leach from her body, leaving her feeling tired and lonely. It wasn't the first time she'd felt that way, but she'd never imagined she could with Alex at court. She'd always been so happy to see him, just as he was to see her. But his rejection pained her in a way it hadn't since he and Cairren became adolescents and thought they were in love. They'd gone for long walks together and refused to allow Caitlyn to join them.

Alex and Cairren eventually realized they weren't in love so much as loved one another as siblings. They'd thought to marry because it seemed natural, since they were the same age and had known each other for so long. Fortunately for Cairren, they'd realized they didn't suit as well as they thought, and now she and Padraig Munro had a blissful marriage. Alex visited Dunure often, even after Cairren left home and became a lady-in-waiting. Alex and Caitlyn had always been close, but she'd been certain something had been developing between them over the last few years that left neither of them thinking they were like siblings. She supposed she'd erred to believe such a thing.

With a sigh that seemed to come from her very soul, Caitlyn turned away from the arrow slit and walked toward the passageway that led to the stairwell to her floor. She paused when she thought she noticed a shadow move. She reached for the dirk she kept at her waist, and her left hand slid along her skirts to assure herself that her other, hidden dirk was in her pocket. She swept her gaze along the shadows

35

before she angled her back to the wall and glanced the opposite way. Nothing seemed to approach from behind where she had stood, and she saw nothing else move in front of her. Nonetheless, she kept her dirk at the ready as she gathered her skirts and hurried down the passageway. She took the stairs two at a time before she bolted to her door, which she locked and barred.

Caitlyn had one too many men make assumptions about her over the years she'd been at court to shrug off any sense of danger. She knew that she hardly overreacted, since men had followed her to her chamber before. She fought to catch her breath as she wondered who she'd seen because she was certain someone was there lurking. Her heritage made many gossip about her, wondering if she were already secretly bedding men or whose offer she would accept first to become a mistress. If the only unique thing about her was her French mother, she wouldn't be a target. But her mother's father had been a Saracen, once stranded in the south of France. He'd married her widowed grandmother and together they had one daughter. Lady Collette Kennedy and her daughter Cairren shared a rich olive-brown skin color that Caitlyn had often envied until she understood the cruelty that came along with it at court. She was far lighter than the other two women, her Scottish father's influence stronger in her than in Cairren. The sisters shared Innes's unusual gray eyes, making their paternity indisputable. But her Saracen lineage made many wonder if she behaved like a woman in a harem.

For all the insinuations and propositions, Caitlyn recognized that having lighter skin than Cairren protected her. But it didn't keep men from pursuing her the few times she moved around the castle alone. She chided herself for letting her temper get the better of her. Not because of the way she treated Margaret, but because it made her foolish enough to disregard her safety.

Alex watched Caitlyn lean against the brick wall and wondered what she was thinking. He'd been unable to hear what caused Caitlyn to throw wine on her fellow lady-in-waiting, but he'd recognized Caitlyn's expression. He feared she might gut the other woman at the table. She'd been a boisterous child who settled into being merely effervescent as a woman. But she had a temper that rivaled her French mother's. Few underestimated Lady Collette more than once. She nearly gelded one of his men a few years ago when Collette learned what the man said to Cairren just before the younger woman left court.

When she glared at him, he suspected whatever caused her ire had to do with him. But she'd barely spared that attention as she breezed past him. Being ignored burned a pit into his stomach, and he wondered if he'd hurt Caitlyn just as badly. He also worried about her moving through the keep alone at night. He'd barely taken a seat when the commotion started, so he slipped toward the wall after Caitlyn passed him and moved along it until he passed through the doors she'd used.

When she left the arrow slit, Alex feared that she had caught sight of him. He wasn't prepared to talk to her, but he could not overlook her need for protection. He ducked into an alcove and peeked around the tapestry. His lips drew tight with annoyance at himself when he realized Caitlyn had nearly seen him. He breathed easier when he observed she carried the dirk he'd given her and trained her to use. He caught sight of her checking for the dirk he was grateful she kept hidden in her skirts. But his heart raced as she took off toward the stairs, then raced to climb them. He feared he was creating too much noise as he followed at a distance. He remained in the shadows until he watched the door close behind her. He hurried after her and arrived at her door in time to hear the lock click.

Alex loathed stalking Caitlyn from the shadows, inadvertently scaring her, but letting her risk her safety was unconscionable. However, he chided himself for the thought as he made his way to his chamber, forsaking the evening meal. He was incapable of doing much if a man really attacked her, or God forbid, several men were there. But too many years of friendship, and a pledge to Innes and Collette that he would always watch over Caitlyn and Cairren, weren't easily cast aside.

Alone in his chamber, Alex stared at the empty bed. He had not coupled with a woman since before his injuries. He never brought women to his chamber in Mangerton, but neither had he gone to any woman's croft or room at the tavern since regaining consciousness. He doubted any of the widows or bored matrons who usually flirted with him would take an interest during this visit. But he couldn't fool himself. He had wanted no woman in his bed but Caitlyn for years. He wasn't a monk, but she was who he always thought of, and who he envisioned sharing his chamber one day at Mangerton.

Alex heaved a sigh as he stripped off his clothes. Knowing the night's inevitable progress once he retired, he figured he should get the scant sleep he could. It didn't matter if he stayed awake for a few more hours or merely woke during the early morning. He only ever managed a few.

Alex spun around. His right hand struggled to grasp his sword while holding his left arm, which was attached to his shoulder by a few sinews. He glanced down at his feet and found Brice unconscious, blood dripping from his temple, although he wasn't searching for Brice. There was someone else he had to find. But when Brice groaned, Alex's attention snapped to his younger brother. He sheathed his sword and grabbed Brice by his collar. Keeping his head on a swivel and praying his left arm didn't fall from his body, he dragged Brice off the battle-field. He found the Armstrong men waiting with their horses and left Brice with them.

There was someone else he had to find though he still didn't know who it was. Once more trying to hold on to his arm, his eyes scanned the pandemonium playing out before him. Rain washed the blood from his injured shoulder, leaving pud-dles of it at his feet. He pushed his sodden ebony hair from his eyes as he tried to catch sight of whoever his mind insisted he find. His gaze alighted on a solitary figure standing in the middle of the melee. It was a woman, and he recognized her even in the dark.

"Caitlyn!" Alex cried out as he tried to run toward her. Agonizing pain rent through him, but he pushed himself to reach Caitlyn. Hearing his voice, she turned to him, her face bloody and her gown torn. He leapt over the bodies strewn be-fore him and weaved past enemy combatants, singularly focused on reaching her. As he neared, he stumbled and pitched forward. He caught himself before he fell, but his half-severed arm swung at his side. He looked back at Caitlyn as his arm seemed to grow until his fingers dug into the dirt. He attempted a step forward, but his mangled arm remained stuck in the mud.

Alex locked his eyes on Caitlyn and watched a swarm of Scotts charging toward her. He peered down at his arm. He knew he had to choose. He knew he couldn't keep both his arm and Caitlyn. It took no thought to decide. He wrenched his body away from his arm, which stood like a solitary tree trunk. Running once more, he was nearly within Caitlyn's reach. She *lifted her arms to him. Fear flooded him, but for a reason he didn't expect. He feared his missing arm might revolt her or that she might pity him. But all he saw was Caitlyn's loving eyes. But he'd paused, and in that moment of indecision, the Scotts reached Caitlyn. He watched as swords thrust through her, and her back arched as she fell forward.*

Alex bellowed his rage as he pulled his sword from its scabbard and charged toward Caitlyn's attackers. Yet he was far too late. Her body hit the ground and seemed to fracture into a cloud of dust that billowed where she'd just stood. Alex swept his sword through the air, vanquishing all of Caitlyn's attackers. But it mattered not that he defeated them. Caitlyn was gone. He'd chosen her over his arm, but what good had it done? She was dead, and naught remained.

Alex woke with a start, sitting upright in his bed. His ears rang with such ferocity that he didn't even notice the pain in his arm. He swept his gaze around the dark chamber, uncertain where he was at first and feeling panicked. As he recognized the décor, he realized he was at court. His breathing slowed, but his pounding heart threatened to steal the shallow breaths he managed. He stared down at his left shoulder, uncertain if he would even find his arm. The dream had been so vivid that it nearly convinced him he'd left his arm behind, and without its normal pain, he felt disoriented.

As Alex recalled every moment of his nightmare, bile rose through his chest and into his throat. He sprang from the bed and barely made it to the chamber pot before it spewed forward. He heaved over and over, only acidic bile coming forth since he'd missed the evening meal. When he was finally through, he wiped his mouth on a drying linen and chewed a sprig of mint. He glanced at the window embrasure, and no light peeked around the corners of the cow hide that covered the opening.

Alex realized it was only the middle of the night.

He'd gotten far less sleep than he did on his usual restless nights. He moved to the opposite side of the bed from where he'd woken. He realized he must have thrashed even more than usual because he drenched the sheets almost the entire width of the bed. He positioned himself on the edge in a dry spot and tried to relax. He focused on relaxing each toe before relaxing his ankles, then his calves. He moved on to his thighs, imagining he could get each muscle to ease as his mind calmed. He kept his eyes closed, praying a miracle might strike, and he could fall back to sleep. On the best of nights, he fell back to sleep by the time he reached his waist. But that night, he attempted to relax his earlobes and was still wide awake.

I have to see her. I have to see for myself that she's safe. I can't go now, but I can be in the chapel before her. I can be in the Great Hall when she arrives to break her fast. But what will I do when she goes for her walk? I won't head to the lists. I won't be going to check a steed I can't mount without a block or help. I'll have to see her in the chapel or the Great Hall. Those are my only chances. But I won't breathe easy until I do.

I know it's only a dream. I know it's not real. But it always feels so bluidy real. Caity has never been in my nightmares. She's filled plenty of my dreams, but they were back when I had happy ones. I chose her, and she still died. I couldn't get to her. I couldn't protect her. She needs—she deserves—a husband who can. If I see her and know she's fine, I don't need to talk to her. I can still avoid her. I don't want to. Not even for a fucking moment. But why drive yourself barmy hearing her voice, smelling her myrrh fragrance, seeing the flecks of green in her gray eyes—the ones I memorized years ago? What good will it do either of you? The sooner she understands she should look elsewhere, the better for her.

Alex lay in bed awake for hours before he rose to dress for Mass. He was among the first to arrive, so he positioned himself in the first pew after the ones the ladies-in-waiting normally occupied. He chose the opposite side from where Caitlyn routinely sat in the hopes of a better view. When he heard people approaching, he slipped to his knees and bent his head as though in reverent prayer. He hadn't entirely abandoned God, nor did he think God had entirely abandoned him. But he felt overlooked, and he wasn't certain if he was prepared to forgive God for that.

He kept his head bowed until the liturgy began. He attempted a surreptitious glance toward the ladies-in-waiting, but his moss-green eyes suddenly locked with a pair the exact shade of pewter. Caitlyn's expression did nothing to warm toward him. He expected to see pity, but after his brusque attitude the night prior, there was no pity, hurt, disdain, or even confusion. There was nothing. It was as though she didn't see him despite looking directly at him. She turned away as though she'd glanced at a stranger, not a lifelong friend and a once-potential suitor. Alex's blood ran cold. He couldn't court her, but he hadn't intended to ruin their friendship.

FIVE

Anger vibrated through Caitlyn's body as she felt Alex's eyes remain on her. She hadn't overcome the desire to stare at him, but she'd kept her expression studiously blank lest she crumble into tears. Heartbreak shot through her as their eyes met, but now only anger remained. She directed it toward herself for not having the willpower to ignore Alex. She directed it toward him for being hurtful and distant. And she directed it to whichever bastard had changed Alex and left him so bitter. She'd seen the change in his eyes the night before when he refused to meet her gaze.

It shocked Caitlyn just as much as it did others when she noticed Alex's scarred face and realized his left arm no longer worked. She understood the two injuries were significant and no one could overlook them. Yet until his disdainful treatment of her, she'd still thought of him as the man she'd adored since she was a child and fallen in love with as a woman. She'd believed Alex's sentiments matched hers, especially since he'd visited court more frequently over the past couple years. She'd written to her parents when Alex seemed to disappear for the past six months. All they knew was he'd been in a battle, and the situation remained tense with the Scotts. The ease with which he dismissed her last night felt like a mockery of everything she thought they shared.

The Mass continued around her, but she barely noticed as she received the Eucharist or as they passed around the pax board. She heard none of the hymns, even though she knew she sang along. By the end of the morning service, her anger dulled to strong irritation. But she refused to allow Alex's foulness to destroy her day. She intended to go riding with her guards, so she hurried to the stables after filing out of her pew and following the other women from the chapel. She forewent the morning meal, knowing her guards carried dried beef and dried fruit that they would share with her. It was a familiar routine.

Caitlyn noticed Alex followed her at a distance to the bailey. He hung back, only watching her, so she made no effort to acknowledge him. Not so long ago, he would have joined her, and they would have raced across the meadow and up to the ridge with a vista of a flower-filled valley and the Highland mountains in the distance. Rather than have her friend join her, she couldn't wait to escape. She mounted with ease and slipped her feet into the stirrups, turning her horse away from the stables and Alex. Her guards formed a ring around her, and she didn't glance back as they clattered through the gates.

Alex watched Caitlyn's rigid posture when she noticed him again. He didn't approach, despite wanting to speak to her. However, he was unwilling to give her a false sense of hope. He was certain it was better to cut their ties so that his intentions could not be mistaken. Guilt nipped at him that he shouldn't make this decision solely based on his desires. But he worried about her safety, and if he couldn't protect Caitlyn with his sword, he would protect her by keeping his distance. While filing out of the chapel, he'd overheard some ladies talking as they glanced back at him several times. He learned what Margaret said in the Great Hall, which explained Caitlyn's subsequent actions. His lips had twitched to witness that Caitlyn's temper and loyalty were as they'd always been: fierce.

However, Alex chided himself since it—*he*—wasn't what he wanted for Caitlyn. He'd feared people disparaging him, and, in turn, humiliating Caitlyn if people linked her to him. He strengthened his resolve to keep his distance. Watching her ride out, knowing he couldn't join her, made that goal easier. It also stung and brought back waves of bitterness. Rather than seek his men and train with his knives as he'd begun doing at Mangerton, he retreated to his chamber. He swore he wasn't going there to sulk. He spared his men the embarrassment of having their incapable tánaiste pretend he could still fight.

Alex hadn't napped since his recovery from the fever that took hold for more than a fortnight when his wound became infected. But he toed off his boots and reclined on his bed. He stared at the canopy overhead and forced himself to think about the outstanding matter with the Scotts rather than a chestnut-haired beauty. He was certain the Bruce sided with the Armstrongs and Elliots, but he also suspected it came with a price. He tried to imagine the various outcomes and consequences and how he needed to handle them.

His mind jumped from one idea to another, a beehive of thoughts, so it surprised him when he woke. He hadn't realized he'd been sleepy or that he was drifting off. Ringing bells permeated Alex's mental fog, and he realized he'd slept through the morning all the way to the midday meal. It was the first time in months that nightmares didn't wake him, and he felt rested after months of physical and mental exhaustion.

I didn't sleep well last night. I suppose I thought seeing Caitlyn at the evening meal, even if I didn't want to speak to her, would make me feel better. This morning was no better. So what else is different?

Alex glanced around the chamber, his eyes alighting on the window embrasure. Light poured through the opening, and the room was bright.

Is it the dark that gives me the nightmares? Is it because it was so dark that day? I can't very well spend my days sleeping. What would I do at home? Prowl through the keep like a wraith? But I've underestimated how much better I feel sleeping without waking in a panic. It's been so long. Mayhap lighting candles to burn through the night could help. If it were brighter in here at night, mayhap then I could sleep.

How many candles do I need? At least a dozen. I can't ask for that many. But I could go into town and buy more. Dare I go alone? Of course you do. You're not a woman fearing a mon accosting her and stealing her virginity. While you don't swing a sword anymore, you're still a mon. And a large one at that. You can manage a trip into town without your nursemaids. Get a hold of yourself.

Alex slid from the bed and donned his boots once again. He swept his eyes over the chamber, noticing where he could place candles and how many might fit on each surface. As long as nothing caught fire and burned down the keep, he might get a full night's sleep.

Don't go being overly ambitious. A few more hours should suffice. Aught must be better than the three or four I usually get. Even one more hour should make a tremendous difference. I need a satchel and my coin.

Once Alex had what he needed, he felt almost

giddy as he left his chamber. The prospect of solving his nightmares gave him renewed hope. If he could put the gruesome images behind him, then he might feel a touch more normal, a touch more like his old self. He made his way to the Great Hall, where he joined his men for the midday meal. They asked if he wished them to accompany him when he explained he was going into town. He declined, and he noticed their skeptical glances, but none naysaid him.

With a slight spring in his step, Alex walked through Stirling. While it was excruciating when people jostled his arm, no one paid him any attention. No one recoiled from his face or stared at his lame arm. They were all too busy going about their business. He found the candlestick maker and slipped into the shop. A distinct scent he would recognize anywhere greeted him. The sweet smell of myrrh didn't come from the candles. It could only come from one woman in all of Stirling. The woman whose grandfather had once been an Arab fragrance merchant, and whose French mother and Scots sister also wore the exotic scent.

Caitlyn glanced over her shoulder as she heard the door open, and Alex registered her surprise when she recognized him. She dipped her chin and flashed him a brief smile that appeared pained. He was at a loss as to what to do. They were the only customers in the shop. As he browsed, he realized he knew nothing about picking out candles. He'd never considered them, since his mother oversaw such household matters. He was aware there were different kinds of candles, but beyond that, he realized he had no clue what to ask for. He glanced back at Caitlyn, who swiftly turned her attention away. Clenching his jaw, he accepted he needed help.

"Lady Caitlyn, good day," Alex said as he approached.

"Armstrong," Caitlyn dipped her head again. She'd never addressed him by his clan's name before. He couldn't think of any greater distance she could put between them, short of running to the northern Highlands. He recognized she chafed at his formality and was making a point. One that he realized was almost as painful as his scar when he nicked it with his razor. If she felt how he did, he regretted his decision.

"My lady, I admit I'm at a loss. Would you please help me?" Alex held his breath, feeling humbled and foolish. Caitlyn shifted away from him, and he thought she intended to deny him. He nearly sighed when she turned to face him. But she said nothing, her head canted slightly to the right, as though she were impatient to finish their conversation. "I came to buy a dozen or so candles, but I don't know what I should ask for or a reasonable price."

"A dozen?" Caitlyn cocked an eyebrow. "That shall make for enchanting lighting."

Alex heard the frigid tone that once held mirth. He would disabuse her of the idea that he was creating a love nest for another woman. "I believe it will help me sleep." He waited for the expected pity. The more Caitlyn learned, Alex believed, the more it was inevitable. Instead, she shrugged.

"Beeswax will be more expensive than tallow, but a dozen tallow candles burning in a single chamber will smell horrid. A pigsty in summer smells better. If you have the coin, I'd purchase tall beeswax ones, but they won't last more than a couple nights if you plan to burn them the entire time." Caitlyn offered her advice and turned back to the candles she examined, dismissing Alex. Despite himself, he found he wanted to continue the conversation.

"Which would you pick?" Alex pressed. Caitlyn glanced at him before pointing across the store.

"There are nice ones over there."

"Caity," Alex said, certain he sounded like a beggar. He regretted it as hurt, then anger, flashed across Caitlyn's face.

"I'm Caity when you need something, Alexander?"

"And I'm Alexander when you're in a snit?"

"In a snit? In that case, good day." Caitlyn abandoned the candles on the counter before her and spun toward the door, her skirts swirling around her ankles. Alex made to reach for her, but his left arm did nothing. She was gone before his right arm could grasp anything but air. The shop door slammed behind her.

Alex examined the candles Caitlyn abandoned. He smelled one, rosemary and lavender. He recalled that was the scent Collette preferred for the rushes throughout Dunure. It was a sense of comfort he hadn't had in years. For a moment, he forgot about his adult life and flashed back to a time when he chased Caitlyn and Cairren through the Great Hall with a toad in each hand. He assumed they ran from him until they crossed the bailey and into the stables. Both girls ran through a pile of hay. He was unprepared for them to each snatch a mouse by the tail and stick it in his face. He'd yelped and dropped the toads.

"Can I help you, my lord?" The shopkeeper approached, but he frowned and glanced at the door.

"My lady needed to depart, but I wish to get these candles for her. Do you have a dozen more?"

"You want four-and-ten candles?" The man's skepticism was obvious. When Alex pulled a pouch that tinkled with coins, the man hurried to count out the additional sticks. He wrapped them in cheese cloth before handing them to Alex in exchange for the money. Alex dropped them into his satchel and thanked the man. When he stepped into the street, he turned toward the castle, but he had no wish to return.

Noise from a nearby tavern drew his attention. He'd never been given to drinking with abandon, but a few drams of whisky tempted him. He arrived at the Merry Widow, surprised at the crowd for the middle of the day. It was a popular place at night, aptly nicknamed the Merry Widow for the women from court who held their assignations there. He recognized no one, which relieved him. A little anonymity suited him as he drowned his sorrows. He found a seat in a dim corner, hoping to not draw attention.

"And what would a fine mon like yourself be having today?" A serving wench with deep cleavage approached him. She leaned forward, and Alex wondered if her breasts might spill loose. They tempted him more than the whisky. The woman's dark hair reminded him of Caitlyn, and he found his right hand rising to touch it. He caught himself and rested his hand on the table instead.

"What're you offering?" Alex countered.

"Aught that you like, my lord." The woman plopped herself onto Alex's lap and brushed the back of her hand against his cheek. She froze when she felt the rigid scar. He watched her peer closer in the dim light. The puckered skin ran from the corner of his right eye down the center of his cheek to just below his chin. His beard covered half, but unfortunately it wasn't the worse part. The woman drew her hand back as though she'd touched something filthy. "A bowl of pottage or some whisky?"

Alex nodded to both as the woman scrambled off his lap and hurried toward the kitchen. His pride stung even though he'd received the same reaction from other women. He'd seen his reflection enough times to understand the scar was vicious and angry. The surrounding skin was red while the scar was white in stark contrast. It had relieved him too much that he hadn't lost his eye to worry about his appearance at first. But it hadn't taken him long to wish he'd lost both eyes instead.

Another wench, with just as ample a bosom and her skirts hiked up on both sides, approached. Alex sat in such a way that his long legs were to the side of the table to avoid bumping it. The brazen woman straddled his legs and ran her hand down his chest and over his abdomen. He recognized her from several visits ago, and he recalled he'd enjoyed an evening with her. From the seductive smile, Alex was certain she recognized him, too. As she shifted, he felt his cock swell. It had been so long since he'd been with a woman that he felt overly eager when her hand trailed down to cup his rod.

"Mmm. You remember me, don't you, my lord?" The woman purred as she leaned forward to murmur in Alex's ear. "I certainly remember you."

Alex rested his right hand on her waist before sliding it to her bottom. He peered at the woman's blonde hair and brown eyes. A pang of disappointment surged through him, since it wasn't the one woman he wanted more than any other. But he'd finally found one after so many months of drought. She was but a mirage when she tried to lift his left hand to place it on her breast. She felt the dead weight and let it go, watching it drop and hang lifeless. Alex squeezed her backside with his good hand, and the women offered him a coy smile.

"Remind me of your name, lass." Alex's deep voice had always been one of his secret weapons to lure women. It rumbled in his chest when he kept it low. The woman rocked her hips forward and pressed her cheek to his, but she recoiled when she felt the scar. Alex watched her turn her head to peer at his face, then shift her gaze to his arm. "You can feel what matters still works."

Alex tried to hide his irritation, but he was growing weary of the women only paying attention to what he couldn't change. The part of him they should be most interested in seemed to get forgotten all too easily.

"Uh, Catriona. Caty," the wench stuttered. Alex nearly pushed her from his lap. He couldn't bear the idea of bedding another woman who shared a diminutive with Caitlyn. It had always felt off to bed other women once he realized he had feelings for Caitlyn, but they'd never declared their feelings or made any agreement that they intended to pursue more than friendship. Yet he drew the line at the same name. While it ensured he cried out the right one, he disgusted himself to even consider it.

"That's my sister's name. It just wouldn't be right," Alex lied, or at least told a half-truth. Catriona shot him a disdainful expression before moving on to another customer as the first woman returned with his food and drink. She returned several more times, but only with more whisky until the room grew blurry to Alex's heavy-lidded eyes. He'd seen the two women who'd approached him whispering to the other whores. It took little imagination to recognize they warned them away from him.

Knowing he was close to growing too intoxicated to make his way back to the keep, he rose on unsteady feet. If he remained, he was certain to pass out and wind up robbed. He staggered from the alehouse and wobbled his way back to the keep. The guards ogled him, and he perceived they struggled not to laugh at him. He could only imagine what he looked like as he stumbled, and his left arm swung beside him. He hadn't bothered to take his sword with him, so he had nothing to turn over.

Alex set a course for a side door he was certain should get him close to the stairs he needed to find his chamber. But a peal of laughter made his cock harden more than it had when the whores rubbed against him. His head whipped toward the sound, and he regretted the quick movement. He caught sight of Caitlyn at the same time she spotted him. She appeared ready to hurry her friends along, but Alex stalked toward her, suddenly much steadier on his feet. He kept approaching, even as ladies-in-waiting had to move out of his path.

"Alex?" Caitlyn hissed.

Alex ignored Caitlyn's repetition of his name as he steered them toward the undercroft. When they entered the secluded area, his good arm snaked around her and pulled her close. He felt her come willingly, stepping toward him the moment his arm came around her. He gazed into her upturned face and recognized the desire that shone in her eyes. He brought his mouth crashing down on hers as he pressed her back to the wall. He swept his tongue across her lips, and she opened to him. A flash of curiosity crossed his mind as he wondered who taught her to kiss with her mouth open.

Caitlyn clung to his doublet, fearing she'd either trip over her skirts or her knees would buckle. She felt Alex's entire body press against her as her back met the stone wall. She reveled in the feeling of finally experiencing her first kiss with the only man who'd ever held her interest. But the moment she opened to him and his tongue slid past her teeth, she could taste the whisky. She shoved at his chest and fought to break free.

"What?" Alex demanded as he reeled back from her pushes. "You wanted it."

"You're drunk."

"So. Drunk or sober, I know what a woman feels like when she wants a mon."

"Then find one who does," Caitlyn snapped.

"Come on, Caity." Alex's words slurred, making Caitlyn's name sound like Casey. "You've wanted me for years, and I've wanted up your skirt since you were auld enough to hike them for a mon."

"Alex," Caitlyn hissed. "I don't understand what's happened to you other than what I can see, but I'm leaving. I won't listen to this, and I'll gut you if I stay." Caitlyn made to step around Alex, but he shifted to block her.

"Stay, Caity. Find out how good what we've both wanted feels."

"You think I want to be with a drunk mon? Find yourself a whore."

"Why find someone else when you're right here?" Something in Alex's inebriated mind kept telling him to stop talking. As his last words spewed from his mouth, he had a feeling he'd really erred. When Caitlyn's knee came up to his groin, he barely backed away in time. It made her pitch toward him. His arm wrapped around her waist and grasped her backside.

"I'm not your whore or anyone else's, Alex. Would you force me?"

Alex released Caitlyn immediately, some of the alcohol clearing from his mind. "Never. I thought you wanted this, wanted us."

"Us? There is no us. You ignore me, then you call me a whore. You are not the mon you once were," Caitlyn spat.

"I know I'm not, Caity. Every woman who glances at me knows that. I'd find a whore if she'd take me. I'd find one who reminds me of you, and I'd pleasure her for a month of Sundays. But who wants a disfigured mon?"

"I would if you weren't such a shite pile." Caitlyn pushed Alex hard enough for him to stumble backward. She bolted to her right, lifting her skirts to her shins. She never thought Alex might force her, but she didn't want to remain for the wretched conversation they were having. Neither would say anything that didn't hurt the other.

"You'd have half a mon?" Alex questioned as he caught Caitlyn's arm and swung her around.

"Half? The only thing I notice missing is your honor," Caitlyn stated as she swept a look of disgust over him. "You know me not at all, Alexander. If you did, you'd understand what matters."

"What matters is that I'm no longer a mon who has any right asking for your hand," Alex stated.

"But you're the right mon to ask for my virginity." Caitlyn thrust her face forward to bring her to eye level as Alex bent over her. "You'd disgrace me. I think you believe *I'm* good enough to marry *you*."

"What the devil are you talking aboot?" Alex demanded, surprised by Caitlyn's assertion.

"I think you're like all the others. You'd proposition me and learn if I'll whore for you like I live in a harem. Like I'd be lucky to catch a mon like you. That you're too good to stoop to marrying someone brown like me. You really have no honor left. None."

"I never once thought that, Caity. I can't believe you could accuse me of that."

"You can't believe it." Caitlyn pointed to where they'd been standing only minutes ago. "What the hell did you mean when you called me a whore and tried to get me to couple with you against a wall?"

"I did no such—" Alex went silent. He was growing clearer headed as he continued to argue, but he suddenly remembered how their conversation started. He stumbled backward and shook his head. "Caity."

Caitlyn watched as shame washed over Alex's face, and she even thought his eyes misted. But the lighting was too dim in the undercroft to see. She watched his shoulders round, then the grimace of pain. He took three more steps back and turned away.

"No, you don't. You don't get to ruin my first kiss and insult me to boot, then walk away because you realize you're an arse."

"Your first kiss? But I thought…"

"You should have remembered that I have a married sister. You should have remembered that my mother has always done what she can to prepare me for life. You should have remembered that I've been at court for years and have seen and heard things that make Sodom and Gomorrah appear quaint. You are the only mon I've ever kissed, and I will forever remember being called a whore for it."

"I don't know what to say other than I'm sorry. That isn't nearly enough. I never should have approached you while I was drunk. I never should have kissed you when I was. I certainly shouldn't have said any of what I did."

"Then why? You have never treated me like this." Caitlyn crossed her arms, wrapping them around her middle as though she could shield herself.

Alex tilted his head back and closed his eyes. "Because I was angrier than I thought. I was angry that I want you when I shouldn't. I thought to drown my sorrows, even distract myself from wanting you and not having you. But the same thing happens when any woman approaches. They can't flee fast enough once they realize what I am. I took that out on you. I preyed on the assumption that you wanted to kiss me as much as I always do you. I wanted to prove to myself that I'm still a mon."

"Alex," Caitlyn whispered. "I don't even know where to start. You are still a mon." Caitlyn held up her hand to keep Alex from interrupting. "You really take to heart the opinions of whores? Not someone who's known you for as long as she can remember? Is bedding a woman really what makes you a mon? My father wouldn't agree, and he never would stand for you to say such. He didn't teach you to think that way. I'm still standing here, Alex. Did I run away last eve? Did I run from you today because of how you look, or was it from the things you said? The only thing making you less of a mon is the despicable things you've said, not because of your face or your arm."

"But I can't be the mon you need. I can't protect you. I'll only embarrass you. People will gossip that you could do no better than me. And I won't even be able to defend you from those who do."

"Just how dangerous is your clan?" Caitlyn asked with a soft smile.

"What? They aren't dangerous to you. You know that."

"Then why do I suddenly need all this protection? If I were at Mangerton, do you need to defend me from your people?"

"No."

"Then you make no sense."

"And to travel to Mangerton? What happens if we're attacked on the road, and I can't protect you? What if someone attacks our clan because our neighbors believe me weak? You'd be in danger."

"Weak?" Caitlyn's gaze swept over Alex's body, and he witnessed the lust spark again before her eyes met his. He even sensed her sway toward him before she caught herself.

"I can't lead my men anymore. I can't ride out in battle to represent my clan. I can't do the things a laird must. Your parents raised you to marry a laird or an heir."

"That's as true as saying the sky is purple. Did *Maman* train me to be a chatelaine? Yes. But neither she nor Papa expected me to marry a laird or an heir. Cairren married a second son, and she's aulder than me. All my parents wanted for either of us was a happy marriage like theirs. That nearly didn't happen for Cairren. Papa promised not to arrange a marriage for me." Caitlyn paused as she swallowed the lump in her throat. "We didn't think he'd have to."

"Caity, you deserve better."

"Who are you to decide for me? You don't want to be my husband, and you aren't my father. You haven't asked once what I want. And you definitely haven't come close to guessing. Alex, you are a fool." Caitlyn's emotions felt too overwrought after all the anger, hurt, and sadness. She needed space. "I'm walking away now. I can't do this anymore. I don't recognize the mon you've become. And you obviously never knew me."

Alex watched as Caitlyn made her way out of the undercroft. He followed at a discreet distance, watching to ensure she entered the keep safely. Her shoulders were rounded and stooped as though she protected herself from a gusty wind, except there was none. He silently acknowledged he'd done that. He'd blown out the spark that had once been between them.

You wanted to push her away. You couldn't have done a finer job if you'd done it on purpose. What the hell is wrong with you? How could you say any of that to Caity? It was —is—unforgiveable. My father and hers would skelp me alive if she ever told them. Neither of them would accept me treating her, or any lady, how I did. Whisky is no excuse. No one else thought me worthless until today.

Alex ran his hand through his hair as he tried to swallow the sour taste in his mouth. He couldn't guess that he could ever repair the damage he'd done that night, and he didn't feel he deserved to. But he didn't want to hurt Caitlyn any further. He intended to apologize again if she'd hear him out, but he resolved to keep his distance like he should have.

I wanted to be alone to spare her. The only thing I got right was now I'm definitely alone.

SIX

Caitlyn perceived that Alex wanted to apologize for his behavior three nights earlier, but she couldn't bring herself to be near him. She wasn't certain if she would cry or pound her fist into his face, but she was certain she couldn't be rational. She avoided him, entrenching herself among the other ladies, knowing he wouldn't approach. She made sure she was with at least two other women any time she left her chamber. Her heart felt hollow whenever he wasn't near. Then, when he was close, it ached with a ferocity that she feared might kill her.

Alex watched Caitlyn any time she was within sight. He accepted he needed to keep his distance, but he worried obliging her obvious request was only making the damage irreparable. His cheek burned in a way it hadn't in months, and his arm ached more than it ever had. He'd left the candles he purchased for Caitlyn outside her door the morning after their argument. She'd gifted him the briefest nod during Terce before turning back to listen to the liturgy. His suspicions that the dark contributed to his nightmares were right. He slept better once he lit six candles on each bedside table. His body felt more rested than it had since before riding out to Hermitage Castle, but his mind was never at ease.

The only distraction came from his summons back to the Privy Council chamber. He'd waited days to hear the Bruce's decision, and he wanted to have done with the matter. He admitted to himself that he wanted to tuck tail and run home to escape the additional guilt that came from being near Caitlyn. He could endure the jarring six-day ride home if it meant he avoided causing Caitlyn more pain. He admitted to himself that his presence only continued to make matters worse.

"Armstrong," Angus called out to him just before he reached the chamberlain. Alex turned back to the Elliot heir, who hurried along the passageway. Alex intuited something wasn't right. With his voice hushed, Angus said, "They're up to something. I don't know what, but one of my men overheard a Scott say that they needed more coin to make whatever they planned work. My mon couldn't tell what the plan was, but he overheard our clan names. He thinks they're planning an attack while we travel home. I would have my contingent ride with yours if you're agreeable."

Alex listened to Angus, suspicious of what he heard and who he heard it from. But he recognized what Angus shared wasn't implausible. He'd avoided the Scott delegates whenever he could, which wasn't difficult, since he didn't go to the lists. If King Robert acted as Alex expected, it would only fuel the Scotts' ire more.

"We can ride together most of the way. It means riding through Douglas land, but we can give them a wide berth. The Johnstones should have no trouble with us passing through. Ride through my clan's land to avoid the Scotts altogether. You and your men can spend the night at Mangerton before continuing on to Redheugh Tower."

"I appreciate that. I wish to avoid the Hays while we're at it. Lady Sarah Anne and Lady Margaret keep looking in my direction, and I keep avoiding them. The last thing I need is their father finding me and trying to match me with one of them. Good God, I'd chew my leg off at the ankle before being shackled to either of those bitches." Angus scowled.

"Armstrong, Elliot," the chamberlain announced. The two men made their way into the king's meeting room. Neither caught sight of any of the Scott representatives, and Alex was sure his sigh matched Angus's. But it was short lived. They'd just stepped up to the table when they heard their nemeses announced. Alex refused to acknowledge the men as they entered. He watched King Robert watch him before turning his eyes to Angus, then resting on the three Scotts.

Once the six men sat, King Robert steepled his fingers and rested his forefingers against his lips and the tip of his nose, as though he studied each man. Alex was certain the king's mind was already made. This was for show, and it irritated Alex. He wanted to be done, so he could be on the road in the morning. If Angus didn't prepare to leave that soon, Alex intended to depart without him.

"Laird Scott violated the Armstrongs' and Elliots' right to settle on their own land when he launched his attacks," King Robert started. "There is no disputing the boundaries or the deeds the Armstrongs and Elliots hold, just as Alexander pointed out. What has given me pause is how to handle this strife. Your clans have been faithful and loyal to my cause since the beginning; however, you cannot seem to get along. Laird Scott will have to take responsibility for his greediness and arrogance."

Alex wanted to gloat, but he forced his face to remain neutral. The fingers on his right hand dug into the back of his left hand as he fought to keep his arm in place when all he wanted to do was cheer, pack, and leave.

"The Scotts will forfeit any claim they have to this contested land. They will not cross the boundaries into Armstrong or Elliot territory. Additionally, the Scotts shall pay recompense," King Robert declared.

Alex shifted his gaze to watch the Scotts, sensing their anger and wanting to laugh. It was hardly justified. When the man closest to him cast an indignant glare, Alex cocked an eyebrow.

"Do not antagonize them, Armstrong," the Bruce warned, and Alex shifted his focus back at the king. "I have given thought to what the remuneration should be."

The five delegates from the three clans froze. King Robert's tone warned that it would displease someone. Alex prayed it would be the Scotts. His mind jumped from one possibility to the other, and he hoped it involved livestock being transferred to at least the Armstrongs. They'd lost cattle from the Scotts reiving and razing villages along the border.

"The Armstrongs suffered greater losses before you fought. They also grieve the loss of more men than the Elliots." King Robert's eyes darted to Alex, but they didn't meet his gaze. Instead, they focused on his arm before he glanced at Angus. "Consequently, the Scotts shall send seven and a half score coos to the Armstrongs. The Elliots receive five score sheep."

"Your Majesty," the Scott delegate in the middle exclaimed. "You shall ruin us."

"*I* shall ruin you, Collin?" the Bruce asked imperiously. "Mayhap your laird should have thought before he took on a set of allies who protect *my* border. I struggle to feel any sympathy for your clan's fool-hardiness. Be glad I don't give the Armstrongs and Elliots half your land."

"Your Majesty," the Scotts representative sitting farthest from Alex intervened. "We do not deny that you are granting the Armstrongs and Elliots recompense, but we do not have that much livestock to spare."

"Granting us?" Angus demanded as he leaned forward to glower past Alex. "You bluidy maggots stole from us. The king isn't granting us aught. He's ensuring we get back what you took."

"I'm certain you have those seven score coos, Scott," Alex waded in. "Because that's how many you've stolen from us over the past two years. Your people couldn't have eaten that many, and they didn't just disappear. Return what is ours."

"But—" Collin spluttered.

"But naught," King Robert boomed. "You will return the branded livestock, which I'm aware the Armstrongs and Elliots have marked, and you will cease your incursion. If I hear even a dickeybird that you've put a toe on their land, I will strip you of half of yours. You will give up all but the cattle you need to feed your weans and elders. Test me not."

"And how can we be sure we can herd the animals to their land and make it back onto ours safely?" the delegate closest to Alex asked.

"Mayhap these are things your laird should have thought aboot before stealing from us and leading us into a battle he lost," Alex suggested.

"Paul," King Robert glared at the delegate beside Alex. "You will not sway me. You will only irritate me further. Tell Laird Scott he has a moon to herd the animals back to their rightful owners."

"Your Majesty," Angus cut in. "There is still the

matter of the razed villages. We lost crofters, not just warriors. Those who survived not only lost their homes, they lost their crops. Mutton alone will not feed them or pay for new homes."

"You shouldn't have——" the delegate at the far end.

"Shouldn't have what?" Alex asked as he turned to face his enemies. "Shouldn't have made use of our own land? Shouldn't have defeated your pathetic arses?"

"Your clan may have won, but you hardly did," the man taunted.

"Christopher," King Robert spat. "Cease, or you three will find your accommodations moved to my dungeon. Accept your defeat, pay your penalty, and stay on your land. If I hear of any more trouble from the Scotts, I swear I will rain down hellfire. I do not need your clan causing squabbles with clans who need to defend our borders, not themselves."

Alex felt his blood pumping through his body as it suffused his limbs. His anger threatened to boil over, but he kept his expression impassive. He refused to take Christopher's bait and make a fool of himself. Besides, he could irritate all the Scotts more if he didn't respond.

"Smug bastard," Collin mumbled.

"I ken Armstrong's father well, and I ken his parents married long before his birth. Can you say the same for your da? I heard——" Angus leaned forward again.

"I'll——"

"You'll what?" Alex interrupted. "Return our livestock and stay off our land. That's the only thing you'll be doing if you wish to live long enough to grow some whiskers."

"Enough," King Robert declared. "The time for measuring your cocks has come and gone. My decision will not change. If you do not carry my word out within the next moon, I shall get involved in a way that will satisfy no one. Leave."

The five men rose, but once more, no one wished to take the first step. But same as the last time, the Scotts sat closer to the door. Alex raised his arm and gestured toward it. He no longer hid his smugness as he nodded his canted head. The Scotts marched toward the door, looking like petulant children trying not to leave in a huff. Alex turned toward King Robert and bowed low, careful not to bang his arm against the massive wood table. He and Angus took their leave together. Once in the passageway, Alex and Angus stopped to watch the Scotts disappear at the other end.

"Will you be ready to leave in the morn?" Alex asked.

"Aye. If it weren't so late in the day, I would leave now. I don't trust that we resolved this."

"We most certainly didn't resolve aught. And if what your mon overheard is right, the Scotts don't believe it is either. We all were aware the Bruce intended to order them to pay restitution. I'd hoped we'd get all our animals back, but I hadn't held my breath. I'm sure they didn't think the penalty levied against them would be that steep. If they were already planning a way to attack us before this, it's a guarantee that they will act now."

"Do you think they might strike here? The king would know they are the likely culprits after what he just watched."

"The Bruce would, but I still think they would do something within the castle."

"We'd do well to remain with our men," Angus suggested. Alex tried not to bristle. He was unsure if Angus's comment was more directed at him, but it felt that way.

66

"I'm going back to my chamber to draft a missive to my father," Alex explained.

"I should do the same, but I will meet with my men first and tell them we leave in the morn."

"I will find mine after I get my missive to a messenger," Alex stated. The men shook forearms and parted ways. Alex wound his way through the keep, his hand on one of his dirks, his senses keen to anyone who might approach. He glanced out of an arrow slit and noticed menacing clouds moving over the keep; a hellacious storm was brewing. He wished to be in his chamber for the night before it began.

SEVEN

Caitlyn noticed Alex entering the Great Hall for the evening meal. She noticed everything about him, even though she still wasn't prepared to make amends. Her feelings remained hurt by the things he'd said, but she scrutinized him, hoping he didn't note her increased curiosity. She noticed the small grimaces and flinches when he moved the wrong way or his left arm bumped into things. She observed how his right cheek sometimes twitched as though he wanted to scratch his scar, but he fought the temptation. But the most painful thing to watch was how others treated him.

Caitlyn told Margaret that Alex wasn't a leper the first night he arrived, but most still treated him as such. She'd once been jealous when other women showered Alex with attention. She'd envied them when he partnered with them to dance, and she'd felt ill when she realized the familiarity he had with some. However, now her chest burned at the injustice and indignity of watching people shun him for his appearance. Women she was certain he'd bedded, or at least used to flirt with, turned up their noses because he was no longer the handsome man he'd once been. Men who'd respected him and even feared him now smirked and made snide comments that Caitlyn overheard far too often.

She fought not to lose her temper on his behalf, but she failed more than once. She hadn't thrown wine on anyone like she had Margaret, but she'd had cross words with Sarah Anne and a few other ladies. She pointed out how shallow they were since not that long ago they fawned over Alex. But none of the women seemed concerned about her observations of their character. She'd refused to dance with men she noticed were rude to Alex or spoke ill of him within her hearing.

She struggled to reconcile her anger on Alex's behalf with the anger she felt toward him. It had peaks and troughs, and it unsettled her. But a lifetime of friendship was hard to overlook, especially when she discovered what Alex's life had become. He was a pariah, and there was nothing Alex or she could do. She recalled Alex denying that he believed she was good enough for him, but not the other way around. However, she'd always struggled with knowing people would speak poorly of Alex if they ever married. She could no more change her skin color than he could fix his injuries.

"Still gawking at him," Catherine MacFarlane commented as the ladies took their seats for the evening meal. "You'd make a fine pair."

The surrounding ladies tittered, but Blythe Dunbar slammed her hand on the table. She wasn't prone to bouts of bad temper, but she was Caitlyn's friend. "At least she'd make a pair. After Laird Gunn's disgrace and your unfortunate ties to him, I don't see your uncle making a match for you. Laird MacFarlane's begging up every tree, but no one wants you. I'd say Caitlyn's closer to the altar than you are."

Caitlyn sat speechless as Blythe spoke aloud a

well-known fact that no one discussed. Laird Edgar Gunn involved himself in a plot to ruin Laird Brodie Campbell's marriage to Laurel Ross, a hellion no one expected to wed. The MacFarlanes were the Campbells' ally. When Catherine's cousin Andrew, heir to Clan MacFarlane, also entered the wagers against the couple, it only made matters worse. The potential match between Edgar and Catherine disintegrated when Laird MacFarlane learned of his son's and potential nephew's-by-marriage perfidy. It left Catherine practically at the altar without a groom.

"A mon doesn't have to marry Caitlyn to get what he's after," Sarah Anne weighed in. "And if they did, which none of them need to do, then the only one who'd shame himself that much is a mon no one else wants."

"I am sitting here," Caitlyn spat.

"So?" Sarah Anne genuinely appeared perplexed that Caitlyn's presence should make her curb her tongue.

"Summon a midwife. Stand at the foot of my bed while she examines me," Caitlyn suggested. "She'll tell you what we all know is the truth: I'm a maiden. But when she's done with me, mayhap she'll have time for your sister. Though I doubt it's even worth it since the woman will find naught."

"At least that insinuates men want me," Margaret gloated.

"You hen-wit," Caitlyn crowed. "It can't be both. Either no one wants me, and I'm untouched, or I'm the whore you claim. Do make up your mind. It grows tiresome waiting."

Margaret glowered at Caitlyn, having no comeback to the obvious. The women lobbed insults at Caitlyn frequently, but Caitlyn reminded herself that, as much as they hurt, they were only half of what her darker skinned sister endured.

"Liam Oliphant is courting my sister," Sarah Anne boasted, but it fell on deaf ears. Everyone was aware the man was hardly a catch. Nelson Mac-Dougall had been courting Margaret, but he'd died in a battle against the Campbells, when he, Edgar Gunn, Andrew MacFarlane and a handful of other men kidnapped Laurel and threatened to kill her to end the Campbell-Ross alliance.

"And tossing her skirts along with every whore in Stirling. I hope you don't catch aught, *Maggie*." Caitlyn stressed the nickname Margaret loathed, claiming only chamber maids had the name Maggie.

"At least I'm not brown," Margaret hurled back at Caitlyn. It was Margaret's fallback insult whenever she could think of nothing better. Caitlyn had heard it from the woman and others enough times that it no longer hurt, but it still angered her.

"Aye, and I can enjoy a summer day without looking like a bushel of shriveled hindberries." Caitlyn grinned as she recalled the sunburn the woman received while observing an archery tournament. She'd matched the raspberries Caitlyn called her.

"That happened because I'm a proper lady. *Ma mère n'est pas une pute française,*" Margaret sneered. Caitlyn had heard her mother called a French whore nearly as often as she'd heard people label her a Saracen harem member. How she wished no Scot ever rode off to the Crusades. They would be none the wiser to how others lived in far-flung locales. "Naught to say now?"

"*Au moins, mon visage n'a pas l'air d'essayer toujours de chier,*" Caitlyn grinned, knowing neither Sarah Anne nor Margaret spoke French well enough to understand, but Blythe did.

"Her face does look like she's always trying to shite!" Blythe giggled. Margaret snapped her mouth shut, realizing she couldn't hurl rivaling insults in either language at Caitlyn. She squirmed in her seat, but Sarah Anne wasn't finished.

"The only thing I can say in your favor is that at least you don't resemble a Saracen as much as your filthy sister. God made her that dark to show the evil within her."

Caitlyn rose from the table and leaned over until her nose nearly touched Sarah Anne's. "The only reason I'm not slapping the smirk off your hideous face is because the queen is present. You'd be wise to stay away from me when her presence isn't there to save you. I have my mother's French temper. My handprint will leave your cheek redder than any summer sun." Caitlyn flashed her gaze at Margaret and the other ladies who'd encouraged her nemeses by nodding and smiling. "The only thing in your favor is that you're not *faux-cul* like some. Your face is always ugly, but never one way in front of me and another behind my back."

Caitlyn left the table as the music began and wove through the diners, preparing for the evening's entertainment. She found a spot in line for a country reel, forcing herself to calm. Her racing heart made heat pour from her cheeks. She glanced at Alex, who watched her. His inquisitive stare told her he'd seen her exchange with Margaret. A dip of her chin was all she gave him before she turned her attention to her partner. She wanted to groan. Liam Oliphant stood before her.

"Lady Caitlyn, you were having a lively conversation with Lady Margaret," the other woman's suitor mused.

"We were of a different opinion on a matter," Caitlyn hedged, wishing the musicians hurried to play the tune that way she could switch to another partner.

"Aboot Alexander Armstrong, no doubt," Liam smirked. Caitlyn said nothing, which flustered Liam. "Am I right?"

"If you have no doubt, then you are certain you are right. Does it matter if I disagree?"

"Not you too," Liam grumbled.

"Me too, what?" Caitlyn wished she hadn't asked once the words left her mouth. She regretted engaging with Liam.

"You have a way with words that's reminiscent of the Shrew of Stirling," Liam stated.

"I would err on the side of caution speaking aboot Lady Campbell like that. Her brother arrived yesterday." Caitlyn pressed her lips together as Liam frantically searched for Montgomery Ross as the music guided them to switch partners. She glanced at Alex, wishing he might partner with her to rescue her from the men, but she accepted it was more likely to snow in hell before he would join the dancers. She realized that despite their heated words, she still trusted him with her wellbeing.

"Lady Caitlyn," her new partner greeted her with a lascivious smile. She couldn't recall the man's name, but she believed he was a Maxwell. It was moments like this when she wished Lowland men wore plaids like the Highlanders. It made it easier to recognize from which clan they hailed. Caitlyn knew birds of a feather often flocked together from the same clan. If she could avoid men she was certain held little value in honoring a woman's reputation, she might have an easier life at court. "You look enchanting tonight."

"Thank you," Caitlyn nodded and forced a smile. She regretted it, since the man took it as encouragement and drew her closer. "You know my name, but I am at a loss to yours."

"Christopher Scott, my lady."

Caitlyn's eyes darted to Alex, who'd risen and glared at her. He must have read her panic because his expression remained angry, but she was certain it was no longer directed at her.

"Worried Armstrong won't enjoy watching us together?" Christopher guessed. "Will he pry you out of my arms? That shall be hard when I have one arm around you and the other swatting him away. However will he move me and take hold of you?"

"Take hold? You assume I wouldn't go to him," Caitlyn stated as she peered down her nose at her partner, which was no small feat since she was at least two heads shorter than him. The music called for her to twirl, allowing her to spot Alex standing near the wall, watching them. A small flick of his hand told her what she needed. When the music called for her to step back from Christopher, she moved far enough that it forced the woman to her right to take her place.

"I'll take you to your chamber," Alex said.

"Thank you," Caitlyn whispered. "He did it purposely to antagonize you."

"Did he scare you, Caity?" Caitlyn hesitated to be truthful, but that hesitation told Alex everything he needed to understand. "I know you didn't want to dance with him, but you must avoid the Scotts, even after I leave. It's no secret that I'm close to your family. I don't want them anywhere near you, especially since I can't protect you."

Caitlyn stopped short, glancing back over her shoulder. "Am I still with him? Did I not know I could turn to you and be safe? Stop saying you can't protect me." She wanted to stomp her foot by the time she finished speaking.

"We're fortunate he didn't follow us. What could I have done?"

"Then what's the point of you even walking with

me, Alex. If you're so worthless, then why bother with me?" Caitlyn didn't wait for Alex's answer. She took the stairs they reached as quickly as she dared in the dim light. She sensed Alex followed her this time, but he said nothing. When she reached her door, she glanced back. She recognized his form at the top of the stairs before she slipped into her chamber.

Alex sighed in frustration and ran his hand over his face. He'd forgotten for a moment that he was incapable of defending Caitlyn like he once had. His need to get her away from Christopher had been so urgent that he hadn't thought about what he might do if the man followed them. It wasn't until they were halfway to Caitlyn's chamber that he realized he might have endangered her more by taking her from the crowded Great Hall into an empty passageway.

He trudged down the stairs and made his way toward the wing that housed the bachelors' quarters. A clap of thunder made his heart drop and his gut tighten. A flash of lightning made him glance toward an arrow slit. Three more rapid rumbles of thunder made him freeze. The brief interval told him they were practically in the storm's eye. More lightning flashed, but he couldn't move his feet. As he continued to gaze out of the gap between the stones, he no longer noticed the bailey but the battlefield that haunted him now during his waking hours.

He was certain he felt his horse's gait beneath him as his steed clomped through the mud until Alex feared the beast getting stuck. He dismounted into the sludge that came up his shins. He struggled to pry his feet free as he twisted toward the hillside that overflowed with Scotts hurtling toward the Armstrongs and Elliots.

His head didn't move while he peered out the arrow slit, yet he was sure he searched for Brice. Part of his mind recognized he couldn't find Brice since he stood in Stirling Castle, not Mangerton, but the need to find where his younger brother fought pinched like a vise.

"Brice," Alex whispered to no one.

Another flash of lightning brought his memory back to the Scott he battled as his back brushed against Brice's, reassuring him that his brother was still there.

He struggled to keep his balance as his enemy sliced his sword through the air, and the impact rattled Alex's bones. He defeated the man before him as he thrust a dirk into the man's throat, but as he did, he realized he no longer felt Brice behind him. Yanking his knife free, he spun around and watched Brice crumple to the ground. He bent to check if Brice lived, so he was unprepared for the man who ran toward them. It was too late when he sensed the warrior's approach. Alex straightened and stepped over Brice, shielding him as he always promised his mother. He didn't raise his sword in time to block the downward momentum that nearly severed his arm from his shoulder. As the force threw him backward, a sgian dubh pierced his cheek. He felt his weight drag the knife down his cheek as much as his enemy's strength did.

Alex's eyes riveted on the lightning that continued to flash, but the thunder was now the screams of pain and clashes of metal. He trembled as memory after memory flooded him, so powerful that he could smell the death from that day. The part of his mind that was still aware of where he was, told him to move, to walk to his chamber, that it wasn't wise to lurk alone in the passageway. But the fear had too tight a grip on him.

"Just who we were looking for," Collin Scott said as he and his fellow Scotts approached. He frowned when Alex didn't acknowledge him. "What's wrong with him?"

"Is he having an apoplexy?" Christopher wondered. "Are we really that fortunate?"

"Nay," Paul responded. "He's terrified. Watch at how he trembles. Are you going to pish yourself, Armstrong?" He sneered at Alex, but it fell when Alex still acted as though no one was around.

"Armstrong?" Christopher tried to gain his attention, but Alex barely registered the voices. He was certain he was hearing men from the battle. How could it be anything else since he was standing on the field in Liddesdale?

"We can kill him, and not only do we not have to worry aboot him defending himself, he won't even know it's happening," Paul pointed out before his fist landed against Alex's left cheek. His head whipped back, and he stumbled. Christopher was next, landing an upper cut to Alex's jaw. Losing his balance, Alex swayed toward Collin, who held a dirk. But unprepared for Alex's movements, Collin only slashed a nick across Alex's wounded arm.

Alex felt the beating and couldn't reconcile the fresh pain with what happened during battle. The enemy had left him for dead, but he'd pulled himself onto his feet and found the strength to drag Brice to the tree line before he collapsed. No one had pummeled and kicked him. Besides the knife slicing his cheek, there had been no other dirks piercing his skin. As his mind cleared from the traumatic fog, he realized he was no longer experiencing a memory. He roared as he pulled a dirk from his belt and rolled away from the men who all stood to his right.

Pressing his weight onto his left arm made Alex bellow once again, but it made his attackers pause. Still agile, Alex came to his feet and pointed his dagger at Christopher. When he observed the men preparing for Alex to charge, he hurled the blade at Collin instead, lodging it above the man's collarbone. Blood geysered from it, taking the other two Scotts' attention from Alex. He flung a second knife that landed in Paul's ribs. Paul hollered with pain as Collin sagged toward the floor.

"I still have plenty more knives. Where shall I throw the next? Christopher, you seem to be the odd mon out. Mayhap you are next." Using his clansmen as a shield, Christopher pulled Paul and Collin backwards until they disappeared into the shadows. Alex waited until he was certain none of them intended to return. He took five backward steps in the opposite direction whence the Scotts came. Then he collapsed; another clap of thunder and bolt of lightning were all he remembered.

EIGHT

C aitlyn rolled in her bed toward the incessant banging at her door. Her roommate, Evina, sat up, rubbing sleep from her eyes. The women glanced at one another before turning back to the door.

"Lady Caitlyn," came an urgent voice. "Lady Caitlyn." Another knock. "Lady Caitlyn, please open the door."

Caitlyn recognized the voice as one of her guards. She bolted from her bed, not bothering to grab her robe. She could think of nothing but horrible news that would bring one of her guardsmen to her door in the middle of the night. She flung it open to find Grant standing before her.

"What's happened?" Caitlyn demanded.

"It's Armstrong. Someone's attacked him," Grant whispered. "It's bad, my lady. Very bad. You need to come."

"Let me get presentable, then take me to him." Caitlyn pressed the door closed and turned to Evina. "I know you heard. If you say a word, I will know."

"Caitlyn, you know I won't say aught," Evina reassured Caitlyn. She mostly believed the other woman. She was a gossip, but Caitlyn had never heard that Evina spoke about or against her. She had no time to say anything more while she pulled a plain kirtle from a peg. It was one she wore when she visited the almshouse to give out bread. It laced in the front. She was still pulling the laces tight when she opened the door, having barely stopped to slide her feet into slippers.

"This way," Grant whispered as Caitlyn finished tying her gown closed. She lifted her skirts and hurried to keep up with Grant's swift pace. She'd never been on the bachelors' floor, and a sense of unease grew, knowing it would destroy her reputation if anyone learned of her presence. She peered over Grant's shoulder and recognized two of her other guards, Duncan and Devlin. She assumed they waited outside Alex's door. When she and Grant reached the other two men, she noticed their expressions. It made her stomach drop. She reached out for Devlin's arm.

"Tell me now. Is he dead?" Caitlyn rasped.

"No, my lady. But they've beaten him badly. Whoever did this wanted him dead. All we can tell is two dirk sheaths are empty. We're assuming he defended himself long enough to scare them away. When we went back to where he was found, there was a puddle of blood, but it wasn't near him, my lady."

"Who found him?"

"His men. They watched him leave with you. When he didn't return, they were going to his chamber to confirm they were leaving in the morn. They found him in the passageway. One of them came for us, telling us you're needed, my lady."

Caitlyn looked at the men, grateful that they'd agreed and grateful that the Armstrong guards sent for her. "You can't all wait outside his door. You'll draw too much attention. Is he alone?"

"Nay. The king's physician is in there. His men

weren't sure what to do, so they sent a message to the king. The physician showed up as I left to fetch you," Grant explained. "His men are there too."

"Go back to the barracks," Caitlyn instructed. "His men won't go anywhere. They'll guard me as well as they do their tánaiste. No one can find you here."

"Aye, my lady," Duncan agreed, but Caitlyn could tell they were all hesitant to leave.

"It's for the best," Caitlyn reassured them before she pushed the door open. Her hand flew to her mouth as she stifled her gasp. Alex lay upon his bed, blood covering his battered face. She noticed patches of blood on his doublet where it leaked through slices to his abdomen. Her initial shock fleeting, she rushed across the room to the bed and climbed onto it without thinking. She cared not that Alex's men and the king's physician stared at her. She brushed back ebony locks from Alex's forehead, wishing his emerald eyes would open and meet hers. She pressed a kiss to his forehead and breathed, "Alex."

Alex groaned and his good hand twitched. Caitlyn grasped it and squeezed. She settled herself to face Alex as she clasped his hand in hers. She swallowed back tears, knowing they did no one any good, least of whom Alex. She peered at the physician.

"Should I step out while you undress him?" Caitlyn asked. She realized Grant must have come for her immediately if no one had removed Alex's clothes yet.

"My lady," one of Alex's men stepped forward. Caitlyn looked back over her shoulder.

"Aye, Stephen?"

"You can't go into the passageway alone, and if anyone noticed you with one of us, there would be even more trouble. Mayhap you could wait behind the screen while we help the physician." As Stephen spoke, two other guards pulled the partition open. With another kiss to Alex's forehead, Caitlyn slid off the bed and ducked behind the screen.

She scrunched her eyes closed and bit back her own cries as Alex groaned with pain. When he bellowed in agony, she assumed someone was moving his left arm. Each sound tore a piece of her heart away. She wanted to demand the men be more careful, but she was certain they were doing the best they could. When she heard no more movement, she peeked around the screen. Stephen nodded, so she emerged and moved back to the bedside. The sheet sat low over Alex's waist.

It had been years since Caitlyn observed Alex without a shirt on, and she couldn't stop her eyes from feasting on him. She took in the broad shoulders, her eyes lingering for a moment on his left shoulder's scar. His chest's rise and fall made his muscles ripple, drawing her attention away immediately. She'd seen nothing like Alex's body. She'd witnessed men training without doublets or leines, but she'd never been so close to spy such intimate details as the path of hair from his navel to what lay beneath the sheet. She had a sudden desire to discover what his back and buttocks looked like. If they were as hewn as his front, Caitlyn feared she'd drool. While she admired the chiseled muscles, she noticed the various wounds he'd gained during the fight.

More cautiously than before, Caitlyn climbed onto the bed and took Alex's hand. It surprised her when his eyes fluttered open, and he gazed at her. His lips separated, but he licked his lips before he tried to speak.

"Caity," Alex croaked.

"Shh. Grant came to get me. I'm not going anywhere, so don't bother starting," Caitlyn said adamantly.

"Thank you," Alex mumbled and squeezed her hand. He shifted his gaze to the physician, who opened a jar of leeches.

"No."

Five sets of male eyes turned toward Caitlyn, her tone emphatic. The physician glowered at her and tsked as he continued to open the jar. "My lady, he needs the bad humors cleared from his body."

"The only bad humor in this chamber shall be mine if you touch him with one of those. He has no sickness. He needs stitches and his bruises cleansed with witch hazel. He's already lost blood from the gashes he has on his arms and that nasty one on his ribs. Sew him up and leave."

"Caity," Alex tried to say more.

"No, Alex. Losing more blood to those vile things will not make you better. If you had the ague or a fever, I might agree. But you know as well as I do, injured warriors don't need leeches."

"Mayhap leeches might have saved his maimed arm and kept him from being useless," the physician stated, his tone condescending to an extreme.

"Get out," Caitlyn hissed. "Get out before I shove you out. You will not touch him. I will sew his wounds and tend to him. How dare you say something so wretched?"

"My lady," the physician said, patronizing her as he reached out to touch her head.

"Pat me like a dog, and you lose that hand. Get out," Caitlyn threatened. She turned to Alex's men. "One of you go to the barracks. There's bound to be needles, thread, witch hazel, and yarrow there. Bring some to me, please."

"Aye, my lady," a man Caitlyn knew was called

David hurried to the door. He didn't turn back before he passed through.

"Lady Caitlyn has made her wishes clear," Stephen said as he stood beside the door and glared at the king's physician.

"King Robert shall hear of this," the man sniffed.

"Be sure that he does," Caitlyn challenged. The man grew red in the face as he collected his belongings and rushed from the chamber. Caitlyn leaned toward Alex and stroked his right cheek, the side easier to reach. His eyes flashed anger as her hand encountered the scar, but she thought nothing of it, too impatient for David to return. When he recognized only worry in Caitlyn's gaze, he pulled his hand free and cupped it over his cheek and closed his eyes once more, relishing the feel of her gentle touch. Dropping her voice to a whisper, Caitlyn asked, "What happened?"

Alex's hand pressed hers more firmly against his cheek. She glanced down when she realized she could feel Alex's heartbeat beneath the other. She was unaware of when she'd placed her hand on his chest, but it felt natural. She waited for him to answer, knowing his men wanted to hear his answer as much as she did.

"The Scotts found me." Alex couldn't say more. It humiliated him too much to admit what happened when the storm was overhead, and he didn't remember everything that happened during the fight. Caitlyn shifted her attention to Alex's men and tilted her head toward the door. Stephen and the third guard, Mitcham, stepped into the passageway. She inched closer to Alex and pressed her lips to his mouth for a breath.

"Tell me what you remember, Alex," Caitlyn whispered before she kissed his marred cheek. "It's only me. I won't repeat what you don't want me to."

"I know you won't, Caity. I trust you more than anyone but Brice. You're tied for it." Alex twisted his head to kiss the palm that cupped his cheek again. "I don't remember everything, but I know I didn't even notice them approach me."

"How can that be? You're always aware of what's happening. You've chastised me often enough for not being aware."

Alex clenched his jaw as he glanced at his left shoulder. "Obviously, I'm not."

"St. Michael's sword, Alex! You survived that day. Something went your way," Caitlyn snapped.

"Bluidy load of good it did me. Everyone would be better off if I hadn't."

Caitlyn grasped Alex's jaw in a punishing hold. "Don't you dare say something so horrid ever again. Do you understand what it would have done to me if you'd died? You may not want me, but I don't think I could survive knowing you're dead." Tears streamed down Caitlyn's cheeks as she released Alex's jaw. She hadn't realized how tightly she held it until her fingers cramped.

"Caity, I've never not wanted you," Alex confessed. "But I proved tonight that I'm worthless to you and everyone else. Not only couldn't I protect you had you still been with me, I couldn't even defend myself."

"Then where are your two dirks that are missing?" Caitlyn demanded. She watched confusion settle into Alex's expression, and she realized he didn't recall most of what happened. "My men said two of your dirks were missing when your men found you. I doubt anyone in the keep would steal them. On the street, definitely. Here, no. You must have defended yourself because they weren't on you or in the passageway."

Alex closed his eyes, his brow furrowing as he

tried to remember. He recalled the storm, then he recalled the first few punches, but nothing else came to mind. "I'm not sure. I don't remember that."

"What do you remember? Please tell me, Alex. Whatever it is, not knowing is scaring me far more."

Alex saw as much as felt Caitlyn's anxiety. He didn't want to keep secrets from her, but it was humiliating to admit a shortcoming that nearly killed him. "I told you I don't sleep well."

"Aye. That's why you have all these candles." Caitlyn hadn't registered that it was the candles that Alex must have purchased in town that lit his chamber, but she recognized the scent.

"I have nightmares. I remember that battle every night. Now that I have the candles, I can sleep through more of the night. I realized when I took a nap and didn't have a single nightmare, it's the dark that causes them." Alex peered toward the window embrasure. He could hear the rain falling, but the fierce storm had passed. "But it's not only the dark that causes me to remember, to feel like I'm there all over again. There was a storm raging as bad as tonight's while we fought. It was so dark that it appeared almost like night. I think that's why darkness bothers me. When I passed an arrow slit, the thunder seemed to reverberate through the passageway, and the lightning was extraordinarily bright. I was there all over again."

Caitlyn listened to Alex as he told her what she was certain few people knew. She tried to envision all that he shared, and her soul ached for the pain Alex endured. She understood the invisible wounds caused him more agony than even his arm. Caitlyn glanced at Alex's cuts, glad to find they'd all stopped bleeding. She felt bad for sending for suturing supplies since she didn't think he needed stitches after all. With space and no blood trickling from him,

Caitlyn lay on her side and rested her hand on Alex's chest. He slid his right arm beneath her and pulled her closer.

"I froze, Caity. It was like I was no longer here in Stirling. I was back in Liddesdale near the Hermitage. I was back on that hill in the storm, fighting the waves of Scotts that descended upon us and the Elliots. We outnumbered them, so I'd been confident from the start that we already claimed the victory, but it was brutal all the same. They had the advantage of elevation while we slogged through bogs and mud. I'm not sure if it was the weather or our enemy, but it was the most brutal fight I've ever been in. And as I stood beside the arrow slit tonight, I was certain I was there. I felt Brice no longer at my back. I felt the sword cut through my shoulder, and the dirk pierce my cheek. I felt the unbearable pain of dragging Brice out of the fray, only caring at the time that my brother was still alive."

Caitlyn rose up on her elbow, her hand sliding to wrap her arm across Alex's chest. Their gazes met; once again, what Alex expected to find wasn't there. Tenderness and concern filled Caitlyn's eyes. He raised his chin, and she accepted the offer. Their kiss was brief, but neither could deny they filled it with love.

"Stop waiting for me to pity you, Alex," Caitlyn said. "You will die an auld mon before that happens. I hate what's happened to you. I sympathize with your pain, and I commiserate with what you've lost. But I do not pity you. You are no less a mon to me than you were six months ago. To have survived what you've told me, to be familiar with the journey you took from Mangerton to here and imagining the discomfort of riding and sleeping on the ground, to watch you in constant pain, and to observe how you endure others. Well, all of that makes me respect you more. I lo—" Caitlyn stopped as the door inched open.

Caitlyn pulled herself away from Alex's embrace, straightening her skirts as she sat beside him. She registered the men's surprise, and she realized she should have been washing Alex's wounds. She prayed none of them became infected, or she might be begging the physician to return with his leeches. She watched Alex and sensed there was more he wished to say, but she understood not in front of his men. She hoped he would confide in her again and finish telling her what happened.

"Could someone fetch boiling water? I need to brew willow bark tea. I see you found some," Caitlyn said as she poured out the sack of supplies on the bed. She moved to the washstand and poured water into the basin to soak a linen square and rub soap against it. She rang most of the water from it and moved to the opposite side of the bed. She cleaned Alex's wounds, thanking the man who brought the ewer and basin closer. There was only one cut that she hadn't seen on Alex's back that she felt warranted stitches. The guards helped hold Alex in position. He swallowed his pride, but he refused to swallow the whisky Caitlyn encouraged him to drink. She struggled not to cry when Alex didn't register the additional pain as the needle passed through his skin over and over. She understood he lived with such pain daily, and other parts of him surely hurt more, that he didn't notice the pricks as she sewed.

Caitlyn finished tying off the thread when Mitcham arrived with the steaming water. She brewed the tea, letting it steep while she spread yarrow paste around and over the stitches. She dabbed witch hazel, which made Alex's breath whistle, on his other cuts and abrasions. But he didn't move during any of her ministrations. Stephen and

Mitcham helped prop Alex up with pillows so he could sip tea. David stood near the door, listening for any noise in the passageway.

"Thank you, Caity. You must be fatigued. I wish you good sleep," Alex whispered. Caitlyn jerked her chin back, her brow furrowing.

"I'm not going anywhere, Alex."

"You can't stay here all night, Caity," Alex argued.

"If being here is going to ruin my reputation, then merely stepping foot on this floor did that. Whether I spent five minutes or the entire night in here with you, any damage has already happened."

"You can slip out of here now with no one the wiser. You can't do that in the morn," Alex asserted.

"Do any of you have the skills to tend a fever or deal with an infected wound before looking for a healer?" Caitlyn asked the guards. The men frowned and shook their heads. "If I leave this chamber, it's only to go in search of more medicinals, Alex. Someone who knows what she's doing needs to be here if you get worse. Is there someone else you'd prefer?"

"Caitlyn," Alex warned, but he realized she wasn't being facetious. She feared he might name someone. He whispered, "You know there isn't."

"I'll sit in that chair if you're worried I'll compromise your reputation," Caitlyn said with a wink as she stood to wash her hands. She glanced around the chamber and realized it was darker than it had been when she arrived. With the candles on the bedside table near her, she'd had enough light to work. But several had gutted, as had ones on the other side. She couldn't fetch more candles in the middle of the night. "Could someone please stoke the fire. I want a blaze."

At Alex's confused expression, her eyes darted to

the candles on each table. Alex's gaze followed hers, understanding her request. Caitlyn watched as David threw extra logs and peat into the hearth until the flames jumped up the chimney. The room glowed brighter, but it also grew much warmer.

"I didn't want the leeches, but I think you should sweat out any ill humors you might have," Caitlyn said to Alex, but she spoke to offer an excuse to the men. Alex nodded, once more knowing why Caitlyn said what she did. His right hand caught her wrist, pulling her toward him. His warm breath wafted across the shell of her ear and made her shiver.

"The few moments of you lying beside me were bliss. That memory shall heal me faster than any medicinal."

"It doesn't have to only be a memory, Alex," Caitlyn whispered. But she wished she hadn't spoken when she watched Alex retreat. Her shoulders slumped, and she shook her head as she rose. She made to carry a chair closer to the bed, but Stephen did it for her. She settled into the chair and rested her head on her fist. "Sleep if you can, Alex. I'll be here if you need aught."

Alex watched Caitlyn close her eyes. He sensed she was no more asleep than he was. But he'd shut her out, and now she did the same. They were making a pattern of this, and it made them both miserable. But the night's attack only firmed Alex's resolve that he was the worst potential husband for Caitlyn.

NINE

A lex's heart raced as he sat upright in bed. He felt fresh pain where there had been none since he returned to consciousness six months earlier. His eyes scanned the chamber, but it was dark. The fire burned low, and wind coming in from around the window hanging blew out the candles.

Where am I? Why am I in even more pain than usual?

Alex struggled to breathe as the walls he couldn't see pressed toward him. He tried to kick his legs free of the sheets but howled as pain tore through his body.

What the fuck happened to me?

Soft hands grasped his shoulder, only increasing his panic. He struck out with his right arm, knocking aside whoever tried to restrain him. A feminine cry as something fell over met Alex's ears. A door flung open, and light poured in from a torch.

"Leave." A woman's authoritative voice rang out. "I'll tend to him."

Caity? Where am I?

Alex heard a crash of thunder, and a moment later a sheet of lightning powerful enough to push light around the window hanging illuminated Caitlyn as she rubbed her arm. He realized Caitlyn was the person he'd shoved away, and she'd fallen into the chair.

"Caity?" Alex reached for her, but without the torch or the lightning, he couldn't glimpse her.

"I'm here, Alex. Wait a moment."

Alex sensed a shape moving across the chamber, and Caitlyn's body suddenly appeared when she stepped before the fire. She tossed in three more logs and two blocks of peat. They caught immediately, and the room brightened. She hurried back to his side.

"I shoved you, Caity. I'm sorry." Alex shuddered, guilt nearly swallowing him whole.

"I know you are. I should have spoken before I approached a warrior in the dark. I know better than that, but I wasn't thinking," Alex grunted at the word warrior but left it alone. "Let me check your stitches."

"Stitches?" Alex reached behind him but felt nothing.

"The other side." Caitlyn kept her voice low. The same soft hands as a moment ago ran along his back. He felt the slight tug as her fingers brushed his sutures. "You woke in a panic. Were you dreaming?"

"I don't know," Alex admitted. "Most likely, but they aren't dreams. There is naught dreamy aboot them. But I don't recall what I was thinking aboot. Usually, I do. Usually, it's still so vivid."

Thunder rattled the candlestick holders on the bedside tables and made Alex jump. He pulled away as though he could avoid the storm if he leaned far enough. More lightning flashed, and Alex felt himself slipping back into his memories. As the images danced before his eyes, it was the nightmare he'd had when he envisioned Caitlyn on the battlefield. Now, nightmares haunted even his waking moments.

He was running toward her, and this time he reached her

before the Scotts. He wrapped his arms around her, shielding her with his larger body. He turned them to run back to where Armstrong guards waited with horses that fled the battlefield.

Alex turned his head in time to catch sight of a Scott charging toward them with his sword raised. Movement on his other side shifted his attention. As another man hurtled toward them, he pushed Caitlyn ahead of him as he raised his sword. But with two men attacking and Caitlyn so close, he couldn't fend off the men without striking her. He felt the moment each sword severed an arm as though it were actually happening. He felt the arms fall to the ground, and he glanced down at the limbs merely lying there. He raised his eyes in time to watch one man grab Caitlyn's hair.

Alex tried to move, but mud mired his feet. He dragged himself free as the man pulled Caitlyn with him. But when Alex made to raise his sword, he remembered he had no arms. The man spun Caitlyn around and ran a dirk across her throat as Alex watched, armless and unable to protect her.

"Alex. Alex." He turned sightless eyes toward Caitlyn's voice. It was calm, and he didn't understand how. He tested his arms and found the right one worked as it reached to Caitlyn. She grasped it and brought his palm to her cheek.

"How can I feel a ghost?" Alex's words were hard to make out.

"I'm not a ghost, Alex. I'm right here. I'm not going anywhere. But where were you a moment ago? You seemed so far away." Caitlyn's voice held a note of concern as Alex focused in her direction, his eyes no longer glazed.

"I was. My mind insisted I stood on that field, and I discovered you there. I couldn't save you. I can never save you." Alex's voice trembled as he tried to pull his hand away. Caitlyn let him, but she climbed onto the bed beside him. Careful not to touch his left arm, she wrapped hers around him. She felt no tears, but the sobs wracked Alex's enormous body. She said

93

nothing, but she stroked his hair and ran her hand over his back until he went still. She wondered if he'd fallen back to sleep. She tried to ease away, but he spoke. "Stay."

The single word changed everything for Caitlyn. No longer was she frustrated and hurt by Alex's rejection. Now determination made her stay. Not only that night, but for the rest of their lives. She accepted she couldn't cure him of the demons that plagued him or heal his arm. But she was determined to remain his confidante and support. She wasn't fooling herself into believing she had a simple path. She understood Alex intended to continue to push her away, and she would give him space when he needed it. But she would keep coming back. He might never marry her, and she knew that. However, she would be a shoulder he could always turn to.

"I'm not going anywhere, Alex. I'm staying."

Alex heard the resolution in Caitlyn's voice, and it felt as though an enormous weight rose from suffocating him and pressing him into the mattress. He held no wish to consider the next day or the ones to follow. He wanted to relish the time alone with Caitlyn. She was a beacon of hope and an anchor for him amid the storm that continued to rage outside the castle and in his head.

"I don't fear the dark or the storms; I just can't control what they do to my mind," Alex confessed. "They take control, and I can't shake the terror or the memories away."

"Does Brice experience these nightmares?"

"Aye. How'd you guess? I didn't find out until right before I left Mangerton."

"Because I know your brother and how close you are. He must suffer such guilt," Caitlyn mused.

"There was naught he could have done." Alex's

decisive tone convinced Caitlyn even more that Alex never realized Brice likely shared his guilt.

"Mayhap. But that can't possibly be what he feels. I remember you both swore to your mother to always protect one another. Brice may live with these nightmares, but you haven't told me he bears the same impediments as you. He must struggle with knowing that because his enemy injured him first, someone injured you."

Alex laid still beside Caitlyn, wondering if he'd been so incredibly self-involved for so long that he hadn't noticed Brice suffered wounds no one saw. Alex's eyes closed as he shuddered. It had taken Brice half a year to admit that he had nightmares too. He'd said he didn't speak of them because he worried about making Alex's own suffering worse. Alex never imagined Brice felt the guilt that he did. A wave of exhaustion swept over him as he thought about how much effort and strain it must put on Brice to be the cheerful person everyone expected if he no longer felt that way.

"You haven't seen Brice in ages, yet you understand him better than I do."

"I have Cairren. I can imagine what it must be like for you and Brice, because that's how it would be for me if something happened to my sister."

"I have been so unconscionably self-centered for months. I've likely made Brice's life miserable, and I still can't forgive myself for what I said to you. How're you even beside me?"

"Because I'm piecing it together, and I'm finding a mon I care for deeply who's still hurting. Everyone else only notices the wounds on the outside. You've hurt me since you arrived, but I suspect it's happened because you know I won't turn away from you. You've needed to vent your feelings, and you know you're safe with me."

"That doesn't make it all right, Caity. That makes it worse," Alex stated as he sat up. "That means I've taken advantage of you in the worst way. I've treated you like shite and expected to get away with it. That isn't a friend. That isn't aught that should be in your life."

"I can decide for myself whether what you've done is too horrible to forgive and whether I want to remain friends with you. Why do you insist on making every decision alone? Is that how it'll be?"

"It'll be?" Alex's tone reflected his confusion. He watched Caitlyn pull away, unsure why she retreated. She slid from the bed and righted the chair. She drew it to the bedside and reached for Alex's hand. She wove her fingers between hers.

"Go to sleep, Alex. We're both tired."

"But Caity…" Alex didn't understand the shift that happened in the matter of seconds. Caitlyn was still by his side, but something was different besides her no longer lying next to him. He watched her rest her head on the mattress and close her eyes. He stroked her hair, much like she had done for him. He could tell she fought falling asleep before him, but eventually she drifted off. Alex lay still and watched her. He wanted to beg her to cuddle beside him again. He wanted to beg that she forgive him for whatever transgression he committed a moment ago. He wanted to beg God to stop being so cruel. Because all he really wanted was to hold the woman he would love for the rest of his life.

Caitlyn woke to light shining around the cowhide at the window embrasure. Her eyes fluttered open as she realized she still laced her fingers with Alex's. When she lifted her head, she found brilliant emerald orbs gazing at her from behind horribly bruised and swollen eyelids. Bruises mottled Alex's face, and it shocked her that he could still open his eyes even a slit. Whoever attacked him hadn't broken his nose or his jaw, but there were bruises along both sides of his chin. She suppressed her gasp as she took in the damage.

Caitlyn's mouth felt parched from the warm, dry air the fire generated throughout the night. She swallowed and swiped her tongue across the insides of her cheeks as she considered what to say. She'd fallen asleep to keep tears from trickling from her eyes. She'd told herself—convinced herself—that she could live without Alex marrying her if they could remain close friends. But when he hadn't understood her reference to the future, albeit a rather ambiguous one, it was a fresh stab to her heart. She had to accept that Alex no longer wanted to marry her, and he didn't intend to change his mind.

"Did you sleep?" Caitlyn's voice sounded husky from slumber. The sound shot heat to Alex's cock, which stirred inconveniently. He adjusted the sheet and sat up, praying the new position hid the evidence that he wasn't immune to Caitlyn. Despite how his body ached from his beating, one part of him still worked without difficulty.

Alex had realized after she'd fallen asleep what her comment meant. She still envisioned a future together. He hadn't understood and he still couldn't agree, but he felt wretched that he'd hurt her yet again. He'd watched a tear slide down her cheek as her eyelids relaxed in slumber.

"Rested," Alex responded. "It's still early. I have heard no one stirring in the passageway. One of the men can escort you back to your chamber."

"I need to check your wounds first. Have you felt feverish?" Caitlyn rose and pressed Alex's uninjured

97

shoulder forward, so she could examine his stitches. "You should cover that with bandages before you dress. Would you like me to help?"

Would I like her to? Of course. Any reason for her to touch me is one I don't want to turn down. But can I hide my poleaxe under this sheet? Dear saints, she's already leaning forward with the linen strips.

Alex tried not to fidget as Caitlyn wound the bandages around his ribs to cover the stitches. He bunched the sheet over his groin, praying it hid his obvious interest. When she leaned sideways to pass the bandage beneath his left arm, he caught glimpses of her cleavage. He felt like a wolf salivating over a lamb. He forced himself not to lick his chops—or worse, her breasts. He didn't breathe easy until she stepped back, and he no longer peered at breasts he wished to make a meal of. His mouth tingled with his desire to knead the supple flesh and suckle them.

"There's enough yarrow here to cover the other cuts. You can put more witch hazel on the bruises. If the pain bothers you, or you feel overheated, have a guard bring you boiling water and brew some tea."

If I feel overheated? As opposed to now? I'd bluidy well go up in flames if I got any hotter. "Thank you, Caity. I appreciate you tending to me." Caitlyn nodded and made to turn away, but Alex grasped her wrist. "Please promise me you won't go anywhere without at least two of your guards. I'm serious aboot this. I don't trust the Scotts not to come after you."

"I promise, Alex. I'll be careful." Caitlyn hesitated, then placed a kiss on his forehead. They'd both noticed David sitting against the door and sensed he was awake. But he was discreet and kept his eyes closed. "David, could someone walk me back, please?"

"Aye, my lady," David responded immediately. He glanced at Alex, who nodded as he rose. The guard eased the door open, revealing Stephen and Mitcham on the other side.

"Are you ready, my lady?" Stephen stepped aside to let her pass.

"Aye. Thank you." Caitlyn turned back to Alex. "I'll come back while everyone is at the midday meal."

"Caity, that isn't wise," Alex protested.

"I said, I'll come back." Caitlyn stepped into the passageway without waiting to hear Alex disagree further.

"Thank you, Lady Caitlyn." Stephen ensured his voice didn't carry as they made their way out of the bachelor quarters. "I'm certain you're now aware of Alex's nightmares."

"You were aware of them?" Stephen's comment surprised Caitlyn, knowing Alex never wanted that.

"I don't think they were aught like last night's, but he was restless every night we traveled. We think he slept little to avoid having any in front of us. But even he needs rest at some point." Stephen studied Caitlyn as they ambled along the passageway. "We know he doesn't want us to know. The others and I wish he would realize no one thinks less of him. Just the opposite. I think most of the men in our clan are in awe of what he's survived and how he continues on as he does. The pain is no secret to anyone. He actually started coming back to the lists the last couple days before we left Mangerton."

"He did?" The news surprised her.

"Brice convinced him to train with dirks." Stephen paused as they reached the ladies'-in-waiting floor. "No one knew what to say or where to look at first. But he knocked Brice on his back repeatedly. You're acquainted with him. Brice stands as big as any of us and is heavier than many. He didn't go down of his own accord. Alex knocked him down.

Brice got the better of Alex a few times, but it was exactly like it's always been. Alex still bests his younger brother more often than the other way around. It shocked the hell out of everyone."

"Thank you for telling me this." Caitlyn remained unsure what to do with the knowledge.

"I'm telling you this, my lady, because no one at home thinks aboot him the way he does himself. And I don't think you've changed how you think aboot him. No one expects you to fix him, so please don't think I'd place that burden on you. But you may be the only person he'll listen to and believe." Stephen met Caitlyn's gaze before shifting to peer beyond her shoulders. "I hope you won't think I'm speaking out of turn."

"I don't, Stephen. I appreciate you telling me because you know he wouldn't. He doesn't view it that way. He's said he doesn't think he's the mon he once was, that he's not enough of a mon."

"Everyone at home knows he thinks that. He's tried to push the succession on to Brice, but the laird and Brice won't hear of it."

"He doesn't want to be laird?" Caitlyn glanced back in the direction from which they came, as though she might see all the way to Alex's chamber and then within.

"He doesn't think he's worthy. He thinks other clans will mock us, and he fears endangering us because he believes others think him weak."

"And being here and hearing all the comments certainly doesn't help," Caitlyn surmised.

"Nor does being attacked. In his mind, it confirms what he's been saying for moons."

"Can I ask you something?"

"Of course, my lady," Stephen raised his eyebrows.

"I'd venture a guess that he can't ride into battle

anymore because he couldn't manage his horse and a sword. But could he still wield a sword? I assume a targe isn't an option either, but can a mon fight with just one arm, or does it really take both?"

"Both is always better, as you can imagine. But Lady Caitlyn, he's stronger than anyone guessed. Far more than I think he knows. He hadn't trained in six months, and the first day back, he beat Brice several times with dirks. I can't imagine what he could do with a sword against a sword, but if I had to wager, I'm putting my coin on him before just aboot anyone. I ken the training pained him. We all witnessed that, but it shocked the devil right out of us to watch him. It was like watching the Alex we've always known."

"You think the warrior is still in him?"

"It always will be, my lady. I don't think he remembers enough of last night to realize how he fought off those men. But we haven't recovered his dirks, and the amount of blood we found didn't come from him. I glimpsed his face this morn, and it's as bad as we all feared now that the swelling's started. I can guess at how his attackers are. They might even be dead." Stephen shrugged.

Caitlyn believed him. She hadn't seen the blood, but she'd seen Alex's bare muscles. His body was still powerful, and she'd seen him train as a young man. She'd never met someone who could be so singularly focused, yet so attuned to what went on around him. She was certain that's what kept him alive on that battlefield. He might not have thought he was aware of the man who injured him until it was too late. But Caitlyn disagreed. It would have only been too late if the man killed Alex, and then likely moved on to kill Brice.

"I'm aware you planned to leave this morning. How long do you think Alex will remain abed?"

"Mayhap a day. Two, at best."

Caitlyn nodded. They both knew he needed longer than that. The chapel bell put an end to their conversation. She thanked Stephen and hurried to her chamber before any early risers made their way to the Mass. Evina still slept when Caitlyn entered. She shucked off her kirtle and climbed into bed. Despite being designed for only one person, it felt empty after lying in a bed beside Alex. Her eyes drifted closed as she fell into a deep, dreamless sleep.

TEN

Alex turned toward the door when there was a brief knock before it opened. He was in the midst of pulling his breeks over his hips when King Robert entered with three royal guards surrounding him. It startled Alex to watch the monarch enter his chamber, but he assumed the king's physician had already tattled on Caitlyn. He frowned at the thought, making the Bruce chuckle.

"Aye. The pugnacious little mon has already been to visit me. But he knows enough to keep me alive." King Robert approached but stepped to the window hanging, which he pushed back. He walked to Alex and examined his injuries. "How are you even balancing on your feet with a face like that?"

"Carefully, Your Majesty." Alex clenched his jaw as he struggled to tie the laces. Knowing the king watched him only flustered him more, but the determination not to appear like an invalid was stronger.

"No one's seen them since the evening meal." Alex didn't need the Bruce to name who he meant. "I suspect it was them, but I have no proof."

"You have the proof that I recognized them." Alex wished he could cross his arms. He refused to put his hand on his hip like a nagging fishwife.

"They're gone, which should suffice." King Robert peered at Alex's face, then shook his head.

"You're disgusted at what you can see. Even with my eyes nearly swollen shut, I can tell. Yet you wish for me to accept a beating, then you want knowing they ran away to mollify me."

"That's politics."

"That's a slight to my clan and me. But more than aught, it's a royal sod off." Alex turned away from the king as he fought not to wince when he withdrew a fresh doublet from his satchel.

"Tread carefully." King Robert's ire rang out in the room.

"Like they did? Och, aye. They didn't put a toe over our borders to assault my people. They took care of it by attacking me here. Sounds like they complied well." Alex felt his anger growing each moment King Robert remained in his chamber.

"Alexander, I can understand you're in pain, but—"

"This has naught to do with any pain I might be in. This has everything to do with the insult they've doled out to my father and my clan. I disagreed with being my father's delegate, but here I am. I warned of this happening, and it did. But just because I guessed the inevitable trouble doesn't mean I have to accept it. If they had the bollocks to attack me in your keep, right beneath your nose, then what confidence do *you* have that they will obey you when they are beyond your reach? Like I said, they told you to sod off just as loudly as they did me."

Alex finished buttoning his doublet, surprised he'd done it with ease while he railed against the Scotts and insulted the king. It was nearly midday, and he expected Caitlyn to return. He didn't want King Robert to linger lest she arrive while he was still there. Alex forced himself to stop speaking. He would let the king say his piece, even if he barely listened and didn't agree.

"I can send an entourage to accompany you to Mangerton." King Robert nearly stepped back when Alex turned his angry face toward him. Even discolored and swollen, he witnessed the disgust in Alex's eyes.

"Is one of them a wet nurse for me too?" Alex sat on the edge of the bed to pull up his stockings. He cared not that the king remained standing. He didn't intend to offer the Bruce a seat, since he wanted him gone.

"Then what do you want?"

"I want their bollocks on a platter. What I'll settle for is their cowardly arses dragged back here and tossed in the oubliette. Don't think of it as a gift to me. Think of it as reminding the Scotts who's king."

"You play a dangerous game, Alexander." King Robert's temper frayed with every antagonistic word Alex spewed.

"One where I might wind up dead? I didn't ask to join in, but I seem to be the only player. Whether it's you or the Scotts, someone's bound to get it right. But I refuse to die before you resolve the matter in my clan's favor. Just like you promised." Alex threw down the gauntlet.

"You seem eager to be the one whose bollocks are on a platter."

"Mayhap, but you won't be able to deny I have the biggest set." Alex cocked an eyebrow, but he didn't think King Robert could tell.

"I'll give you that. I will not bring them back to court, nor will I insist upon an escort for you. But I will send men to make my position clear to Laird Scott since his men have proven untrustworthy. The royal livery might make them take notice."

One can hope. "Thank you, Your—" Alex turned

his attention at the door as a soft knock sounded. He was certain who was on the other side of the portal, and he wanted to groan. He couldn't avoid Caitlyn or the king finding her, whether it was on his doorstep or in his chamber. "Enter."

Caitlyn stepped across the threshold carrying a basket but stopped short when she caught sight of King Robert. She dipped into a low curtsy. When no acknowledgement came that she could rise, she did so anyway and closed the door behind her. She didn't think anyone noticed her, but if word circulated that she was in a chamber with the king and Alex, not only would her reputation be beyond repair, she feared the queen would send her to the gallows.

"Lady Caitlyn, you've returned." King Robert scrutinized Caitlyn, but after years at court, she no longer grew uncomfortable under the intimidating gaze. She wondered how he'd heard that she'd already been to visit Alex. Then she recalled the physician. She said nothing, knowing the king didn't expect a response. "You risk much coming here, not only at night, but in the middle of the day."

"Lady Caitlyn promised to check in on me in case I need more bandages or willow bark, then be on her way." Alex turned to face Caitlyn who, to her credit, didn't show her shock at how much worse Alex's face appeared. "I have what I need, thank you. Mayhap I'll see you at the meal."

Alex watched Caitlyn's jaw set, and he prayed she didn't argue. She cast him a warning glare before lowering her head as she dipped into another curtsy. She rose gracefully, looking at the king rather than Alex.

"Good day, Your Majesty." She shifted her eyes to Alex. "Until I see you at *tomorrow's* midday meal, Alexander."

"Lady Caitlyn, do you not approve of Alexander

being up and moving around? Did you expect to find him abed, waiting for you?"

Alex opened his mouth to defend Caitlyn, aghast at the Bruce's implications. But Caitlyn was swifter. "Aboot as much as I expected to find him beaten, Your Majesty."

Caitlyn resented being the brunt of King Robert's taunts. She wanted to check Alex's stitches and ensure he ran no fever. Deciding not to play the royal game any longer, she crossed the chamber, making a straight line to Alex, which forced King Robert to step out of her way. She placed the back of her hand to his forehead before stepping around him to raise the back of his doublet. She pulled down the bandages, dissatisfied when she found inflammation around the edges, and red lines were creeping away from it.

"Alex, I need to take these stitches out and clean your wound again. I need to pack more yarrow into it. You're too warm for only the layer of clothing you have on, and I suspect the wound is getting infected. I shouldn't have let you sleep on your back."

"Let him sleep on his back?" King Robert crowed, but he snapped his mouth shut and jerked his chin back at the scathing expression Caitlyn cast him. He knew he should have expected as much from his wife's lady-in-waiting. They were, as a whole and individually, fiercer than any of his men for those about whom they cared. He was certain something existed between the pair, and he suspected Caitlyn would be as steadfastly protective of Alex as her former peers were of their husbands.

"You already knew I was here, Your Majesty. I'd wager you were informed of when I arrived and when I left. I'm aware there are secret passages in this castle, so it surprises me not if you knew exactly what happened—or didn't happen—in here last night." Caitlyn placed her basket on the bed and rapidly unbuttoned Alex's doublet without a second thought. She eased the garment from his body before carrying a candle to the fireplace and lighting it. The men remained silent as she moved around. She cared not if she interrupted their conversation.

David slipped into the chamber with the boiling water Caitlyn had requested before knocking. She brewed two cups of willow bark tea, insisting a man Alex's size would do well to have both. She brewed another tea, but Alex didn't recognize the scent. When she returned to him, she kept her voice low but knew the Bruce could still hear her. She did it for Alex's sake. "Can you lie on your stomach?"

"Aye." Alex moved onto the bed, so he could roll over his right arm as he positioned himself for Caitlyn to work. She was efficient as she snipped the stitches from the night before. He pressed his face into the mattress to keep anyone from witnessing his pain. Caitlyn's cool hands eased some of his anxiety as she cleaned his wound with a wash she'd brewed into a tea from alder leaves and primrose. When her examination satisfied her that it was clean, she packed it with more yarrow. She passed her needle and thread through the candle's flame, then ran a soft palm around the wound before she began the first stitch.

Much like the night before, Alex tensed with each pass of the needle, but he made no sound. She glanced at King Robert and found him staring at Alex's head. Their eyes met, and she glimpsed not a monarch viewing his subject, but a warrior leader watching one of his men. She found a man who understood what it was to be in Alex's condition, but she could tell Alex's lack of reaction discomfited the Bruce. He nodded to her, respect in his gaze for them both. She slathered a poultice made from yarrow and burdock. She applied it more liberally than she had the night before. When she finished, she wiped her hands on a linen cloth.

"I shall let this breathe for a while, but you can't put any pressure on it. I think pressing it against the sheet made sweat get into it last night. I didn't find aught else in there to make it get infected. Can you stay like this, Alex?"

"Aye." The single word was all he'd said since he answered Caitlyn's last question. He turned his head, so his left cheek rested on the bed, having pushed the pillow out of the way.

"Do you want me to send for some broth? Are you hungry?" Caitlyn knew Alex was in pain, even if he showed no signs, so she didn't want to bombard him with questions. But she doubted he'd eaten anything yet that day.

"Yes, please."

"I'll send one of his men." The Bruce stood beside the door. "Alexander, let Lady Caitlyn tend to you as she sees fit. It's clear she knows what to do. I'll ensure naught disrupts your rest."

Caitlyn assumed that was as close to consent and discretion that the king would offer. She pulled the chair close to the bed as she had the night before. "With the light in here, do you think you could sleep after you eat?"

"I think so." Alex reached out his hand to Caitlyn, his silent request clear. She took it, wrapping her forearm around his before he drew it close to his chest. "Thank you, Caity."

Caitlyn kissed Alex's temple, remaining quiet until Mitcham arrived with beef bone broth. She helped Alex sit up and held one side of the warm bowl while Alex held the other and sipped the liquid. He asked for his flask and swallowed a tot before lying back on his stomach. Caitlyn watched as he drifted back to sleep. She wondered how long it would take to recover, and she wondered what Alex discussed with the king. If it were anything short of the Scotts being punished, she wasn't certain she could remain quiet.

Alex felt arms wrap around his waist as he gazed out from Mangerton's battlements. Without turning his head, he was sure it was Caitlyn. He rested his right hand over hers as she pressed her cheek against his back. He could feel the rounded swell of her belly brushing his hips. He guessed his expression softened since his face relaxed. Twisting in her hold, he wrapped his arm around her waist and drew her around until he could bend and kiss her upturned face. Their lips fused together, and a bolt of heat surged through Alex.

They drew apart, and both beheld the land before them. It was spring, and the crops flourished in the distant field. A pair of doves called to one another from the orchard just beyond the bailey wall. Happiness swelled in Alex's chest as he stood with Caitlyn at his side as he gazed at their clan's land.

"How do you feel this morn, Caity?"

"Enormous." Feminine laughter filled the air as Caitlyn grinned and rubbed her belly. "This bairn shall be the largest of the three, I swear."

Surprise yet a sense of rightness made Alex shift his eyes from Caitlyn's face to her belly. He hesitantly placed his hand over it and felt a succession of sharp jabs before the bairn seemed to perform a somersault.

Three? We already have two weans? I'm certain Caity is my wife. We could never hold one another if she wed someone else. We couldn't have kissed if she were. But when did this happen?

Alex's mind attempted to sort through the scene in his dream, where he continued to converse with Caitlyn.

110

"Will you ride out today, Alex?" Caitlyn's furrowed brow appeared to Alex more like she was planning for her day rather than concerned that he left the keep on horseback.

"Aye. I need to visit the crofters again. They still haven't recovered all that they lost during the last raid."

"I wish I could go with you, but I fear the wagon ride jostling this bairn right out of me." As if the babe wished to make a point, Alex watched as Caitlyn's belly shifted and rippled.

"I don't enjoy leaving you here when you're this far along, but Brice is on patrol."

"I'll be well. Coira spoils me rotten." Caitlyn grinned and leaned in conspiratorially. "When you leave, I get all the apricot tarts."

"I shall miss kissing the leftover sugar from your lips." Alex drew Caitlyn in for another kiss, this one filled with searing passion. "Would that we could slip away for ten minutes."

"When has it ever been so quick as ten minutes?" Caitlyn offered a saucy wink to which Alex squeezed her bottom.

"And that's why we're having our third bairn in five years. You are too much temptation, mo ghaol."

Caitlyn stretched to peck a kiss on Alex's cheek before she grew serious. "Things were quiet for so long that I thought the Scotts finally realized the futility in continuing this feud. When you became laird and Sully inherited the lairdship, I thought he was willing to put the past behind us. How can any clan face so many defeats and still antagonize their enemy?"

"They do just enough damage to feel victorious, never mind that they lose each battle. I thought things were quieter now that Sully is laird, but he's worse than his father. And I don't know how mine put up with the auld laird for as long as he did. I respect my father's diplomacy more than I ever did when he was alive. He was wiser than I thought."

"And you learned more from him than you realize. You're a fine laird, and we're more prosperous than ever because of it. They can't stand it."

"Nay, they can't. But that prosperity is your doing as much as it is mine. My mother was an admirable chatelaine, but you are far more frugal than she is. You make our coin stretch further, and so we are better able to provide for our crofters when they lose their property after the Scotts raid. Angus will arrive tomorrow. He's been having troubles with the Kerrs, so they distracted him from the Scotts. They've taken advantage of it. He was spitting mad the last time I met him at our border."

"He's too hot-tempered by half. Don't let him get you killed." Caitlyn bit her bottom lip, and Alex was certain she had more to say about their neighboring laird. He shared her sentiments, but they both understood the alliance with the Elliots was what both antagonized the Scotts and ensured they defeated their troublesome neighbors.

"I'll be back by tomorrow afternoon. Be ready for me to lock our chamber door and not let you out until next sennight." Alex's wolfish grin made Caitlyn tug on his doublet before they exchanged another passionate kiss.

"I believe that's how I got with child each time."

"And such braw bairns we make. I'll look in on the lads before I go." Neither Alex nor Caitlyn needed to voice what every warrior and his wife understood: it could be his last goodbye, so he refused to miss the opportunity to kiss his sons one last time. "Have I told you what a happy mon you make me, mo ghaol?"

Caitlyn glanced toward the sun before looking back at Alex. "I think it's been at least three hours since you have. When was the last time I told you how happy you make me, mo ghràidh?"

"I believe it was this morn while you rode me." Alex offered Caitlyn a lascivious smile before they walked hand-in-hand to the steps. Alex guided Caitlyn, always nervous when she descended while pregnant. They entered the keep together but went separate directions after Alex dropped a kiss on Caitlyn's cheek.

. . .

"Caity."

"Aye, Alex. I'm right here. Do you need some water?" Caitlyn reached for the cup before she rested her hand on Alex's forehead. "You've cooled."

Alex grimaced as he rolled over and sat up. He rubbed the sleep from his eyes. "I feel better for sleeping." Alex accepted the mug, relishing the liquid sliding along his parched throat.

"You were smiling in your sleep." Caitlyn watched Alex, wondering what he dreamed about. A part of her dreaded the notion that he was dreaming about a woman.

"Was I?" Alex's eyes locked with Caitlyn's. He reached out his hand and cupped her cheek. "It was the first time I didn't have a nightmare. I had a dream, a pleasant one."

"Oh?" Caitlyn still wasn't sure what to make of Alex's expression or the vague comment.

"We were happy." Alex watched as Caitlyn tried to decipher his comment. "But it was only a dream."

Caitlyn pulled away, her heart breaking after a moment of hope. She gave a jerky nod before she rose and pressed Alex's shoulder forward. She couldn't bear for him to watch her face as she fought back tears. She peeled back the bandage, pleased to find the wound already appeared better than it had when she arrived.

"You must continue to sleep on your stomach." Caitlyn readjusted the bandage and turned to gather her medicinals. She couldn't meet Alex's eyes. While she appreciated knowing he hadn't been happily fantasizing about another woman, his comment felt like a cruel tease.

"Caity?"

"I've been here too long. I should have let your men mind you."

"Mind me? Am I suddenly a child who needs watching?"

Caitlyn straightened and looked at Alex, but her expression was inscrutable. He wished he could reach out and pull back his earlier comment. He'd found solace in his dream, but opening his eyes brought him back to reality. A reality that didn't have Caitlyn carrying any of his children or standing beside him as they gazed out at their land. Gathering her basket, Caitlyn nodded to Alex before she walked to the door.

"Caity?"

Caitlyn glanced back at Alex but shook her head. She had nothing left to say to him. She was angry and hurt that he continued to draw her in only to push her away. She wanted no one else, but she wasn't certain she could continue to endure this back and forth. She wanted a life with a man who wanted her as unconditionally as she wanted him. She opened the door and greeted Mitcham, who stood guard.

"Send one of your men or one of mine if you need aught." Caitlyn kept her voice low as she peered in both directions. When Alex called out to her again, she ignored him before slipping away.

ELEVEN

A fortnight in limbo passed for Caitlyn and Alex. She checked on him early each morning before most of the castle's occupants woke. She slipped back while the court danced the night away. But neither had much to say. Alex slept through most of the day but remained awake at night, too anxious about having a nightmare and ripping his stitches. When he slept, it was with the window hanging drawn back and light streaming into the chamber. While he had the occasional nightmare, they were nothing like what he experienced before seeing Caitlyn. Instead, their being together, happy and with a family of their own, filled most of his dreams.

Alex chided himself over and over for the wishful thinking that one day the dreams could come true. He could neither be Caitlyn's husband nor Clan Armstrong's laird. It was folly to think otherwise, but as much as his conscious mind nagged his subconscious to cease, the dreams came back nearly each time he closed his eyes. He knew Caitlyn could tell he was better rested than before the attack. He suspected she deduced why, but she never asked. Neither did he offer, understanding he'd hurt her the one time he'd confessed that his dreams were about them as a couple.

Caitlyn was eager to see Alex before each visit, but she dreaded them as she walked into the chamber. While it relieved her to watch Alex improve daily, it pained her to tend to him and know nothing would come of her dedication. His face was no longer bruised, and the swelling around his eyes had disappeared after a sennight. Now the brilliant green orbs watched her every movement. Their gazes locked over and over, the temptation to say more than they should obvious in their expressions. But she always hurried through his examination and application of more salve before leaving as quietly as she arrived. They barely spoke during those two weeks, despite seeing one another twice a day.

Alex accepted he was to blame for the tension between them, but he was at a loss for what to do. He knew he should apologize, but he feared only re-opening the festering wound. He considered how Caitlyn removed his stitches and cleaned his wound when it became infected. He wondered if he should treat the wound to their relationship the same way. But each time he opened his mouth, he watched Caitlyn withdraw. When another three days passed, Alex was unwilling to leave things unresolved. He intended to set off for Mangerton the next day.

"Caity, will you go riding with me this morn?"

Caitlyn froze as she leaned behind Alex to inspect his injury. She'd removed the stitches four days earlier, but she was unconvinced Alex should spend five nights sleeping on the ground. But she understood he couldn't remain at court forever. She hadn't expected his request.

"Wouldn't a walk be better?" Caitlyn spoke before she realized what she was saying. While she knew the walk would be better for Alex, she realized she might have insulted him, and she'd implied a willingness to go with him.

"Likely. But I know being here with me keeps you cooped up. A walk won't afford you the distance from the keep that you'd like. And I'm leaving tomorrow."

"Are you?" The casualness in Caitlyn's voice fooled neither of them.

"I have to return home. I dispatched a missive to my father the first day I could see well enough to write. He's aware of what happened, but I must meet with him to give him the details of my meetings with the king. You know those are things I can't put in writing for anyone to read."

"I understand."

"Will you go riding with me, Caity?" Alex waited as Caitlyn considered his invitation.

"I'm certain you'd enjoy escaping this chamber. I'll go."

"You sound as though it's a duty, an obligation. Do you think I need a nursemaid? Do you fear it will overtax me, and I shall need you to put me to rights?" Alex's tone was bitter. He resented yet another thing that made him feel like half a man. Caitlyn threw the linen square she'd used to wipe her hands on the bed.

"What do you want from me, Alex? You come here and treat me like shite. You push me away while I try to take care of you, angry that you need someone's help. Now you want me to enjoy your company after you've been surly for a fortnight. Did I misunderstand how I'm supposed to react? Am I supposed to be overjoyed that you wish to spend time with me now that you've decided not to be an arse?"

"All of that is true." Alex pushed back the covers

and rose from bed, wearing only a pair of breeks. "But you haven't been very approachable of late. Everything I say, even when I try my damnedest to get it right, only aggravates you. I don't want to leave here tomorrow with us both upset with one another. You've been my friend for nearly as long as I can remember."

"Friend?" Caitlyn blew a puff of air from her nose in disgust. "As a friend, I will tell you, you're more spoiled and selfish now than you were when you arrived at Dunure, believing yourself a fine little lordling because you're an heir. As a friend, I will tell you that the only pity to be had is what you feel for yourself. And as a friend, I will tell you that the misery you think you feel now will only grow worse each year you insist upon pushing away people who love you no matter whether you lost all your limbs or just one. You want to be alone? Then keep it up. You will have your wish soon enough."

Alex stood with his mouth agape, shocked at the vehemence in Caitlyn's tone. She had said nothing untrue, but he realized that he'd pushed her to where she might walk away and not come back. The constant push-and-pull he felt whenever he was near Caitlyn was driving him to the brink, but he was punishing Caitlyn as much as he was himself. Only she had no control over his sulkiness.

"I'm sorry, Caitlyn." Alex watched as her chin lifted, and he could tell she was uncertain how she felt about him using her full name. "I don't know how to come to terms with everything that's happened. But I know you are the last person I want to walk away and not look back. I know what I want, but I can't reconcile that with what I believe is right. I don't know that I ever can, and the guilt is swallowing me. I'm different from I was, and not just because of my arm and my face. I don't like who I am, but I don't know how to be any different."

Caitlyn listened to Alex's heartfelt words, knowing the confession cost him his pride. She stepped closer to him and cupped his cheeks. "Mayhap neither of us is going to have the future we wanted. But don't punish me for that, Alex. I swore to myself that night you got hurt that I wouldn't turn my back on you, but you make it mighty hard. If a friend is how you view me, then a friend I will be. But let me do that. Don't blame me for the choice you've made. You know it isn't the one I would make."

Alex cupped Caitlyn's hand before he turned his head to kiss her palm. "Thank you, Caity. Not only for tending to me, and not only for putting up with me. Thank you for your friendship. Thank you for seeing me the way you always have when I can't do it."

Caitlyn swallowed the temptation to tell him she did it because she loved him. It would only cause her more pain. Whether or not he returned the sentiment, they would go no further with their romance. She drew in a fortifying breath.

"I can be ready to ride in fifteen minutes. I'll join you in the stables. Can one of your men find my guards, please?"

"Of course."

Caitlyn offered a tight smile before she gathered her belongings and passed through the door. Alex watched her go, and it was as though a vacuum sucked all the light from the chamber despite how the sun shone.

Am I wrong? Each dream has made it seem more and more possible to have a future with Caitlyn. They feel so real. But they're just dreams, you fool. You might think aboot the trouble with the Scotts, but you're too busy swanning around with your make-believe wife to recall what life is really like. It's all fantasy. One that is likely to get Caitlyn and half your clan killed. Be realistic, mon. This attack proved I'm not strong enough to defend myself, let alone Caitlyn or lead a clan.

Go for the ride with her, enjoy as much time as you have, then mount your horse again in the morn and leave. Leave Stirling and leave Caitlyn to find the mon she deserves. It might be what finally kills me, knowing she's with someone else, but try to be bluidy decent for the first time since you arrived here.

Alex struggled into his doublet, having not worn one since the morning King Robert visited and Caitlyn arrived to check on him. He glanced at his scabbard and gritted his teeth. If he rode out without it, anyone who spotted them would think him an easy target. They would be right, but he hoped carrying his sword would be a deterrent. He pulled the strap over his head and settled the empty sheath on his back. It felt as natural as breathing, and for the first time since the battle, it felt right to wear it. That only made him feel even more conflicted.

Alex joined his men in the bailey after claiming his sword from the guards at the gate. He'd held it in his hand long enough to make people stare even more than usual. When he slid it into the scabbard the sound was reassuring, when it had been humiliating and bitter for the past six months. He spotted Mitcham, Stephen, and Grant, who stood with his men as Caitlyn's chaperone on their outing. Alex ordered David to remain at the keep and listen for anything said about him once he was through the gate. He expected more gossip once people thought he wouldn't hear it.

Alex watched as Grant helped Caitlyn into the saddle, an act Alex had done countless times over the years. His palms tingled and his chest burned knowing he couldn't do so anymore. Caitlyn glanced at him, but beyond that, she studiously kept her eyes averted. He understood she was attempting to preserve his dignity as he struggled to mount. Alex examined his saddle, dreading how ungainly he appeared. He considered whether there was a better way than what he'd been doing. He'd kept the reins in his right hand rather than his left while trying to use his right hand to grip the saddle. It felt uncoordinated, and it had irritated his horse, Strong, the first few times. But he'd aptly named his mount when he was two-and-twelve. He'd chosen the name because he thought it was the better part of his clan's name, but it was a fitting moniker for the enormous beast.

Taking the reins and passing them to his left hand, he wrapped his fingers around the leather leads. It surprised him to find he could grip them better than he expected. He glanced around him, sensing people watched him. He doubted it was a wise time to attempt mounting a different way, but somehow, he felt braver than he had since he started riding again. He lifted his left arm until his left hand could grip the saddle with the reins still in his hold. Slipping his foot into the stirrup, his right hand wrapped around the saddle where it belonged. Pushing with all the strength he could muster in his legs, he heaved himself into the saddle with such force that he nearly slid off the other side. He hadn't expected the ease with which he could move. He grinned to himself before regaining his bearing and nodding to the others.

Caitlyn tried to pretend she wasn't watching Alex, fearful of how he planned to mount without tearing his stitches and curious about how he overcame the lack of his left arm to help him. It surprised her to watch him use it to hold his reins and help him balance. The doublet pulled tight across his back as the muscles strained beneath it. She glimpsed the hewn muscles of his expansive chest as he leaned for-

121

ward for a moment as he mounted. The collar was unfastened and afforded her an unobstructed view down his doublet. She caught herself before she licked her lips. She was ready for them to spur their horses and clatter out of the bailey. It gave her something to concentrate on rather than ogling Alex.

When Caitlyn had returned to her chamber to change into a gown better suited for riding, she sent her maid to fetch a picnic lunch for the party. They rode well beyond where Caitlyn and her guards usually stopped when they went north of Stirling. In silent agreement they ventured away from Scotland's borderland rather than toward the Scotts' territory. They rode past the midday hour and stopped to eat midafternoon. Their journey back to Stirling would be easier since much of the ride would be a descent. Neither Alex nor Caitlyn worried about returning at a reasonable hour.

Caitlyn spread out a blanket and unpacked the basket while the guards scouted the area. Alert but more at ease, the men joined Alex and Caitlyn and shared the repast. It surprised Caitlyn how much food the kitchen staff fit into the basket without it overflowing. There was ample food for four men and Caitlyn. As the group jested and bantered, it was the most normal Caitlyn and Alex felt while together since Alex arrived at court. They teased one another with stories from their childhood that the guards had never heard. They trod more carefully when Grant asked what happened between Alex and Cairren. He recalled the two had once appeared in love and likely to marry.

"It was puppy love," Alex explained. "We're the same age, and so after a while, it just seemed like that was the natural progression. I suppose no one really expected us to, but we thought so. Fortunately, we realized it wasn't more than a lifelong friendship."

Caitlyn listened in silence, but she caught Alex's eye as he spoke. What he didn't include was how Caitlyn suffered her own case of puppy love for Alex as the starry-eyed girl who wished she were her sister. He didn't mention that after Cairren left for court, and Alex still came to visit when his fostering ended, it was he and Caitlyn who went for long walks and paired for nearly every evening dance. While others still thought of them as childhood friends, it had ceased feeling that way for them years ago. But Caitlyn had been too young, and Alex had struggled with guilt for lusting after a woman barely out of girlhood.

While they'd never shared a kiss before that day in the undercroft, they'd held hands on their walks and pressed shoulders together when they whispered at meals. It had been a slow progression over a handful of years, but they seemed to have made headway and silently agreed to a future during Cairren's trip to court not long after she married. Caitlyn was aware her sister noticed there was a difference in how Alex and Caitlyn acted together. After that, it had seemed like Alex was courting Caitlyn whenever he came to court, which was more frequent than it had been when Cairren was a lady-in-waiting.

Caitlyn half-listened to the conversation around her as she watched the breeze make the meadow flowers sway. She closed her eyes for a long blink before gazing at the lazy clouds shuffling by overhead. She was more content than she ever was within the castle's walls. Things were still tense with Alex, but it was the first time in weeks that she'd relaxed. It finally felt like they were friends again instead of enemies. She inhaled, filling her lungs nearly to bursting with the fresh air as the sun warmed her cheeks.

"You shall get more freckles." Alex's voice was so close to Caitlyn's ear that she jumped. Its softness sent a shiver along her spine. "Do you think there are too many to count?"

Alex reminded her of the childhood game they'd played after passing hours outside. He spent much of his day in the lists, while Caitlyn helped in the gardens and visited clan members in the village with her mother. Alex used to tease Caitlyn and Cairren, who were both prone to freckles despite their olive skin.

Caitlyn grimaced, which surprised Alex. At his frown, Caitlyn shook her head. "I wasn't thinking. All this sunshine will have darkened my skin. I should have worn a hat."

"One of those straw peasant hats Cairren insisted upon?"

"Aye. I never wore one at home, but I do when I'm outside without the other ladies and can't hide in the shade. They'll have plenty to say."

"Like they did to Cairren?" Alex felt his jaw clench as he recalled the vicious and dangerous things he'd overheard the Munros say about Cairren when she first arrived at her husband's clan. He'd heard similar things while he'd visited court when she was in residence.

"Not as bad as that. I'm still lighter than Cairren, even when I'm out in the sun. They'll be unkind, but not as hateful as they were to Cairrie. I feel guilty that I have an easier time than she did. It was by chance that she has darker skin than I do. I used to ask God when I was younger to give me the same rich color as *Maman* and Cairrie. Now I admit I've thanked Him for not. Being lighter makes me more acceptable." Caitlyn shrugged. Thinking about it only made her feel worse than the comments.

"Are you safe?" Alex asked every time he visited. He couldn't remember if he already had during this visit.

"Aye. I've had untoward offers, and people assume what they did with Cairren. One of these days, I'll become some mon's mistress and live up to their low expectations." Caitlyn's rueful smile hid the pain the ethnocentric comments caused, but there was little she could do. It was the queen who invited Cairren, then Caitlyn, to serve as ladies-in-waiting. When she first arrived, Caitlyn wondered if Queen Elizabeth took perverse pleasure in having the sisters, with their Saracen heritage showing in their complexions, in her entourage. While she never got that sense during her stay at Stirling, she also knew she would find no champion in the queen.

"How much longer must you remain?" Alex stared to the south as though he might view the malicious royal court from where they lounged.

"I don't know. Until Papa arranges a marriage or the king decrees who I'll wed. It could be years or only sennights. I'm not part of that decision."

Alex loathed the resignation he heard in Caitlyn's voice. He almost wished there were anger or bitterness. It told him during their ride she'd accepted that he would never offer for her. She'd given up, and he was the only one to blame.

The sun passed behind a cloud, casting a dark shadow over them. Alex realized it was later than he thought. He knew they should have started back sooner, but he estimated their arrival at the keep before sundown. But it would be close.

"We need to ride back, Caity."

"I know." Caitlyn's mouth twisted as she accepted that her brief taste of freedom was over. And so was the brief time she had with the Alex she'd known since she was five. The man he was now planned to leave the next day, and she didn't expect him to return. She expected his argument to be that he had no business back at court after being attacked, and she suspected his father relenting—likely after his mother insisted. "Thank you for bringing me out here."

"I think we both needed it." Alex watched as Grant helped Caitlyn once more, but he felt at ease once he mounted, not having struggled now that he had a better method. He found confidence he didn't think he still possessed.

TWELVE

"A lex." Caitlyn tried not to look back.

"I know. I saw them as we rounded the last bend. We need to outrun them. Can you manage?"

Caitlyn glanced at Alex, and he wondered if she questioned whether he was the one who would slow them. She nodded as she pressed her thighs firmer against her horse's flanks. The men already rode in a circle around her, like they always did. But the circle tightened as all their mounts increased their paces.

"No matter what, stay inside the circle."

"Yes, Alex. I know. Who are they?" Caitlyn chanced a glance back and wished she hadn't. Their unknown pursuers were gaining ground and creeping closer.

"I don't know. But we must push forward. We're too far away to reach Stirling and use the castle for protection. We can try to lose them in the woods coming up, but I don't like the idea of leading our horses through there while they're running."

"I'll go wherever you tell me." Caitlyn's voice rang with trust and confidence. Alex prayed he proved worthy of it. He suspected the men following them weren't merely highwaymen hoping to rob them. The glances he'd gotten made him think trained warriors followed them. The horseflesh was too fine, and the men appeared too well-fed. If that was the case, they were after no one but him.

They turned off the road and entered the trees, slowing their horses as man and beast avoided low-hanging branches. They weaved through the tree trunks, the animals cautious not to step on exposed roots. Caitlyn's heart pounded as they rode further into the woods, praying the dim light and uneven terrain slowed the men chasing them. No one spoke as they guided their horses to a walk, attempting to make less noise.

Alex wasn't sure where they headed. He was unfamiliar with the land they were on, having relied on the road to be their guide. He knew none of the guards knew the area, since he knew his men had never traveled this far north, and he wasn't sure about Grant. He supposed Grant might have accompanied Caitlyn on her few brief visits to see Cairren. Alex himself had taken a different route the one time he traveled to Foulis.

It wasn't long before they emerged from the forest and found themselves in another meadow. Unfortunately, steep hills on three sides bordered it. The only way out of the valley seemed to be turning back the way they came. Alex scanned their surroundings, looking for anywhere to hide Caitlyn when the inevitable fight started. He spied a boulder that could at least hide her. He prayed her horse could fit behind it. He didn't want to sacrifice the mount, but he wouldn't let it give away Caitlyn's hiding spot.

"Caity, go behind that rock." Alex pointed out where he meant. "Do not come out. No matter what you spy or hear. Do not leave that hiding place."

"Yes, Alex. I promise." Caitlyn spurred her horse and raced across the short distance. She made it around the far side of the rock only moments before the pack of men broke through the trees. She prayed they hadn't spied her from a distance. She wondered if she should dismount and try to keep her horse quiet or remain in the saddle in case she couldn't keep her promise. No one had trained her mare for battle. The animal sensed the danger and was becoming agitated.

"Shh, Goldie." Caitlyn tried to sooth her fawn-colored mare, who only became more anxious. Keeping her voice low, Caitlyn talked to Goldie as she climbed down from the saddle. She pressed her face against the horse's long nose and stroked her mane. Goldie settled until the first clash of swords, when she reared and tried to bolt. Caitlyn barely hung onto the reins without getting trampled. "You shall make them hear us. They will leave you for dead and take me. I know you favor Alex's horse. If you wish to flirt with that destrier again, you'd do well to be quiet."

Caitlyn whispered as she coaxed her horse, but she was aware Goldie sensed her rising fear as the battle noises grew louder. She dared to peek around the rock and wished she hadn't. There were more of the enemy on the ground than the men who rode with her, and she recognized Mitcham laying supine. She couldn't tell if he still breathed. Her eyes jumped to Alex and was shocked, then pleased, and finally terrified as she caught sight of him wielding his sword where he stood. She knew he hadn't trained with it in months. He fought off two combatants, and from what Caitlyn witnessed, to her eyes, he appeared as though he'd never left the lists. The sword was an extension of his right arm, thrusting and parrying with ease. She winced when he drove his left shoulder into one man's sternum. She wondered if he felt the pain or if it would come later.

Caitlyn searched for Grant, fearful for her guard,

but the experienced warrior fought with confidence. Movement caught her eye, and she watched Mitcham roll onto his hands and knees, shake his head, then rise. Mitcham glanced toward Alex, and Caitlyn felt a moment of relief that the guard would help Alex, but Mitcham dashed it when he turned away and helped Stephen instead. Caitlyn turned her attention back to Alex as he slayed one man, running his sword through his opponent's chest. The other man raised his arm wide to slash at Alex, but the latter was faster. Alex practically cleaved the man in half. Caitlyn had never seen such strength in a man's single arm.

Caitlyn ducked back behind the boulder when a man charged between Mitcham and Stephen, running toward her. His bellow, closer than she expected, spooked Goldie. The mare shot out from behind the rock, eyes wild as she bolted away from the fray. Caitlyn swept her gaze around, but there was nowhere for her to go without a horse. She couldn't outrun the man or climb any of the rocks without her skirts slowing her.

Alex spun around as a man darted past him, headed toward Caitlyn. Without thinking, Alex whistled for Strong, and the ever-faithful animal galloped toward him, having taken shelter near the trees. Alex gritted his teeth against the pain that ricocheted through his body as he hauled himself into the saddle. His need to get to Caitlyn was greater than his concern for his discomfort. When noise came from behind, Alex glanced back to find five more men breaking through the tree line. They were mounted and following Alex. He understood the men had remained hidden, assuming the first wave's victory. But now that Alex was on horseback and galloping away from them, they emerged to give chase.

Alex spurred Strong until he neared the boulder

where Caitlyn hid. He held the reins in his left hand, surprised once again that his hand possessed the strength that it did. He pressed his sword into his left hand, curling his fingers around the hilt. As he held the reins and his sword with his weaker side, he leaned far to his right. He wrapped his arm around Caitlyn's ribs and yanked her off her feet and pulled her across his lap.

"Lay flat." Alex's command wasn't one Caitlyn would disobey. She'd known he would come for her. Her trust and faith in Alex were implicit. She clung to the stirrup, careful not to give the horse the wrong signal. "Keep your head down, Caity. Trust me."

"Always." Caitlyn's voice was nothing more than a puff of air, but still enough for Alex to hear. He transferred his sword back to his right hand, prepared to defend Caitlyn. They barreled toward the only way out of the valley which meant they raced toward the enemy. Slashing and striking the men who rode too close to Caitlyn for Alex's comfort, he fought his way past them. A moment before they entered the forest, he whistled a signal he knew his men understood meant he was safe. Their only choice was to trust that he could get Caitlyn and himself back to Stirling on their own. He would have preferred riding with more men to help protect Caitlyn, but he couldn't risk waiting when their enemy still outnumbered them.

Alex worried about what they might find if they escaped the forest. He didn't think the group of attackers was larger than the dozen he'd seen, but he couldn't be certain. He slowed Strong before they reached the road. He was proud of Caitlyn for remaining quiet and still. He strained to hear any movement that didn't come from nature before inching his steed forward until he could view the road in both directions. When nothing stirred after waiting for a few minutes, he prepared to move back onto the thoroughfare, but Caitlyn tapped his shin. He looked down to find her wiping blood away from her cheek. He helped her struggle to move into a seated position.

"Alex, your arm is bleeding." Caitlyn pointed to a gash on his left arm. Fear and urgency had kept him from feeling it, but now pain burned along his bicep. "I need to see if I should stitch it."

"It doesn't matter if it does. Unless you're hiding a needle and thread somewhere, there is naught to suture it with. What we need is to find shelter for the night and get off the road."

"But what aboot the others?" Caitlyn peered around Alex's shoulder but could see no one.

"They know I left safely with you. They will have won, judging by the men who are already dead, but I couldn't risk what might happen to you in the process. They'll try to meet up with us, and when they don't find us, they'll go back to Stirling. With luck, we will get there before them, and they won't send out a search party."

Caitlyn wanted to argue, but Alex had asked her to trust him, and she did. She held faith that he always believed her safety was paramount, so she remained quiet. She nearly didn't hear him when he spoke again.

"Are you all right, Caity? Did Goldie hurt you?" Alex brushed hair away from Caitlyn's face and ran his thumb over her cheekbone.

"Nay. She spooked and reared, but I was already standing. She's not used to the noise."

"I spied her run; that's what made me race to get to you before that mon." Alex swept his thumb over her cheek several more times before they leaned in. Their lips pressed together as Caitlyn clung to the front of Alex's doublet, and he wrapped his good arm around her. He swiped his tongue across the seam of her mouth until she opened for him. She flicked her tongue, welcoming him into her mouth. He couldn't stifle his needy groan as her breasts pushed against him as she squirmed to get closer.

The rustling leaves brought Alex back to reality, chiding himself for losing his common sense while Caitlyn's kisses drugged him. He scanned their surroundings before nudging Strong. Caitlyn swung her leg over to sit sideways, inspecting Alex's arm while he maneuvered their horse onto the road. Satisfied that the gash needed sewing but wasn't life threatening, she leaned against his chest and sighed. Caitlyn's eyes drifted closed with a sense of security even when she knew they were far from safe. She felt Alex adjust his position until his injured left arm wrapped around her. It surprised them both that he held her against him with ease. They continued south toward Stirling, but the late afternoon light faded rapidly.

"Caity, we passed a group of crofts near here while we rode north. Mayhap we can shelter with one of those families." Alex wouldn't admit how his energy drained from him now that they no longer faced an immediate threat. His arm pained him more than he wanted to let on, and Caitlyn was right: he needed stitches. But his only priority was getting her somewhere safe and sheltered for the night. They rode in silence for a half an hour before Caitlyn pointed to the white smoke puffs to their right. They entered the cluster of crofts as the sun set.

"Who goes?" A man's voice called out. Male heads poked out of each doorway, and Caitlyn realized the cluster of crofts was likely an extended family living together in their own dwellings.

"Alexander Buchanan." Alex's voice rang out clearly in the still air. To his relief, Caitlyn didn't blink as he named another Lowland clan rather than his own. With men pursuing him, Alex neither wanted to risk these people's lives nor Caitlyn's by telling the truth.

"And your wife?" The same man demanded.

"Sorcha." Caitlyn spoke up before leaning back against Alex. She appeared meek, and it wasn't far from how she felt as more strangers stepped outside to observe them.

"My horse stumbled a ways back. I kept Sorcha from falling, but I wasn't so fortunate. I landed on a rock and cut my arm. We hoped one of your women could lend Sorcha a needle and thread, then we'll be on our way."

"Nay. You can't be on the roads this late. Not with your wee wifey." An older woman pushed past a man who could easily have been her grandson. "I'm Helen. Come inside."

Caitlyn glanced at Alex, who nodded. He climbed down awkwardly, hoping it appeared like he tried to avoid jostling Caitlyn. But he paused when he stared up at her. She rested her hands on his shoulders and leaned toward him, making it easier for him to wrap his right arm around her. He pulled her from the saddle and eased her to the ground. Without thinking, she wrapped her arms around him, finally able to embrace him. She buried her face against his chest.

"You gave your bride a right scare, didn't you, lad?" Helen bustled forward, tutting as she approached. She peered at Alex's wound and shook her head. "Come along before that gets infected. And your wife looks ready to drop."

"Gram, there's no room in your croft, but there is in ours." A woman who appeared older than Alex stepped forward. She ushered Alex and Caitlyn toward her open door. "I'm Mary, and this is my husband, Benedict. You're welcome to stay with us. Our Matthew is married now," Mary pointed to the first man who spoke, "and has his own croft with his family. We have space for you."

"That's kind of you. All we really need is some boiling water and the needle and thread, please." Caitlyn leaned heavily against Alex as they approached the kind woman's home. "We don't wish to be any trouble."

"We were just aboot to sit down to sup," Benedict said as he opened the door wider for them. Caitlyn glanced at Alex, who looked just as weary as her, but she knew he was vigilant. They appreciated the hospitality, but how easily the families offered it unnerved them.

"We may not sound like some, but you're in the Highlands now, lass." Benedict spoke as though it explained it all, and Mary's expression led Caitlyn to believe there was something she should understand but didn't.

"Och, Highland hospitality," Benedict elaborated. "You're clearly in need, so we won't turn you away. Share our hearth and our supper. You'll be right as rain by morn."

"You're very generous." Alex's warm tone didn't match the suspicious gaze that took in every detail within the croft. Curtained areas took up opposite corners of the back wall. The kitchen lay to the right of one of them, and there was a large wood table with benches in the center of the croft. The fire blazed, and the scent of cooking pottage wafted toward Alex. His stomach grumbled, which elicited a giggle from Caitlyn.

"You still growing, Alexander?" Benedict teased. Standing closer, Benedict was several years older than Mary and likely close in age to Alex's father, Tavin. When Caitlyn ducked her head to hide another giggle, her body pressed against his hip. He could think of something that would grow if he didn't put some distance between them.

"The meal is nearly ready, but there is plenty of time for you to get cleaned up and for Sorcha to mend your arm." Mary nodded toward a ewer and basin. Caitlyn fetched it and placed it on the table while Mary fetched a sewing kit. "I can get you fresh water before you clean your husband's wound."

Caitlyn and Alex exchanged a long look, a range of emotions flickering across each of their faces. First to break their gaze, Caitlyn lathered a linen square and washed Alex's face and neck. She'd helped him throughout his fortnight convalescence, and it felt natural now. When she was through, she washed her own hands and face. While Benedict poured out the dirty water from the basin and refilled the ewer, Mary worked in the kitchen. Caitlyn helped ease the doublet from Alex's wounded arm, trying not to stare at his bare chest. She knew the effort was pointless. She'd yet to overcome the temptation even once.

"C—Sorcha." Alex caught himself but only barely. "It can wait until after we've eaten. You look exhausted."

Caitlyn ignored Alex as she washed the gash and inspected it. She accepted the jug of whisky Benedict offered. She tried to pass it to Alex, but he refused. It was she who winced when she poured the alcohol over Alex's wound. Her eyes watered when Alex didn't seem to register any pain.

"I can feel it, *leannan*. But there is naught either of us can do. I know you're doing your best." Alex squeezed Caitlyn's hand as he called her sweetheart. Caitlyn nodded, appreciating his reassurance. Once the needle and thread were ready, she angled Alex toward the fireplace, needing the extra light. She was quick and efficient, wanting to cease adding to Alex's pain.

"Seems like you've stitched your mon up before." Mary pointed to the beginning of a scar on Alex's back. "Accident prone, are you?"

"Aye." Alex nodded but kept his eyes on Caitlyn as she worked. She applied the salve Mary offered and accepted the linen strips to bandage Alex's arm. When she finished, Alex feared she might fall asleep on her feet. He made room for her on the bench and held out his right arm. She slid onto the seat next to him, sagging against him as his muscular body seemed to shelter her from the world. "Can you stay awake long enough to eat?"

Caitlyn nodded as she struggled to stifle a yawn. She didn't understand how Alex appeared as though they'd done little more than go for an afternoon jaunt. She ate without tasting the food, even though the sustenance helped revive her. She watched as Alex struggled into his doublet. She wished to help, but she didn't want to embarrass him by appearing to coddle him. But she didn't know if she made it worse by making it obvious that Alex couldn't easily dress himself. At her confused mien, Alex kissed her temple.

"I'm going to check on Strong. I won't be away long." Alex ducked out of the croft, and Caitlyn turned to find Mary stood watching her.

"Strong?"

"Aye. Alexander was still a boy when his horse was born. He was enormous even then, so he figured it was the right name." Caitlyn shrugged, recalling not to mention the entire reason for the animal's name.

"Then you've known one another a long time."

Caitlyn grew cautious as she responded to Mary.

"Since I was five, and he was seven. We grew up together in the same village."

"No wonder you're so in love. You've been sweethearts since the beginning." Mary smiled as she led Caitlyn to one of the cordoned off areas and drew back the curtain. The bed was made with fresh sheets, which Mary turned down. "I can lend you a chemise if you wish for something else to sleep in."

"I don't want to inconvenience you anymore. You and your husband have been so generous already." Caitlyn shook her head but smiled.

"Then I'll help you unlace your gown. I'm sure your husband would rather have the task, but I think his arm needs the rest."

Caitlyn's cheeks radiated heat as she considered Mary and Benedict expected them to share the bed beside her. Many married lairds and ladies didn't share a chamber, but peasant couples shared their bed. She offered a jerky nod and turned her back to Mary. She hung the gown on a peg as she heard the door close and realized Alex returned from the stables.

"Your wife is in bed, lad." Mary's soft voice floated to Caitlyn just before she scrambled to get under the covers before Alex could catch sight of her in only her chemise. They'd swum together countless times as children, but it had been years since he'd seen her in her underclothes.

"Sorcha?"

"Aye, Alex. You can come in." Caitlyn watched as Alex eased back the curtain, cautious not to expose her to Mary and Benedict. But she pushed back the covers and climbed across the bed to kneel before Alex. She undid his doublet's buttons, then nudged him to turn around. She eased the garment over his bandages. She ran her fingers over the healing wound on Alex's back.

"I'm all right, Caity." Alex kept his voice so low that Caitlyn barely heard him. He turned to her and offered a reassuring smile before he pulled the covers back up on his side of the bed. To lie on his right side, he had to turn away from Caitlyn. It also forced him to be farther from the door, leaving Caitlyn as the first person anyone stumbled upon. He would have to lie on his left arm. "Switch sides."

"What? Isn't this side easier on your arm?"

"I won't sleep with my back to the door and have you closer to it. I can't prevent one, but I can solve the other. Switch with me, Caity." Once Caitlyn slid across the bed, Alex laid down on top of the covers. He prayed Caitlyn would face away from him because he didn't trust himself to withstand the temptation not to kiss her. She lay on her back for a long moment before she turned her head toward Alex.

"Do you want me to open the curtain enough for the firelight to shine in?" Caitlyn whispered.

"No. You deserve the little privacy you have, with me in here."

Caitlyn made to argue but swallowed her words, choosing instead to offer Alex a warm smile. "Alex, before everything went to hell, I had a wonderful day. I realize it wasn't easy for you, but you did it for me. Thank you." Caitlyn leaned to kiss his cheek, but he leaned to do the same, making their mouths brush against one another. Her cool fingers slid along his chest until they wrapped around his neck. He twisted to rest his weight on his right forearm as his body hovered over hers. But he grew frustrated when he couldn't touch her because his one working arm bore his weight. Sensing his annoyance, Caitlyn pressed him back until she could drape her body over his. His warm palm covered one globe of her backside.

Their kisses grew more heated as Caitlyn shifted to straddle Alex's thigh. Her breath hitched as the pressure from her weight pressing her onto Alex's muscular leg rubbed her mound against him. Curious about the sensations, she rocked her hips. Alex's fingers bit into Caitlyn's bottom as he guided her to move against him. She felt the air brush the back of her legs as Alex gathered her chemise in his fist. She kicked the bed covers down to their feet while her right hand trailed over his chest until she cupped his rod. Need and frustration grew as Caitlyn tried to get closer to Alex, but his breeks were in the way. She rubbed her hand over his length, and she heard as much as felt his groan.

Pulling away, Caitlyn pressed her lips close to Alex's ear. "Make love to me, fuck me, do whatever, but be with me, Alex. Just once."

Alex's arm tightened around Caitlyn as though he might never let her go, even though his words meant the opposite. "If I could be sure without a doubt that I could marry you tomorrow, I would. I'd bury myself within you and not pull out until the sun comes up. But the attack today was aboot me as much as the one in the passageway. I won't die and leave you without a maidenhead and no way to marry."

"I don't want to marry anyone else."

"That might be true now, but once I was dead, you'll think otherwise."

"Once?" Caitlyn pushed away from Alex. "Do you intend to let them kill you? Are you giving up?"

"I'm being realistic that they might succeed. I'm scared for you, Caity. I'm scared to have you too close lest they hurt you, too. And I fear what would happen to you if I took your virginity, then died. Your mother and father might understand, but few grooms would. I know you wish for a family of your own."

"Of our own," Caitlyn corrected. "I've never

wanted—not even imagined—having a family with anyone but you."

"We already know—"

"You are the only one who seems to know everything, Alex. You've decided how everyone else's life will be, even though you feel you have no control over yours. You've decided your father will pass you over. You've decided Brice will take your place. And you've foisted me off onto some unknown suitor." Caitlyn grasped her chemise and pulled it to her waist as she straddled Alex's hips. She pressed her sheath against his sword. "I've decided I want one night in your arms. If you won't make love to me or even fuck me, then you can at least hold me and let me enjoy being close to you."

"Caity..." Alex didn't know what to say. He cupped the back of Caitlyn's head and eased her mouth toward his. When their lips met, he widened his legs and slid his hand over her bare bottom. His fingers slipped along her seam, growing wet from her dew. "Let me bring you pleasure, Caity. I won't enter you with more than my fingers, but let me show you what I wish I could do every night for the rest of our lives."

Caitlyn nodded as she squeezed her eyes shut. She wanted to tell him he was the only thing keeping them apart, that he was to blame for them not having every night together. But neither would relent, and she didn't want to ruin the moment. Caitlyn's breath hitched at the feel of Alex's fingers dipping into her entrance. He rubbed a spot that made her want to moan and writhe. She shifted against him, the feel of his cock rubbing along her slit adding to her body's excitement. Moving together, Caitlyn felt her core tighten before a wave of sensation rolled through her. She recognized what she felt since Cairren had described it to her.

Still floating in euphoria, Caitlyn tugged at the laces to Alex's breeks. She pulled them open, freeing his cock. "Tell me what to do."

Alex's chin tilted back as his hips rose when Caitlyn's hand wrapped around him. He lowered them, then raised them, rocking into her palm. Without waiting for him to explain, she stroked him, matching his rhythm. She felt him twitch, making her look at him. In the dark section of the croft, neither could see the other's eye color, but Caitlyn knew what the emerald windows to his soul looked like without needing to see them. Alex's hand cupped her skull again and guided her mouth back to his.

The moment their lips touched, passion overruled common sense, and restraint flew away. Neither knew who moved first, but Caitlyn released Alex's cock as his hand returned to her buttocks. She lifted her hips as his hand pressed against her. The tip of his rod glided through the dew on her petals until need pushed them together with an invisible hand. Caitlyn sank down as Alex thrust up until their bodies joined. Alex registered the feel of breaking through Caitlyn's barrier, and she felt the twinge of pain, but lust and love coalesced into consuming desire. They moved together with synchronicity and ease; their bodies already attune to one another. Alex reached between them to cup Caitlyn's breast, prompting her to press against his chest as she rode him.

"Let me taste you," Alex whispered as he brought his mouth to her breast, suckling as Caitlyn ground her pubis against his. Her body ached in a way she never imagined it could. Alex caused it, and he would be her only relief. His scorching mouth wrapped around her nipple as he drew the puckered flesh along his tongue. He kneaded her other one as Caitlyn kissed his neck and nipped at his earlobe. She felt the shiver that ran through Alex's body before his hips thrust harder and faster. She squeezed the muscles within her core, holding him in place as the friction against her pleasure button turned her need into a frenzy. She recognized the same tightening low in her belly as she'd felt before her first climax.

"Alex," Caitlyn breathed before kissing him to muffle her scream. It was only as his seed surged toward the tip of his cock that Alex regained enough sense to lift Caitlyn from him and pull out. His seed spilled across his belly, and they both froze. Reality crashed back down onto them as they panted in the darkness. Caitlyn made to roll away, but Alex couldn't bear to let go. He pulled her down against his chest, and she went willingly. He felt her tears against his shoulder and her shudders.

"Caity, no matter what, I love you. Not just as my friend. That wasn't a mistake. I will never think it was a mistake. Ill advised, mayhap. But I will never regret it, even though I'm certain I should. If that's the only time I'm with you, understand that it's the only time I've ever made love to a woman. I didn't fuck you or tup you, Caitlyn. I loved your body just as I love your soul."

"You know I love you, Alex. You know I wanted this and don't regret it. What I regret is that you won't relent, even now that we discovered what it's like. You won't accept me. That's why I cry. You gave me heaven only to put me in hell."

They lay together in silence, both lost in their thoughts. Despite being at odds over the future, neither pulled away, instead pressing closer. Alex stroked Caitlyn's hair as her hand rested over his heart. They fell asleep in one another's embrace as though there hadn't been heartache after bliss.

THIRTEEN

Alex awoke with a start, hands pushing at his chest. He inhaled, recognizing Caitlyn's scent immediately. He realized he wasn't protecting Mangerton Tower from a raid like he'd been in his dream. He was safe in a cottage with Caitlyn sharing a bed with him.

"Alex, wake up." Anxiety filled Caitlyn's voice as she shook his shoulders again.

"I'm awake now, Caity. Was I dreaming?" Alex was certain he had been.

"Aye. I think it started out nicely, but you grew restless and breathed heavily."

"Do you think I woke them?"

"Nay. I roused you soon enough." Caitlyn hesitated, realizing she was stroking Alex's hair as he held her against his chest. "Do you need aught?"

"Just you." Alex confessed, his words so quiet that he nearly didn't hear them. Caitlyn slid her arm around his waist and nestled closer, a contented sigh escaping as her head found a comfortable spot on his shoulder. "It started out like my other dreams have lately. We were together at Mangerton. I don't remember what happened though because suddenly the bells were ringing, and I was running to the battlements. Brice and I stood together as we watched a massive force ride toward us. I couldn't tell if they were Scotts. That part was unclear for the first time since these nightmares started."

Alex glanced down at Caitlyn, who nodded against his shoulder. Her arm tightened, but she said nothing. Her silence was the encouragement Alex needed to confide in her. They'd shifted during the night, so the only arm that reached her easily was his left. She was hesitant, but she drew it around her. She felt his fingers splay, so she slid hers along them until they held hands. It was an awkward position for her, but she would not deny him the comfort he sought.

"Brice went to the barracks and the armory to ready the men while I ran to the keep, searching for you and to warn the servants to hide. In my other dreams, you've always been with child. Usually we already have two sons, but sometimes two sons and a daughter. Right as I spot you, I hear the attackers battering the front gate. I glanced toward the sound, then when I turned back, you and the weans were gone. I ran out to the bailey as the attackers burst through. I was the only person standing there, trying to block them. A mon—I didn't recognize who he was—called out to me as the enemy poured in around me. When I searched for whoever yelled my name, I found this mon had a knife to your throat. Before I could say aught, he ran it across your neck. He did the same to five children standing around him. I tried to run to you, but my legs didn't move. I was standing in a bog. I reached for my sword, but there was naught there. I stood and watched this mon kill our entire family, and I could do naught to stop him."

145

Caitlyn pushed onto her elbow when Alex shuddered at the end of his tale. She stared at him in the dark, unable to see his expression, but she could feel how his emotions roiled within him as though they were her own. His body was rigid, his heart pounded, and he felt warm beneath her. She pressed the back of her hand to his forehead, wondering if a fever had set in and caused the nightmare. He wasn't feverish, only overheated.

"Caity, I never want to let you go. I'm convinced it's having you here that's keeping me from panicking. But I'm also certain it was a warning. I have no business taking you to Mangerton Tower nor becoming laird."

"Alex, you've decided that a future you think might happen is already destined to be true. You can't be sure of that. No one can. Mayhap not a single thing you've dreamed will come to pass. Mayhap you will live to be an auld mon who could have grandbairns hanging off you. Mayhap we could grow auld together. Or mayhap I have only a few years with you, but that's better than none."

"Better than none?" Alex hissed. "There would be far many more for you to enjoy if you married someone who can take care of you. But I ruined that last night."

Caitlyn froze. Her chest ached, then burned. She understood the consequences of their actions, but she hadn't regretted them. She accepted she'd made it nearly impossible to marry, and that with Alex's ongoing refusal, she'd likely end up a spinster. But it was hearing Alex's regret that felt like a knife through her heart.

"The only thing ruined, Alexander, is my memory of the only night I'll likely spend in your arms." Caitlyn turned away, putting space between them, but her voice sounded detached when she spoke again. "Wake me if you need aught. I'll be here."

"Caity…" Alex closed his eyes and pressed his palm to his forehead as tears stung behind his lids. He hadn't meant to ruin anything, but once more he'd spoken without thinking about how it made Caitlyn feel. He didn't regret making love to her, but he regretted stealing her future. That made him feel even worse.

They lay in silence, both still awake, for another hour. Eventually, Caitlyn relented and reached her hand behind her until she found Alex's arm. He took her hand and wrapped his arm around her waist when she pulled it over her. Neither said more, but they both fell back to sleep. They woke to Mary and Benedict moving around the cottage. Temptation told Alex to drop a kiss on Caitlyn's cheek and pretend as though they hadn't exchanged words after his dream. He wanted to pretend as though they were a blissful couple who'd joined for the first time, a couple with a future together. Instead, he drew his arm from Caitlyn's waist and rolled off the bed with a grunt.

"I'll saddle Strong while you get ready." Alex couldn't guess how to do that. It had been a challenge to unsaddle the animal the night before, but with one good arm, he pulled it to the ground. He feared he couldn't hoist it onto the beast's back.

"Give me a moment, and I will go with you." Caitlyn rose, keeping her back to Alex while grabbing her kirtle. She sighed in frustration when she recalled the gown closed in the back. Someone had to lace it, even if she could tie it. She suspected Alex couldn't, so that meant Mary. She would only do it if Alex wasn't there, otherwise, the woman would wonder why the husband didn't help his wife.

"I know you're offering help, and I can't even do

147

something as simple as tie a bow." Caitlyn turned her head toward Alex's despondent voice. He was looking at the back of her kirtle, and his expression was so defeated that Caitlyn wanted to cry. His misplaced guilt frustrated her, but in raw moments like this, she understood the depth of what the Scotts stole from Alex when he lost the use of his arm. She understood why he felt useless. It was an ingrained sense of duty and loyalty that urged him to convince his family to set him aside as a leader. It was the nightmares that haunted him that made him question himself. He wasn't being awkward on purpose. He was lost.

"Can you pass the laces through the eyelets from top to bottom? I've seen you tie your breeks closed. Could you help me if they ended at my waist?" Caitlyn held her breath, praying she hadn't set Alex up for failure.

"Aye." Alex stepped behind Caitlyn. It took him what felt like forever, but he passed the ribbon through each opening and cinched it tight. He concentrated as he worked on the tie. When he finished, he flexed the fingers of his left hand, feeling more sensation than he had in months. He stared down at his breeks as Caitlyn turned toward him. Determined to not need a nursemaid for himself, he pulled his pants closed and managed the fastening with less trouble than he ever had.

"Alex?"

"Hmm." Alex remained looking at his breeks, pleased with his accomplishment.

"You're doing more with your left hand." Caitlyn pointed to the extremity. "Do you think using it is making it easier?"

"I think so. I've always been able to move my fingers, and I can even make my arm move slightly—

twitch, really. But I hadn't tried to hold aught before yestermorn. I tried when I was first recovering but couldn't. I dropped everything. I assumed it was still the case."

"Alex?"

"Aye, Caity. You don't have to keep saying my name as though you're afraid to talk to me."

"I don't want to say the wrong thing." Caitlyn's anxiousness was easy to read in her expression. Alex's mouth turned down, but he nodded. "I watched you fight yesterday. I—I don't understand how you made it seem so easy. I mean, I know you haven't been going to the lists. Stephen told me you started training with dirks a couple days before you left—and please don't be mad that he told me. I just didn't exp—didn't rea—wasn't—"

"You didn't think I could do it."

"Sort of. I remember you've been wielding a sword since you were two-and-twelve, and you'd watched the men for years before that. I'm not so surprised that you can do it. It must feel natural. I'm more surprised at how strong you are. I figured any mon who hadn't trained in six moons would be rusty or weaker. But, Alex, you were not weak out there. You managed Strong and fought. You controlled him and lifted me off the ground. If you are weaker than before the battle, then I can't fathom how much power you had back then. It's almost scary, but I never once felt threatened by you. You've always been gentle with me."

"Because I've never wanted to hurt you, Caity. Even if that's all I do these days. I intended for my strength to protect you, never to intimidate you. As for how I am now, I suppose it's from close to a lifetime of practice. The sword is just part of me when I hold it."

"But your strength?"

"I don't know. I don't feel that different from before my injury, but I also thought I was just a large mon."

Caitlyn's gaze flickered to his waist, and her cheeks felt on fire because she knew Alex watched her. She hadn't intended to take his words as an innuendo, but she hadn't been able to stop herself from what his words brought to mind.

"You flatter me, lass." Alex grinned as Caitlyn gazed everywhere but at his eyes. He grew serious as he continued. "I can't explain some of this. I think I should have tried using my hand sooner, but I didn't know. Mayhap it will improve with use. But I don't think my arm will ever be useful again. It's only skin sewn tight that's keeping it on. Even if I can't use my arm, having use of my hand makes life seem a little easier to bear."

Caitlyn reached out a tentative hand. "I know your arm pains you all the time, especially when you jar it, or someone bumps it. But does your hand hurt to be touched?"

"Nay." Alex was unprepared for Caitlyn to slide her hands into his. It felt normal. It felt like it had the innumerable times they'd done it since they were children.

"I'm not saying yesterday proves your worries wrong." Caitlyn squeezed his hands. "But I will say that I never—not for a single breath—doubted you could protect me. I just knew. I was worried something would happen to you, but at the same time, I was positive I was safe because you were there."

"I will never give up protecting you, even if I'm holding on by my fingernails. There is naught I wouldn't do for you, Caity. I love you."

"I love you, Alex. I always have." Caitlyn's green-gray gaze met Alex's green one. "I understand that doesn't change things. Don't fear that I expect aught from you now."

"Now? Do you mean after you watched me fight or after I bedded you?"

"Either." Caitlyn shrugged. "Both."

Alex didn't know what to say. He wanted her to expect a great deal from him, but he recognized the perverted selfishness in that when he had nothing he could give. They left the sleeping area together and accepted the warm bannocks and honey Mary offered. Benedict came inside, brushing his windswept hair from his forehead.

"I guessed your wife likely needed the sleep but that you'd want to be off soon. I hope you don't mind, but I saddled your horse. I thought to give you more time to eat." Benedict explained casually as he gathered his own bannocks. He'd saved Alex the embarrassment of trying to maneuver the large leather object, and his casual tone downplayed the help he offered. Neither Mary nor Benedict knew for certain that something more than a gash was wrong with Alex's arm, but it was obvious they'd noticed he favored his left arm for everything.

"I appreciate that. Sorcha needed the rest, and I admit, so did I. You've been so gracious to us."

"You two haven't been married long, have you?" Mary asked. At Caitlyn and Alex's surprised expressions, she explained, "I can tell from how close you stand without realizing it. If my Matthew and his wife were ever in need, I would hope someone would take them in. It was the least we could do for you. Mayhap you will offer the same hospitality one day to a young couple."

Caitlyn stepped forward and embraced Mary while Alex and Benedict clasped forearms. They left the older couple in their croft and made their way to the stables. Alex felt a surge of trepidation when he remembered he couldn't help Caitlyn mount. He watched as she clicked her tongue and grasped Strong's bridle. She led him to a stump where Benedict chopped wood. She swung the horse to block anyone's view and used the stump as a mounting block. She cocked an eyebrow at Alex. Swallowing his pride, he followed suit, and they were on their way.

"People will talk if they aren't already. How do you want to explain why you were away from the keep with me overnight?" Alex held the reins lightly in his hands, his arms resting at the sides of Caitlyn's waist as she rode before him.

"The truth?"

"Do you think people will believe it? If they learn someone attacked, they will wonder why I'm not dead."

"You believe everyone assumes you're an invalid. I don't think that's how others view you."

"Then you are hard of hearing or short of memory. You've heard what's been said. But I don't care aboot that. I'm more worried aboot what people will say aboot you."

"They'll crow over being right, that I'm a fallen woman, who is only suited to being a mistress." Caitlyn didn't want to consider how close to the truth the assumptions were. But it wasn't her skin color that made her only suited to be Alex's mistress—albeit for one night—rather than his wife. It was his stubbornness.

"It makes me uneasy to leave you at court. I'm

worried aboot what men will do if they think you aren't a maiden anymore."

"Half the court assumes I'm not, while the other half assumes no one will touch me. They'll gossip aboot me being gone, but I doubt it will change aught. Their opinions can't get any lower."

"I loathe that. Can Innes and Collette not request you return home? Come up with some reason?"

"Nay. My parents don't want me near the border anymore. That's why they married Cairren to a Highlander. They would only agree to me going south for one reason." Caitlyn didn't need to articulate that the one reason was marriage to Alex.

"Then discretion is best."

"You mean not being seen together. Won't that make us appear guiltier?"

"We've been—uh—rather distant while I've been at court. People might think we've had another falling out."

"Or that you tupped me and are no longer interested. But discretion is best." Caitlyn sighed, but neither said any more. It took them an hour to ride back to Stirling. They entered the bailey while it was still early. Men were already in the lists, but few members of court were awake. Alex and Caitlyn's guards met them in the stables.

"What happened?" Grant demanded as the couple dismounted. Alex raised his chin and cocked an eyebrow, reminding the guardsman that his tone wasn't appropriate to his lady.

"We sought shelter with a couple in their cottage. It was the cluster of crofts we passed. It wasn't safe for Lady Caitlyn to sleep outdoors last night." Alex's hardened expression dared any of the men to speak against Caitlyn or him.

"Thank the merciful saints. We feared that's what

you'd had to do when we couldn't find you. We rode until after sundown but found no trace of you. We did find Goldie." Stephen shifted his gaze to Caitlyn, one of his eyes swollen shut. "We all survived, but not all of them did."

"That means there are still some of them alive to chase me again." Alex glanced down at Caitlyn, who was looking back at him over her shoulder. "You need to keep your distance from me, Caity."

Neither noticed the informality, and it barely registered with the guards. But the other men sensed something was different between the couple and wondered what happened in the hours they spent separated from the nobles they were tasked to defend. The men nodded and slipped away, allowing Alex and Caitlyn to whisper.

"I know. That doesn't mean I like it." Caitlyn glanced nervously toward the stable doors. "Please promise you'll have at least one of your men with you. You never rode out from Mangerton without men, even before. You're a laird's heir, and that obviously still means a great deal to some."

"I know. But I need you to promise me you won't venture away from the keep for the next few days."

"Are you still leaving tomorrow?" Caitlyn needed to know, even though she didn't want to hear it.

"No. I will delay a day to ensure you're safe here and to see if aught comes from yesterday's attack. I'm certain the Bruce will demand to meet with me. Perhaps he'll have some insights." Alex shifted, thinking to kiss Caitlyn, but he stopped himself in time. "You should go inside."

"Be careful, Alex. I'm scared." Caitlyn strained on her toes, dropping a kiss on his cheek before hurrying out of the stables. Alex watched Caitlyn enter the keep before turning toward the lists. He was exhausted and sore, but curiosity was stronger. He would either surprise himself and prove Caitlyn right, or he would make a fool of himself. But he had to find out whether he still possessed the strength he once had. He wanted to learn if he could train and still stay on his feet or if it was sheer luck and stubbornness that kept him alive in the valley.

FOURTEEN

A lex spotted the Armstrong and Kennedy guards
training together as he entered the lists. He
nearly turned back since they were in the center of
the training ground. It made it all the easier for
people to watch him knocked on his arse, and he had
to walk past half the warriors to reach the men. He
knew people were watching him, wondering what he
was doing on the field. He weaved and avoided sparring partners until he came to the Armstrongs and
Kennedys.

Keeping his voice low, Alex leaned forward. "You
can imagine it surprised me as much as it did you
yesterday. But apparently I haven't forgotten how to
fight, nor am I completely incapable. I need to know
whether it was only the heat of battle or if I can still
hold my own. There's nowhere else within the walls
to test me, so here I am." Alex reached back and
withdrew his sword from its sheath. It felt as natural
as it had the day before; it felt as it always had. As he
stared at his men, he noticed a couple targes laying
nearby. He put his sword back into the scabbard before he picked up the wide leather shield. Cautiously,
he slid it onto his left arm. He tried to move it, but it
only made him wince. He angled it higher than nor-

mal, but it blocked most of his upper arm and forearm without having to raise it. He stepped into position with sword in hand.

David, the unofficial leader of the Armstrong group, stepped forward. He raised his sword and moved into a stance that could put him on the offensive or defensive. Like he'd done with Brice, Alex circled, waiting for a chance to strike. David lifted his sword and prepared to slice toward Alex, but the latter rammed his shielded arm into David's chest, pushing him back several steps. Pain burst through Alex's arm, but it wasn't as bad as it had been when he rammed his shoulder into the man the day before.

Alex and David repositioned themselves and circled once more. They feinted and moved, testing one another until they both went on the offensive. Their swords clashed, the sound ringing out over the din of other fighters' weapons. Alex twisted his wrist, bringing the flat side of his blade against David's ribs. He danced away before his opponent could reach him. They continued thrusting and parrying until Stephen stepped forth. He raised his brow in question, and Alex nodded.

Alex now faced two men who were still a little uncertain about the force with which they should use against Alex, but when he knocked Stephen off his feet by sweeping his legs out from under him, then made David's head ring when his targe bashed into it, both guardsmen held nothing back. Alex fell more than once, but no more than he pushed the others off their feet. For the next two hours, the men rotated amongst themselves, and Alex trained alongside them. He was certain he would likely regret the pain that increased with each jarring movement, but he didn't regret regaining some of his self-worth.

"Bluidy hell, Alex." Mitcham rubbed his thigh where he could feel a massive knot and bruise forming. "Brice wasn't exaggerating. You've been holding out on us. It was just practice. You didn't have to be so rough."

The men grinned together as they left the lists. Alex and the others made their way to the well, where they passed a ladle around with cool water. When everyone was through, the men headed to the barracks while Alex turned toward the keep. He sensed the men wondered if at least one person should accompany him.

"The sun's up, and the passageways are busy. I'll have one of you with me this eve." Alex decided for them and didn't wait to see if they agreed. He crossed the bailey and entered the keep.

"Armstrong." The youthful voice belonging to a page echoed in the passageway. "The king requests your presence."

Alex nodded but frowned. He peered down at his filthy clothes and noticed the increasing pain in his arm. He supposed he should go to the Privy Council chamber immediately, but he was not presentable, and he would be in a foul mood if he didn't soak his shoulder. He hadn't figured out how to manage that without getting his stitches wet. But he was more inclined to experiment than to meet with the king. He called for a bath when he arrived at his chamber. By the time he'd stripped down and moved behind the screen, servants arrived with the tub and buckets of steaming water. The women still avoided him, which was fine by Alex.

When the chamber was empty save for him, he eased into the scalding water. He rested his left forearm on the rim of the tub and tried to slip lower in the water. He couldn't find a position that allowed him to keep his bicep out of the water while submerging his shoulder. He settled for getting his shoulder close to the water and letting the steam ease some of the burning pain. When he could stand the awkwardness of the position no longer, he hurried to scrub himself before struggling into fresh clothes. A healthy dram of whisky from his flask gave him the fortification he needed to face the king.

It surprised Alex that he didn't have to wait long to gain his audience. He worried how angry he made King Robert by keeping him waiting. When he entered the chamber, it shocked him to find it nearly empty. It was the middle of the day, and it was usually teeming with people. Alex glanced around until he noticed King Robert observing him.

"I suppose I should be grateful that you took the time to refresh yourself after hours in the lists." King Robert's sarcasm rang in the air. The snideness caught Alex off guard. He wondered if it merely annoyed the Bruce to be kept waiting, or if Alex's return to training was the source of his ire. He bowed and waited for the king to motion for him to sit. "You disappeared with one of my wife's ladies yesterday."

"We went for a ride and picnic. Lady Caitlyn has sacrificed much to tend to me. I wished to give her the chance for some fresh air."

"Half a day's ride from here. A ride where you obviously didn't take enough men."

"You've heard." Alex didn't pose it as a question.

"Of course I have. Your men and Lady Caitlyn's guard returned after sundown with the two of you nowhere to be seen. Everyone noticed your absence." King Robert narrowed his eyes at Alex. "You've just made my task immeasurably more difficult."

Alex's heart pounded. A sick sensation told him to what task the Bruce referred. He didn't want to hear it. He wanted to run back to his chamber, lock the door, and stick his head beneath his pillow.

"I see you've guessed. You don't want the lady, so it's time she married someone. Now I shall have to find a mon willing to take an already less-than-desirable bride with a reputation hanging by a thread."

King Robert glowered at Alex as the younger man bristled. "You can be offended all you want, but I have said naught that isn't true. I *thought* you would step up and ask for her hand. Rather than do that, you refuse her and your duty. She deserves a home and a family."

"With someone who will spend her dowry and resent her for the rest of her life?"

"Assuming I can find someone. I had a bluidy hard time with Lady Munro, and we're aware of how that nearly turned out."

"You intend to send another lamb to the slaughter," Alex growled.

"Glare all you want, Armstrong." King Robert's use of Alex's surname was a warning, one of the few he would get. "I can ask the lady myself, or you can be honorable and tell me the truth. Is she still a maiden?"

"You believe I would dishonor her, then cast her aside?" Alex avoided answering one question by posing one of his own.

"I believe that's precisely what you've done, whether it was last night or during some other visit. It's been obvious to the entire court that until this visit, you were courting Lady Caitlyn. You disappear with her overnight. Yet you aren't asking me for her hand nor are you rushing to send Laird Kennedy a missive asking for a betrothal. So I ask you again: is she still a maiden?"

"That is Lady Caitlyn's business, and no one else's."

"You made it your business—and mine—when you tupped her."

"I did no such thing." Alex refused to consider what he shared with Caitlyn as something so trivial as tossing her skirts. He hadn't tupped her. He'd made love to her, and he held tight to that technicality.

"Mince words all you wish, Armstrong, but your time has come and gone. I have a list of men at court who are interested in Lady Caitlyn."

"For more dishonorable purposes than that which you accuse me." Alex's hands gripped the armrests. He'd placed his left arm there and wrapped his fingers around it, hoping it wouldn't fall while he sat. Now it was clenched as tightly as his right hand. In the most unwanted ways, Alex was discovering he hadn't lost as much as he thought that day near Liddesdale.

"If they marry her first…"

"Padraig married Cairren first, and it nearly got her killed. More than once."

"Caitlyn has more men interested in marriage than Cairren did. She's lighter, so it's easier for her." King Robert shrugged, his comment blasé.

"You just said you would have a hard time marrying her off. Now you have a list of men. Either you are trying to play me for a fool, or you'll punish Caitlyn for what you believe are my offenses. Either way, you would sentence her to a miserable life."

"You have tried my patience since you arrived. You were sullen even before the passageway attack. Then you issued me orders. Now you flout my decision. You will not be long for this world if you continue. One day back in the lists doesn't make you the mon you were. You've said as much yourself. Mayhap you've been right all along. You've survived both attacks, but you bring naught but trouble now. Mayhap Brice is the better choice."

Alex sat stunned. His mind whirled as he processed what the king said and his own idiocy for arguing with the monarch. He nodded his head, mute.

"What happens to the succession is your father's problem. But you've made it clear you don't want Lady Caitlyn as your wife. Mayhap swinging your swords last night and this morn are making you think differently." King Robert sneered. "But I've decided."

"Decided to punish Caitlyn," Alex whispered.

"What do you want? You've made it clear that you are casting her aside. You no longer have a say. Or do you only want her now that you discovered what you can expect in bed with her?"

Alex saw red. He rose from his seat and leaned forward. His posture was so menacing, guards moved away from the walls. "I can't touch you. But I also can never forgive you. Say what you want aboot me. Malign me, impugn my honor, but never speak that way aboot her again. It will cost you more than you are willing to pay."

"Are you threatening me?" King Robert's ruddy complexion blazed red.

"No. I'm promising you." Alex didn't wait to be dismissed. He stormed out of the Privy Council chamber with King Robert's oaths echoing behind him. He was angry at the king for his disparaging comments and callous plan for Caitlyn, but he was just as angry at himself for taking the bait. King Robert wanted him away from court, that much was clear. He'd used the best means he had to make Alex leave: he infuriated Alex to where he had no choice but to depart, lest he face King Robert's wrath. He wasn't certain he could leave, though. Not when he didn't know what might happen to Caitlyn.

He stormed through the passageways and slammed his door shut before flipping the lock. He stalked across his chamber and dug through his saddlebag until he retrieved a full flask of whisky. Throwing himself into the chair before the fire, he used his teeth to pull the plug free. He swallowed most of the contents in one swig. It took a second swallow to empty the flask. Disgusted, he flung it aside and went back to the door.

"More whisky," Alex demanded to any page or servant who might hear. He didn't care who arrived with the alcohol, but it appeared on the table beside him. He poured one dram after another into the mug that appeared along with the amber liquid. He didn't keep count, but he felt himself growing even more intoxicated than he'd been when he came across Caitlyn and hurt her while they argued in the undercroft.

He drank until the room was a slowly swirling blur, and his arm no longer pained him. He felt nothing. Not the headache that had pounded behind his eyes while he argued with the Bruce. Not the throbbing pain in his arm that was worse from overexerting himself two days in a row. Not the dull ache that was always around his right cheek's scar. Not the desperation he felt for having his life ripped from him only to be forced to watch the king give Caitlyn to another man. He drank until the only thing he had were his morose thoughts.

Caitlyn glanced over her shoulder, certain someone followed her and the other ladies. She'd hurried to her chamber upon her return to the castle and quickly changed in time to meet the queen for Terce. Her mind had been on everything but the prayer service. She recalled every intimate detail of sharing a bed with Alex, both the good and the bad. She thought about how things stood between them and accepted that as unresolved as it felt to her, there was no other outcome than Alex leaving her behind.

She'd spied him in the lists as she followed the queen on her morning constitutional. It shocked her to watch him sparring with his men, but warmth spread through her as she wondered if he was feeling more like himself. She chided herself for not accepting that there was a new Alex, and the old one would never really come back. Even if he felt more confident after defending her and spending time in the Mangerton and Stirling lists, that didn't mean he felt any differently about marrying her.

As she moved through the passageways with a heavy heart, she thought her initial sense of unease came from hurt and rejection. It wasn't until she heard a heavy tread on the stairs below her that she was certain they were being followed. She glanced over the rope railing and down the spiral staircase. The men following her and the other ladies weren't in the royal livery. They were as large as most of the Highlanders she'd met, but none wore plaids nor leines.

The men dressed as Lowlanders. The only Lowlander men she'd met who rivaled their size were Alex and her father. Both were unusually tall and broad, even among warriors. Innes had always teased Alex that he was trying to catch up to his foster father until Alex knocked Innes off his feet for the first time. Innes returned the favor by getting Alex drunk for the first time.

Caitlyn didn't want to alarm the other ladies, but she silently encouraged them to move faster as she picked up the pace. When they reached the third floor where the queen's solar lay, Caitlyn glanced back. The men were out of sight, but she sensed they were there. She breathed easier when they reached the queen's chamber and flowed through the doorway as a group. She spent the next three hours pretending to listen to the other ladies gossip, sing, and read aloud. All the while, she wondered who the men were and whether they followed her or someone else in her group. Her mind railed against the latter. She was positive she was their target.

"Lady Caitlyn." Queen Elizabeth broke through Caitlyn's foggy thoughts and beckoned her over. "The king informed me this morn that he is considering your suitors."

My suitors? I only had one, and he won't marry me. Caitlyn kept her expression neutral despite being disconcerted.

"Since Armstrong isn't pursuing his courtship anymore, it is time to cast the net elsewhere. The king asked for my opinion, but I'm wary to name anyone. I'm not confident any mon here makes a sound choice for you." Queen Elizabeth's pointed stare at Caitlyn's exposed arms said more than words could. Not for the first time, she wondered why Queen Elizabeth summoned first Cairren, then Caitlyn, to court if she assumed they couldn't fit in and couldn't find suitable husbands.

When Caitlyn said nothing, the queen pushed forward. "Is there someone you fancy? Other than Armstrong?"

"Nay, Your Majesty."

"Does that mean you might be amenable to whoever I suggest?"

Amenable? I don't get a ruddy choice in this blummin' situation. What can I say? "No. Please don't make me marry anyone but the love of my life." A love who doesn't want you beyond making love to you once.

"I'm certain Your Majesty will recommend only men you believe are suitable."

"Hmm." Queen Elizabeth pursed her lips at the not-so-subtle point. "I shall give this matter serious consideration. No one wishes for you to experience what your sister did. Fortunately, you're lighter skinned than she is."

Caitlyn clenched her teeth so hard she feared cracking them. It was one thing when she made that observation since it was fact. But when others said it, the words were so condemning to Cairren and made Caitlyn feel ashamed for having an easier experience than Cairren. Though she could hardly say she was well-received herself. Caitlyn dipped into a curtsy and stepped back from the queen. She wondered who would tell Alex. Part of her hoped someone else did, so she wouldn't have to bring it up. But eventually, he would have to learn that the royal couple were playing matchmaker again, and it would finally sever their connection.

"You need to be more mindful of the sun," Sarah Anne Hay mused. "You're as dark as a Saracen." The malicious lady-in-waiting laughed at her own comment, before looking at the women who surrounded her and Caitlyn. They laughed uneasily, but their haughty expressions were genuine.

"You're nearly as brown as your sister. We shall lose you in the dark." Margaret came to stand beside her sister, Sarah Anne. It was a ridiculous comment, so Caitlyn merely stared at Margaret as though the other lady-in-waiting were a simpleton.

"I believe Lady Caitlyn and Lady Munro have magnificent complexions," Blythe Dunbar stepped beside Caitlyn. "Even her freckles are evenly spaced. Not like your blotchy red spots." Blythe smirked at Margaret, whose complexion was rarely clear.

"But you can see the lily-white skin beneath." Sarah Anne attempted to defend her sister.

"Aye. The red is the only thing that keeps her from looking like the harbinger of death." Blythe mocked both with her words while she pretended to swing a scythe around the group, as though she were an ancient banshee.

"Where were you last night?" Margaret changed the subject and returned the focus to Caitlyn.

"Unable to join you for the evening meal," Caitlyn hedged.

"Och, aye. You were out gallivanting with Alexander Armstrong. You spent the night with him." Sarah Anne raised her chin and attempted to peer down her nose at Caitlyn. It failed since they were of a similar height.

"You've answered your own question, so what does my answer matter?"

"Because when we watched you ride out yester morn, I swore you'd lift your skirts for him before you returned. I'd even guess you lifted them for all the men you rode—" Sarah Anne sneered "—with."

"Mayhap we should have that midwife examine you like you always suggest." Margaret cocked an eyebrow.

"So you're willing to be examined after me?" Caitlyn's smug expression matched Margaret's. "Do tell, which butcher sells the cheapest chicken blood?"

Margaret huffed and opened her mouth, but Queen Elizabeth's throat clearing made the ladies fall silent. Caitlyn stepped away from Margaret and Sarah Anne before she said something she couldn't take back or that the queen overheard. But such caution was not part of the sisters' ladylike comportment.

"They should send her and her people back where they came from," Sarah Anne whispered dramatically to all around them to hear.

"There's a reason our Crusaders were victorious over those demons. God made us white, so that we might shine with His light. He made them look like mud." Margaret stared at Caitlyn as she spewed each word.

"And yet, Christ, the Lord's only son, was from there and resembled me more than you," Caitlyn pointed out, wondering for the umpteenth time why no one else had reasoned that out.

"He did not!" Sarah Anne squawked. "He was naught like those disgusting savages God sent him down to tame."

"Tame?" Caitlyn guffawed. "I've noticed you sleep through most Masses, but have you never listened to a priest? Tame?" Caitlyn's laughter trailed behind her as she glanced at the queen, who nodded her head. Caitlyn left the solar before she got into an argument where she said things she regretted. She appreciated Her Majesty sparing her.

As she wound her way through the passageways, the same sense of danger consumed her. She hadn't considered the foolhardiness of leaving the solar alone when someone had already followed her. She glanced around as she slid her hand into her hidden pocket. Her other hand went to the dirk at her waist.

She rounded a corner to her right and glanced back. Five men didn't try to be inconspicuous. When her gaze met one man in the middle, he gestured to his comrades. They hastened their pace toward Caitlyn, who lifted her skirts to her knees. She counted on knowing the keep better than these men. She bolted along the corridor, then slipped through a servants' door. She raced down the stairs, nearly tripping over her skirts twice. She gathered all the fabric and lifted it entirely to her knees.

Caitlyn heard the door she passed through slam only moments after she made it to the bottom of the stairs. She assumed they'd gone past the door, but when they didn't find her at the end of the passageway, they'd doubled back. She burst through a door on the second floor. Looking in both directions, she turned away from the path that took her to her chamber. There was only one place to go where she felt safe. She would lead the men to their actual target, but it was Caitlyn's only chance not to be attacked or taken.

FIFTEEN

FIFTEEN

Alex's head lolled to the side as a noise made him blink. He turned his head toward the door as something banged against it. He closed his eyes, determined to ignore whatever it was. His head felt as though its weight was pulling him from the chair as he sagged farther down.

"Alex! Alex!"

Caitlyn's desperate voice permeated the door and his fog. He recalled his argument with the king and assumed Caitlyn heard of it. He was in no mood to see anyone, least of all the woman he wanted, but had squandered his chance with.

"Alex! Please! Let me in! Alex!"

Alex stared back at the door as his mind cleared a little more. Caitlyn wasn't knocking. She was pounding her hand against the door and sounded frantic.

"Alex! They're almost here. Let me in. Alex! Please."

Alex hoisted himself out of the chair as the room spun around him. He stumbled over his own feet as he swayed with each step.

"Alex!"

"I'm coming, Caity. Hush." Alex called out, but

170

he doubted she heard him as she continued to pound on the door. He unlocked it and started to pull it open when Caitlyn shoved it open and practically fell into the room.

"Alex, help." Caitlyn clung to Alex, finally feeling safe even though she could hear the men approaching. She spun around and slammed the door shut, turning the lock before reaching for the bar to drop it into the brackets.

"Caity?"

"Och, Alex, you're drunk. Why now?" Caitlyn wondered if she'd erred, and whether that would cost them both their life.

"Wujsh happening?" Alex slurred as he thought to reach out his left arm to steady him. He pitched against the wall and banged his head. He straightened as Caitlyn froze at the sound of someone trying to open the door.

"Those men followed me." Caitlyn prayed the men couldn't hear her low voice. "They followed me when I was with the others, but I forgot aboot them when I left the queen's solar alone."

"Who?" Alex cupped Caitlyn's cheek, mostly to figure out where she was amid the blurry image before his eyes.

"I think they're the men who attacked us in the meadow. I didn't know where else to go but to you."

"And you think I can protect you? I'm the reason they're following you. And you brought them to me."

Caitlyn stared at Alex before turning toward the door. "I'll take my chances with them."

"No, you don't." Alex pulled Caitlyn away from the door. "I may be drunker than I've ever been, but I still have a smidge of sense. I don't have my sword, and I don't know if they have theirs. You are not leaving here until I'm certain no one is waiting for you."

"Alex, I'm scared." Caitlyn confessed as she landed against Alex's chest. She was unsure if she fell against him or he pulled her, but the moment his arm draped around her back, her heart slowed.

"Crouch down on the other side of the bed. Have your dirks in your hands. If they get in, there is little I can do but hope to keep most of them from you. You must be ready to fight like I taught you."

"I am, Alex. I knew that coming here. But this is the only place I feel like I have a chance."

"With the cripple," Alex muttered.

"We can argue aboot that later." Caitlyn followed Alex's instructions and knelt beside the far side of the bed. She was prepared to strike, but she kept out of sight. She heard Alex draw a dirk from his waist, then she listened to the faceless menace at the door. Whoever was there jiggled the handle, pounded on the door, and it sounded as though they kicked or rammed their shoulder into the portal. It shook in its frame, but it didn't open. Caitlyn estimated her would-be assailants attempted to break in for nearly five minutes before they abandoned Alex's door.

On silent feet, Alex came to help Caitlyn stand. She dropped her knives on the bed and sagged onto it. Alex sat beside her, uncertain what to do.

"Alex?" He beheld Caitlyn's tearstained face as she whispered his name. He lifted his arm, and she collapsed against him, her arms wrapped around his waist. "Just hold me."

They sat together in silence for a long time, both looking out of the window, lost in their own thoughts. Eventually, Caitlyn sat up and brushed the hair from her face before wiping away her tears. The moments of lucidity and sobriety Alex felt while he was guarding Caitlyn disappeared when she seemed to no longer need him. He walked back to the table that held the whisky decanter he'd been drinking straight from, having abandoned the mug.

"Were you coming here to tell me who you're marrying, and they followed you?"

"Marrying? You heard aboot that?"

"So you are marrying someone. The king already chose. Who is the lucky bastard?"

"No one that I know of." Caitlyn pried the decanter from Alex's hand and took a healthy swig of her own. "Whoever it is will get a hefty dowry that comes with an unwanted wife."

"Who wouldn't want you, Caity?"

"You're a cruel bastard." Caitlyn pulled away. "Who wouldn't want me? You. You're at the top of the bluidy list for who doesn't want me. More fool am I for still thinking you're who I should turn to in my time of need. I would have been better off running into the barracks naked looking for my guards than dealing with you."

"You know I want you. But I can't."

"I swear to you, Alexander. If I hear you say that pile of dung anymore, I will cut off your cock. You want to believe you're half a mon, I'll make you so. I'm so tired of hearing you say all the things you can't do. I understand as best I can why you feel that way. But you are the only person who does. No one who matters has said you're not enough. No one who matters wants you to step aside."

Alex shook his head, but Caitlyn's narrowed eyes, warning that her temper was on the verge of exploding.

"Do you really think your father is so fucking foolish that he would risk every clan members' life just to make you feel better aboot yourself? If he didn't think you could lead, he would be the one telling you Brice is his heir. He might not like it, but his sense of duty is just as strong as yours. He'd put your people first, even if it killed him. You are not the only valiant member of your family. But you're the only fucking martyr."

"You don't know what you're talking aboot." Alex was fuming. He was too drunk, too tired, and still too scared about Caitlyn's safety to have this argument.

"Don't I? My father is the one who has no sons. You know I love Jamie. He's my cousin and your friend. He's a fine tánaiste, but I also know Papa wished you weren't the aulder son. If you weren't and you'd married Cairren, he could have passed the lairdship to you. He trusts Jamie implicitly and has faith in him, but he's always wished it were you. My parents love me, and I've known that my entire life. But don't you think sometimes I wish I'd been a son? You have two men who would sacrifice to have you lead their clan. My father can't have that, but your own can."

"But—"

"Nay. I don't want to hear it. You thought you couldn't fight anymore, and that it made you weak. But you've proven you can. What more do you need? You fear people will think your clan is weak if they have a so-called cripple leading them. Why are they determined to kill you now? Why not wait until the weakling is in charge, then raid your keep? You daft bugger. They don't want you to be laird because they fear you already. So whores don't want to fuck you. Save your coin. You know I do." Caitlyn snapped her mouth shut, stunned by her last comment. She hadn't intended to be vulgar or that honest.

"Quite the romantic bard, aren't you?" Alex glowered at her.

"You can wipe that expression off your face before I do it for you. It didn't scare me as a wean, and

174

it doesn't scare me now. It only makes me angry, just like it did when we were younger."

"Caity, you deserve—"

"Do not finish that thought, Alex. You are making me angrier than I have ever been. I've had enough. I can't do this anymore. Can you guess what the wretchedly selfish part of me wants to keep telling you? Do you have any idea?"

"No."

"Give up the bluidy lairdship. Let Brice have it. Whether it's the keep or a croft, let someone else deal with it all. Then we can be together. You wouldn't have to worry aboot being a good enough warrior or a good enough laird. You could be my far-better-than-just-good-enough husband. I'd live in a croft like the one last night if I shared it with you. Stop deciding everything for me." Caitlyn picked up her knives and shoved one back into her belt and the other into her pocket. "Maimed or not. I've wished that since I fell in love with you at three-and-ten. I wished you didn't have to become a laird. I didn't want to share, and I still don't. But looks like neither of us gets what we want."

Caitlyn cast such a look of disgust at Alex that the last of the alcohol drained from his mind. She turned toward the door, but Alex's larger body moved to block her. "You don't care if I'm laird?"

Caitlyn's chin fell forward. "After all these years —a score of them—you think I care aboot you because you're supposed to be a laird one day? I watched you talk aboot marrying my sister, and there was naught I could do. I know how you've whiled away your time. You made sure I do. After the heartache you've caused me during this visit and in the past, you think I only want you because you're going to be a laird. Just how petty and pretentious do you think I am? Mayhap we aren't so well suited

175

after all. You seem to know me not at all. All I've ever wanted is the mon."

Caitlyn shook her head as she stepped back and tried to move around Alex, but he shifted to keep blocking her. "People already say such hideous things to you *aboot* you. It would only be worse."

"You think an awful lot aboot yourself to believe so many other people will be that concerned aboot what you and I do. Once I leave here, I won't hear the gossip. Let them say what they want. I already know your people accept me. I've been visiting your clan since I was five. I'm certain people believe—or did, before you fouled this up—that we would marry. Who in your clan would speak against you to me? Who would insult me to you? Who would do it and think they would survive to tell the tale? And if people outside your clan gossip, let them. I don't care."

"But I care. I care that I can't protect you."

"Stop. We are going around in circles. You keep saying that, and yet, here we are, yet again. You have protected me. Alex." Caitlyn sat on the edge of the bed and patted the spot beside her. "The nightmares may never go away. Neither you nor I can control what goes through your mind in your sleep. But you can control what you think when you are awake. I don't expect your guilt and fear to merely disappear. I truly do understand why you feel the way you do. But it's needless. The reasons you believe exist don't. They just don't."

Alex closed his eyes, trying to piece through the conflicting thoughts racing through his mind. "I've heard what people think of me here. What if that is how people view me?"

"You're going to let a group of mealy-mouthed gossips—both men and women—who live off the king's coin and spend their lives here flattering one another decide what you do with yours. Tell me this: Have any of the Highlanders looked down at you?"

"No. They don't seem to notice after the first time they see me."

"Because they're Highlanders. They bluidy well fight one another before bed each night. You aren't the first mon they've seen changed from battle. It doesn't matter to them because either they know you or they know your reputation. They respect you. Besides the Scotts, which Lowland delegates have spoken against you?" Caitlyn held up her hand. "I don't mean the courtiers. I mean the real men, the ones you're likely to face on a battlefield."

"They eye it, but no one has said aught to me."

"What aboot in the lists this morn? I noticed you there. How did people act?"

"They stared. I think many waited for me to make an arse of myself."

"But you didn't. Alex," Caitlyn puffed a breath, "I know Brice is large too, like Papa and Tavin. But do you truly not realize just how imposing you are?"

Alex shrugged with one shoulder, mindful not to move his left. "What good does the size do me now?"

Caitlyn's lips flattened as she closed her eyes. "Blessed saints, one of these days I will keep my mind from falling in the gutter, but it seems today is not that day."

"Caitlyn!"

"What? I'm not allowed to appreciate what I discovered last night? What I've wondered aboot for *years.*" Caitlyn's tone was unabashed as she swept her gaze over Alex, appreciating what she found. "Before I completely distract myself, the point I was trying to make is that you are still a colossus. That you have lost the use of one arm but still fight like the devil doesn't go unnoticed. I think you will find men fear and respect you even more for it."

"I just don't see it that way."

"Because you refuse to look in the right places. Do their opinions mean that much to you? You've proven you're still a warrior who can fight and win. You feared that wasn't the case and that would be a danger to your clan. Now we know. You know how I feel aboot you, Alex. You know what I want. What I don't want is to marry someone I don't love who will barely tolerate me. What I don't want is to bear a mon children he will despise. Did I seem doubtful or disgusted at all last night?"

"No, but you couldn't see."

"The only part of you I couldn't see that I haven't seen before is the part of you I liked best." Caitlyn grinned and waggled her eyebrows. "I've seen your shoulder and arm before. I look at your face every day. I haven't run into the mountains yet. I'm certain you have other scars, but the ones that trouble you the most don't trouble me at all. You're still the most attractive mon I have ever seen."

"I drank myself into a stupor today because I can't bear the idea that you'll marry someone else. That thought hurts more than my arm or face ever has. You came here because you trust me. You trust me even when I have no confidence in myself." Alex glanced away, embarrassed for a moment, before his eyes locked with Caitlyn's. "I love you. This may be the most selfish and reckless decision I've ever made, but it's the only one I can live with. I'm not letting you go. You are not marrying someone else."

"What're you saying, Alex?" Caitlyn's heart was in her throat. She didn't want to discover he meant something other than what she hoped, but she had to know.

"Before I answer that, I need you to believe I'm not drunk. I'm saying this clearheaded, even after I

178

drank as much as I did. I need you to not fear that I will wake up tomorrow and change my mind."

"I can hear it in your voice, Alex. I know you're sober."

"Will you marry me, Caitlyn?" Alex held his breath, which whooshed out of him when Caitlyn knocked him backwards onto the bed. He wrapped his arm around her hips as she smattered kisses across his face. Alex chuckled. "Will you not tell me?"

"Aye. I'll marry you." Caitlyn brought her mouth to his. The kiss was tender and sweet, with a lifetime of love poured into it.

"I'm certain God made me to love you. I've been a fool to think I know better than Him. I will spend my life cherishing you, Caity, whether it's in a castle or a croft. I love you. I want to make your dreams come true. I pray the ones I've had of us as a family come true, too."

"You can make one of my dreams come true." Caitlyn flicked her tongue against Alex's lips until he parted them and slipped his tongue into her mouth. She sucked lightly on it and pressed the length of her body against his, feeling his rod caught between them. "Alex, I want to marry you more than I want aught else."

Alex caught Caitlyn's hand and placed it over his heart. "You only need to say it once more for it to be so." The couple gazed at one another. Caitlyn understood Alex meant that by stating three times that she wished to marry him, they would be married by consent. While not appreciated by the church, and while there should have been a witness, it was more binding than even a handfast. There would be nothing temporary about the commitment.

"I want to marry you this very moment."

Alex exhaled a shuddering sigh. "Wife."

"Husband." Caitlyn closed her eyes. "I've never said a finer word."

"Naught has ever sounded finer."

"Not true. I'm partial to hearing you call me 'wife.'"

"Every day for the rest of our lives."

They rose and undressed one another before climbing into bed. Alex kissed a moist trail along her neck to her collarbone, nipping at the protrusion. He slid his tongue over her right nipple and swirled it until the skin drew into a tight dart that he suckled. His right hand kneaded her other breast before his mouth sought it. He alternated until Caitlyn's heaving breaths pushed her chest toward him. She moaned in frustration when he pulled away and inched down the bed. He drew her left leg over his right shoulder, glancing up at her. She understood what he asked silently, but she didn't understand why. She hooked her right leg over his left shoulder but ensured her foot bore its weight on the mattress.

Caitlyn gasped with the first swipe of Alex's tongue along her seam. It flicked out and tapped her nub. The needy pulse that shot through her core urged her to lift her hips in offering to him. He laved her entrance over and over while his thumb rubbed at the pearl that appeared from within its hood. Caitlyn moaned as the need for more grew. She ran her fingers through his hair and didn't realize she tugged as he drew her bud into his mouth and sucked. She shifted and sat up partially to find his other hand.

Tentatively, she reached for his left hand as she watched him. He nodded, and she eased his arm upward until she could entwine their fingers together while she laid back. Alex's fingers flexed, giving her hand a squeeze before he turned his attention back to her sheath. It wasn't long before Caitlyn's body tensed as waves of release rolled over her.

"Please, Alex."

"No more waiting, Caity."

"You told me you wanted to bury yourself and not pull out until sunup." Caitlyn swallowed, hoping she hadn't taken too seriously something that had meant the world to her.

"I am going to bury myself within you, and it will be several days before anyone sees or hears from us. I'm going to make love to my wife until you beg me to let you rest."

"The only thing I shall beg for is more."

Alex thrust into Caitlyn, who tilted her hips to receive him. They moved together over and over, Alex always cautious not to squash Caitlyn. She marveled at the muscles that rippled across his body, running her hands over the grooves and ridges. Alex watched the desire flare in her eyes as she explored him. There was no hesitation. She didn't even ignore his limp arm, only cautious when she skimmed her fingers over it, more worried about not hurting him than disgusted by what she felt.

"I love you, Caitlyn Armstrong." Caitlyn dragged Alex in for a kiss with such ferocity that it shocked him. He slid his good arm beneath her and rolled them, so he was on his back. "I couldn't spy nearly enough last night. I want to watch my wife as I make love to her."

Caitlyn rocked against him as they experimented with various movements until they found the motion and rhythm that pushed them both over the precipice. They flew through ecstasy together before collapsing, breathless and blissful. Too hot to care about the covers, they drifted to sleep wrapped in one another's embrace.

SIXTEEN

$\mathbf{A}$ lex glanced down at Caitlyn, who slept at his side, when knocking roused him from his early-evening daydreaming. They'd spent the rest of the morning and all afternoon in bed together. Neither believed all their troubles resolved merely by agreeing to marry. They discussed what they intended to say in a missive to Innes and Collette, and they worried about King Robert's impending reaction. They considered when they should depart for Mangerton Tower, both nervous about being on the road again with days of travel ahead of them. They made love in between the discussion; their bond, created from a lifetime of friendship but endangered by circumstance, grew stronger as they planned for their future together. Joining their bodies was as much about pleasure as it was sharing an undeniable love and devotion to one another.

However, reality refused to remain at bay, and Alex had little choice but to slip out of bed. He drew the bed curtains closed, ensuring Caitlyn's privacy. He pulled his breeks on as he crossed the chamber to the door. He hesitated, not lifting the bar or unlocking the door as he recalled what brought Caitlyn to his chamber that morning.

"Who goes?"

"Alex, it's David. We need to speak."

Alex sighed as he lifted the bar, but he turned back to the bed when he heard it creak. Caitlyn poked her head through the gap in the curtain, searching for her chemise. She scurried off the bed and grabbed the garment before diving back onto the bed and drawing the curtains closed. Alex unlocked the door and opened it a crack.

"The king is livid. The queen doesn't know where Lady Caitlyn is, and neither you nor the lady have answered when people knocked at your chamber doors."

"I have heard no knocks until now." Alex's brow furrowed. They'd dozed a few times, but he didn't think he'd slept that deeply. He hadn't dreamed once, and as best he could tell, neither of them shifted in their sleep. They'd remained pressed together in one another's embrace. He wondered if having Caitlyn beside him might finally allow him to slumber in peace.

"Mitcham came up here earlier but got no answer. Lady Caitlyn's maid went in search of my lady more than once, but never found her. People are saying you ran off together again. It's worse, since everyone knows the men and I are here."

Alex turned back to glance out the window embrasure. The sun was nearing the horizon, and it would soon grow dark outside. They would use that to their advantage when they slipped out of the keep. "Gather the others and Lady Caitlyn's guards and wait for us outside the postern gate. We have an errand to run."

"Alex—"

"Now. We must be back before they lock the gates for the night."

David nodded and backed away from the door.

Alex shut the door and locked it once more as Caitlyn emerged from the bed. She gathered her clothes and dressed as she waited for Alex to explain what he meant by an errand. She was uncertain if it included her. She'd donned her clothes before Alex explained his intentions, so she stepped before him and helped button his doublet while asking, "Where are you going?"

"*We* are taking a pouch of coin to the kirk in town and getting married."

"But no one has read the banns." Caitlyn doubted even a generous donation could sway a priest into marrying them.

"We married by consent and consummated our marriage," Alex grinned, "several times. This is a formality, but it's one that will keep King Robert from punishing you or keeping us apart. We must try."

"But can we really claim that? There were no witnesses."

Rather than answer her question, Alex stepped away from Caitlyn and went to the chest that sat against the far wall. He rummaged through the few belongings he'd brought until he found two pouches. One clinked with coins, but Caitlyn couldn't guess what was in the other. He handed her the silent one.

"Open it." Alex waited as Caitlyn poured an emerald ring into her hand and looked up at him, eyes wide with shock. "Mayhap the Lord already intended it, or mayhap I am a sentimental fool. I've carried that ring with me for the last three trips here. I've known all along that I would only ever ask you to marry me. That ring belongs on no woman's hand but yours. Even coming here this time, I couldn't leave it behind. I never imagined offering it to you. It was more of a comfort to me. But I want to slip it on your finger this eve and know that it's finally found its home."

"It's your mother's ring." Caitlyn stared at the jewelry, remembering how she'd embarrassed herself at five-and-ten by blurting out that it reminded her of Alex's eyes. She and Coira had been in Collette's solar while Caitlyn's mother and Cairren visited the village. She and Coira were sewing, and the sunlight struck the stone, making it sparkle. She'd spoken without thinking. Coira had been gracious enough to nod and hum her agreement, but it had mortified Caitlyn.

"Aye. Mother told me aboot what you said that day. I already wanted to marry you. After that, I was certain which ring to give you. I asked Mother for it nearly a year ago. I should have asked then."

"Alex." The single word was a reverent whisper as Caitlyn wrapped her fingers around it and pressed the ring against her palm. She stepped forward, tilting her head back in an invitation Alex eagerly accepted. The kiss was brief but fueled by years of longing. When they pulled apart, Alex drew a cape from the chest and wrapped it around Caitlyn. It was enormous on her, but it shielded her identity. They wound their way through the keep, using back stairways and corridors until they entered the bailey. There were few people left working, the evening meal drawing close. The couple met their guards on the other side of the postern gate and slipped into town.

Caitlyn kept her head down, the hood of Alex's cloak covering her entire head and half of her face. Alex's arm rested lightly around her lower back, a reassurance to Caitlyn and sign of possession to any they passed. The guards encircled them as they hurried through the streets, not daring to tarry. When they reached the town kirk, Mitcham darted up the stairs and tried the door. The group heaved a collective sigh when it opened. Mitcham and Stephen remained at the doorway, sentries on either side, while the rest of the party made their way down the aisle.

A middle-aged man poked his head through a door leading to the sacristy. His brow furrowed and eyes narrowed as he watched the group approach. "I have no coin here. Take what you wish and leave."

When Caitlyn gasped at the announcement, the priest stepped through the door, surprised to find a woman amongst the men. The men's towering height shielded her, but the sound she made was too feminine to have come from Alex or the guards. Caitlyn pushed back her hood as she glanced at Alex. His hand gave her waist a reassuring squeeze before releasing her so his hand could enclose the coin pouch Caitlyn had tied to his waist.

"Father Barret," Alex greeted the suspicious priest. "I realize we've missed Vespers and are early to Compline. We request your aid. My wife and I married by consent when a priest wasn't available. We ask that you perform an official ceremony."

"How far along is she?" Father Barret asked, the skepticism clear.

"She isn't." Alex had no interest in explaining their circumstances any further. He hadn't lied. There was no priest available in his chamber that morning. "A group of thieves chased us while we were on our way to town. It made me realize how important it is that we have our marriage formally blessed. If aught happens to me, I need to have my wife protected."

Caitlyn swallowed, knowing Alex spoke the truth. As his wife, she would have two clans to protect her should he die. An alliance through marriage, rather than just fostering strengthened the bond between the Kennedys and the Armstrongs, making any attack on Alex also an attack on the Kennedys. Her father would rouse their army without hesitation. But without a formal marriage, she was likely back where she was when they left the croft, unchaste and un-marriageable.

"Handfasted?" Father Barret cocked an eyebrow. "You aren't Highlanders."

"We aren't. As I said, we married by consent. Our families are aware of our relationship and have long expected our marriage." Alex knew that wasn't a lie either. His parents and Brice had attempted to bring up the topic several times, but Alex stormed away.

"Have you posted banns? Without them, I cannot marry you."

"We are already married. Fully married." Alex raised his eyebrow in a matching expression. "We would have the church's blessing to ensure the rest of the world sees it as we and our families do."

Alex swept his gaze around the kirk and noticed a few needed improvements. His gaze met the priest's as he pulled the coin pouch free. The guards parted, allowing Alex to pass through. He approached the altar, making the sign of the cross, grateful that his right arm was the one that worked. He ensured the priest could view the pouch before he turned toward the man.

"Before I forget, I offer this to you to aid in the repairs to the mortar along your east wall and for that thinning thatching over the Mary altar." Alex extended his arm and held the coins over the priest's outstretched hand. But he didn't release it. He waited for the priest to announce his decision.

"I will lock this away as soon as we complete the service." Father Barret accepted the pouch and tucked it away in his chasuble before picking up the stole that hung over the communion rail. He kissed the sacred garment and placed it around his neck. He turned his attention at Caitlyn for the first time, surprise clear on his face. She tried not to flinch, knowing the priest recognized her. "Lady Caitlyn?"

"Yes, Father." Caitlyn stepped forward, accepting Alex's hand when he moved it away from his side, a slight gesture but one that gave her immeasurable reassurance. "Alexander and I married privately. I hope to seal our commitment with proper vows and a blessing."

"Why not marry at the kirk within the castle?" Father Barret prodded.

"Because I don't wish my wedding to be a spectacle." Caitlyn's chin set as she dared the man to ask what she meant. Father Barret cast a quick glance at Alex's limp arm and the skin that showed where her cuff ended. He nodded, and something akin to sympathy filled his expression. He motioned them to approach the rail. He used the end of his stole to bind their clasped hands.

Alex heard the priest speak, and he was aware he repeated the vows. He spoke them with reverence and a soul-deep honesty, but he was lost in the depths of Caitlyn's gaze. There was no reservation as she made her pledge to remain faithful and loyal, and to love him for the rest of their days. He found happiness and eagerness where he'd once feared disgust and pity. He chided himself for not having given Caitlyn enough credit and for not respecting her character more. He realized he'd lived the past six months in constant fear of rejection, and the few instances he'd experienced jaded him. He'd nearly pushed away the one person who he should have known he could count on most.

"I will always be by your side, Alex. I will not turn away from you, in this life or the next." Caitlyn's whispered words filled his ears just before they exchanged their first kiss as an officially married couple. The kiss was soft, passion put aside to share an abiding love that would survive the trouble that no doubt lay ahead. Alex's steely arm kept Caitlyn pressed against him as she clutched his doublet, unwilling to step away. When their kiss finally ended, they rested their foreheads together. Alex kissed the tip of Caitlyn's nose as they reveled in the moment of bliss.

"I love you, Caity. Never once has that wavered since the first time I realized it. I've erred and wronged you. I did it out of callousness and selfishness, but no more. I will show you how much I cherish you, and I will be the husband you deserve. Always."

"I love you, *mo chridhe*."

Alex's own heart stuttered as he listened to Caitlyn call him her heart. She was everything to him, and he wanted to be sure she understood. "*Mo h-uile càil.*"

"If you would be so kind, I would have you sign the parish registry." Father Barret's voice permeated the haven they'd slipped into with the practical task of recording their marriage. It was nearly as important as the vows they exchanged and was the reason they'd sought the priest. It was the definitive proof that neither king nor man could separate them. It surprised Father Barret when Caitlyn took the quill from Alex and signed her name, "Caitlyn Marie-Cybèle Armstrong" beside Alex's. She supposed he expected her to place an "X" to make her mark.

"You write that with ease." Alex teased as she straightened.

"You've given me plenty of time to imagine it." Caitlyn's lips twitched, and her eyes sparkled.

"And I shall make it up to you over and over, in our bed and anywhere else we can think of."

Father Barret cleared his throat, having overheard the newlyweds. Alex winked as Caitlyn struggled to smother her smile. But her heated gaze made Alex want to toss her over his shoulder and race back to the castle, where he could lock them away for a week.

"Father, thank you." Caitlyn dipped a shallow curtsy before accepting Alex's invitation to hold his hand. The newly married couple and their guards left the chapel as quietly as they'd entered. Alex adjusted Caitlyn's hood, enjoying the husbandly task. When they joined hands again, his thumb brushed over the emerald ring now where it belonged on Caitlyn's finger. A few steps before they reached the postern gate, Caitlyn stopped and titled her head to the side. She and Alex stepped off the path, their guards discreetly giving them space but still vigilant.

"We both know there will be trouble when we arrive and announce we're married." Caitlyn glanced down at her hand, a soft smile playing at her mouth as she caught sight of the ring. It felt both odd and natural at the same time. "If we must, I learned the ways through the secret passageways to get to the bailey. We can hide in the passageways until the gates open and we can leave."

"How do you know?" It intrigued and horrified Alex, thinking of Caitlyn traipsing through the castle's bowels.

"Elizabeth Fraser grew up here and learned her way throughout the castle. One of her former roommates discovered that Elizabeth used them. She demanded Elizabeth show her how to get to the bachelors' chambers, and even the married couple's chambers, and how to get to the bailey. While no one knows all the different paths within the walls, the knowledge of how to get to those three places isn't a well-guarded secret. Laurel was my roommate when I first arrived before the Mistress of the Bedchamber assigned me elsewhere.

Laurel made sure I learned how to escape the keep if ever there was an attack. I think she felt guilty aboot not warning Cairren better aboot her sister's involvement with Padraig before he and Cairren married."

"Do you suggest we retire to your chamber? Is that the only way you're aware of to get to the bailey?"

Caitlyn shook her head. "Laurel insisted I learn how to enter the passageways from near the Great Hall and the queen's solar. I don't know from your chamber, but if we can make it to my chamber or either of those places, I can get us out."

"Do you really believe it'll come to that?"

"I believe neither of us should put aught past the Bruce. We've defied him now that he said he intended to match me to someone else." Caitlyn didn't mention that she feared Alex winding up in the dungeon. She had only a vague sense of how to navigate the hidden tunnels if she had to reach him there.

"What would you have us do?" Alex trusted Caitlyn's judgment. While he visited Stirling multiple times a year, he realized that Caitlyn was more experienced with surviving life at court.

"Go to your chamber and pack. I will go to mine and pack a satchel with what I most need. I will make sure my riding gown hangs from a peg in case I must change quickly, but I will dress for the evening meal. It's surely happening now. If we hurry, we can make it before it ends."

"Should we enter together?"

"Absolutely. There is naught anyone can do to end the marriage, short of death." Caitlyn's cheeks flushed crimson, and Alex wondered about Caitlyn's unexpected embarrassment. "My chemise from the other night." Caitlyn's cheeks burned hotter. "It proves I was a maiden. I hid it in my chest before my maid could find it. The kirk registry proves a priest officiated. There can be no annulment."

Alex kissed Caitlyn's cheek, regretting the circumstances around how they consummated their relationship. Sensing his shift, Caitlyn shook her head. "Don't feel badly. I wanted it, and I accepted what might have happened if you hadn't changed your mind. Passion or love didn't blind me. It was my choice as much as it was yours."

"I know, Caity. And I don't regret making love to you. I thank the saints that we did, or I might have died a fool. I only wish it were someplace where I could have introduced you to passion without fearing we'd be overheard or hadn't been rushed."

"I think you made up for it today." Caitlyn's grin was pure seduction, but it was fleeting. "We must hurry."

SEVENTEEN

Caitlyn threw open the lid to her chest, taking in the various items and making an immediate decision about what she needed to pack. She prayed it didn't come to them slipping away in the middle of the night, but she knew not how the royal couple would respond. She also didn't know who pursued her that day and whether they continued to pose a threat. Her three guards stood in the passageway waiting for her. It disturbed all three to learn strangers chased Caitlyn through the castle that morning. She hadn't needed to ask that they accompany her to her chamber. It was irregular for the men to be there, and it would have caused a scene if everyone weren't in the Great Hall.

Caitlyn tossed three chemises, six pairs of stockings, a pair of slippers, and two of her plainest kirtles into the satchel, making it nearly burst at the seams. She pulled her riding gown from her armoire and hung it on a peg before placing her riding boots beneath it. She yanked at her gown's laces and shed the garment, barely taking the time to lay it on her bed before she pulled a fresh gown from the armoire. It laced on the sides, making it possible for Caitlyn to dress without needing help. She scrubbed her face and hurriedly put her hair up, appropriate for her status as a married woman.

She was ready in less than a quarter hour and breathed easier when she spotted Alex waiting for her in the passageway leading to the Great Hall. He slid his hand into hers before leaning in to drop a petal-soft kiss on her lips. Hands still clasped, Alex wrapped his arm around her waist and drew her against him.

"There is no woman more beautiful than you, *mo ghràidh*. I don't doubt that there will be few kind words, but I confess I'm excited and proud to enter that chamber with you beside me as my wife. I've never cared what anyone said aboot you or Cairren, and now that I've seen my wife as I make love to her, I'm certain there is no one more alluring than you. We will leave here in the morn, if we can, and you will not suffer another insult."

"Alex, you know I feel the same, don't you? You know I desire you as I always have, and you are no less handsome to me. I'm proud that you're my husband, and I wish I could crow it from the rooftops. I wished no one cared aboot our appearances, and I don't believe leaving here will protect either of us from ever being insulted aboot our own appearance or each other's, but I am excited to go. Let's get through this meal, hopefully be able to take our time tonight, then leave this den of iniquity in the morn."

They shared another kiss before a royal guard opened the door for them. The meal was nearly at its conclusion, but people remained at their tables, conversing during the last course. As the couple moved toward a table with space for them and their entourage, it was as if a wave passed through the crowd. Heads turned toward them, followed by a pause in conversation; then the diners they passed exchanged a rapid fire of words. Caitlyn kept her chin up and eyes on the king and queen, who watched them approach. Their expressions were inscrutable, so Caitlyn paid attention to the table as they neared.

Alex sat beside Caitlyn as a handful of servants scurried to bring trenchers to the late arrivals and the last course. Caitlyn was starving since neither had eaten since the morning meal. She prayed they could get through their food before whatever awaited them befell them. She forced herself to slow when she realized she inhaled her food lest she miss her only chance to eat. Alex passed her the chalice whenever she reached for it, and when she realized her eyes were bigger than her stomach, she pushed a healthy portion onto his side of the trencher.

"You shall make me go to fat, wife." Alex's warm breath tickled Caitlyn's ear. "I will have to work up an appetite if this is how you shall feed me."

"Fear not, husband. Both dessert and exercise await you this eve." Caitlyn's hand rested on Alex's thigh before her fingers skimmed toward his groin. She stopped before anyone could notice, but she felt Alex shift.

"Caity, unless you wish for me to drag you out of here and really make it obvious, spare me."

"Tempting as that is, I have enough restraint—barely—to recognize that isn't wise. King Robert has been glowering at us since we arrived, and it feels like everyone is still staring." Caitlyn glanced at the tables nearby, noticing the conspicuous gazes that remained on them. When the meal ended and servants cleared the tables, Caitlyn wondered if they could make their escape or if that would be when the Bruce summoned them to account for their actions. When the music began a dance that kept partners together, Alex nudged her.

"It's our wedding day, and this is as close to a

feast as we shall have. I wish to dance with my wife."

Alex led them among the dancers. Caitlyn rested her hand on Alex's right shoulder as his hand rested on her waist. She used her other hand to hold her skirts away from her feet. It was all she could think of to not draw even more attention to their unusual positioning. They'd danced together so many times that they moved with a natural grace and synchronicity. It was easier than either expected, and Alex relaxed in a Great Hall for the first time in half a year. He never imagined he could dance again, let alone with Caitlyn, but he found he rediscovered his bravery when she was at his side.

"Alex, hold me closer. I wish I could lean my head against your chest while we dance." Caitlyn sighed when Alex's arm wrapped around her waist. The dance didn't call for the man to hold the woman in that posture, but it was what they wanted. They drew strength from one another and enjoyed a pastime they both had feared they would never share again. "Can we go? Dare we?"

As if to answer the question for them, a royal guard came to stand beside them, announcing the king requested their presence. Caitlyn shot Alex a panicked expression. They'd both known the summons was coming, but now that the time came for them to explain their unsanctioned marriage, Caitlyn feared one of them losing their temper, and she was certain King Robert had already lost his.

"Armstrong, Lady Caitlyn." King Robert cast a gimlet gaze at them when they both rose from their genuflection. "You absented yourself today, Lady Caitlyn. The queen wondered if you'd forgotten where you are."

Caitlyn kept her gaze cast down, but her eyes flickered up to meet the queen's. There was none of the chastisement she expected. Rather, Caitlyn found humor. She wasn't certain she appreciated being laughed at.

"Armstrong, you test the bounds of any mon's patience, and I find mine has worn out. I made it clear this morn that Lady Caitlyn was to marry, yet you enter my Great Hall as though we never spoke. You spoke to me of the Scotts' blatant disregard for my orders, but you stand before me guilty of the same offense. What say you?"

"My wife and I spent the day together."

"Your what?" Queen Elizabeth snapped before leaning back in her seat, remembering to defer to her husband.

"Explain, Lady Caitlyn. I neither want to hear Armstrong's voice nor trust his words." King Robert glared at Alex before turning his attention to Caitlyn.

"Strange men followed me this morning while I was with the other ladies on the way to Your Grace's solar." Caitlyn flicked her gaze to Queen Elizabeth before she met King Robert's. "Your Majesty, men chased me through the keep when I left Your Grace's solar. I knew the only place I would feel safe is with Alexander. I went to his chamber, barely entering before the men arrived. They banged on the door and tried the handle. When they left, Alex and I had a much-needed conversation. It resolved what was unsettled. We married and registered at the Stirling kirk. Father Barret conducted the ceremony."

"That does not explain where you have been all day." The Bruce didn't relent.

"I spent it with my husband as any newly married couple does when they care for their partner."

King Robert turned his attention to Alex. "So you did tup her and did the honorable thing."

Alex inhaled deeply to keep from blurting the first words that came to mind since they would indubitably wind him in the dungeon. The breath expanded Alex's chest, making him appear as the intimidating warrior he'd always been. King Robert blinked as he realized he'd gone too far, and that Alex's pledge not to forgive insulting the man's wife might not have been bluster. But neither did he intend to apologize.

"My marriage is my business, but it is a marriage by law and by God's blessing. My wife will receive the respect she's due. No one will speak as though she's little more than a tavern wench. That ceases as of this day. We will all discover just how well I protect those I love if anyone utters one more disparaging word aboot Lady Caitlyn."

"You're threatening me?" King Robert spluttered.

"I don't recall saying 'you' or a name."

"Armstrong—"

"Lady Caitlyn, you said men chased you." Queen Elizabeth cut off her husband, stating what seemed to have gone unnoticed by the king. "Who were they?"

"I know not, Your Grace. They wore breeks and doublets like Lowlanders, but they were the size of most Highlanders."

"Then how did you escape them?" King Robert demanded.

"I counted on knowing the keep better than they did, and I do. I used servants' stairs and passageways to make it to Alex's floor. Then I ran as fast as I could."

"You are fortunate Armstrong was there." Queen Elizabeth shifted her gaze to Alex.

"I was. I didn't know for sure, but he is who I feel safest with. He was the only person I considered."

Alex's heart swelled as he listened to Caitlyn and heard the certainty in her voice. He knew she didn't exaggerate. He had a pang of guilt for nearly not opening the door and for how intoxicated he was when she found him. He guessed she sensed his thoughts because her hand squeezed his.

"Would you recognize these men if you saw them again?" King Robert's gaze swept the dancers before returning to Caitlyn.

"I searched when we entered. They aren't here. They didn't strike me as the type who could find chambers in the keep, and they were not guardsmen. I'm certain to recognize them if I spied them again." Caitlyn looked up at Alex. "I believe they're the same men who chased us when we were returning to the keep."

"Your Majesty, I've given that much thought. I—"

"How have you had time to think of much of aught when you seem to spend all of it with your... wife?" King Robert spoke the last word with hesitation.

"Caitlyn is never far from my mind, and these men endangered her twice now. How could I not give them much thought? I imagine any mon would spend a great deal of time thinking aboot the men who threaten his wife." Alex spoke without blinking, daring the king to disagree while his wife sat beside him. Queen Elizabeth endured eight years of house arrest under the English King, Edward Longshanks, as a punishment for Robert the Bruce's pursuit of Scottish independence. "I suspect they are gallow-glasses."

Alex named the elite cadre of warriors who were mercenaries. Many hailed from Argyll and the Western Isles, but Irish men of Norse-Gaelic descent also joined the ranks. These were trained fighters who often wore heavy armor like English knights and foot soldiers.

King Robert failed to hide his shock. He rose

from his chair and titled his head toward the antechamber next to the Great Hall. Queen Elizabeth made no move to join King Robert, which surprised no one. But when Alex guided Caitlyn to turn toward the door, King Robert barked, "She stays."

"She does not. I will not leave her side and abandon her to these rabid mongrels. We're discussing someone chasing my wife, and you're aware of what your courtiers are like. Caitlyn comes with me." Alex refused to relent, even if the Bruce threw him in the dungeon. He trusted no one now. Between the hateful things the courtiers would say and realizing who the unknown assailants were, he feared leaving Caitlyn even with their guards. The men might protect her from a physical attack, but they could do nothing to shield her from the courtiers' barbs.

"Fine." King Robert stormed from the dais, not waiting for Alex and Caitlyn. They entered the antechamber to find King Robert pacing before the fire. "Why would gallowglass men be after you? And how do you know who they are?"

"They wore no armor when they attacked us, but someone clearly trained them as warriors. Their clothes and horses were too fine to be highwaymen, and they fought together like they've known and trusted one another in many battles. Beyond that, they carried claymores and axes. Lowlanders don't favor those." Alex recounted what he'd noticed from the fight in the meadow.

"They spoke Gaelic," Caitlyn added. "I heard them today, but I didn't understand them. I can't imagine how they entered the castle with their swords, but I spotted them as I climbed the stairs ahead of them with the other ladies. One of them carried a short-handled axe when they chased me. I feared that more than the swords. It scared me that he intended to throw it."

"One of Angus's guards heard the Scotts discuss needing more coin to afford something before they left." Alex remembered that detail, but he'd never learned to what the man referred. Now he had his suspicions. "They hired mercenaries to kill me when they couldn't. They knew they couldn't remain at court, and their laird wants to keep his clan's hands clean. I believe the Scott delegates only attacked because they stumbled upon me."

Caitlyn leaned her shoulder against Alex's, knowing he didn't want to articulate why the Scotts overpowered him. She prayed King Robert had the decency not to ask. The monarch flashed Caitlyn a glance before he nodded. She sensed he recalled what he observed when he visited Alex. She remembered his expression while she stitched Alex's wound. It made Caitlyn wonder if he understood ghosts haunted Alex's mind and if they did the same to the king.

"If that's the case, you are safe nowhere but on your land, and in your keep," King Robert surmised. "They obviously found how to enter the castle, and you will be in danger while you travel. I will not stake my crown on it being the Scotts, but it certainly appears they are responsible. I'm sending you with a score of my men, if for no other reason than to protect Lady Caitlyn. I'm still on rocky terms with Laird Kennedy, despite Cairren's marriage improving. I don't need another one of his daughters in danger because I send her from court. Tavin won't be any better if aught happens to you when he didn't wish to send anyone to court."

Alex's brow furrowed, and his head tilted at the king's last statement. King Robert grimaced when he realized what he let slip. He sighed and crossed his arms.

"Tavin didn't trust any Armstrong being safe coming here. He warned that the Scotts wouldn't hesitate to make trouble even under my nose. But I insisted that someone represent your clan because I didn't wish to try to resolve the issue with missives going back and forth and every which way. I was certain he would send you, Alex, because you are the most diplomatic representative he has. I also suggested that you should visit Lady Caitlyn."

Caitlyn wondered if the king and queen would ever cease playing matchmaker. The few couples they directly arranged marriages for had rocky starts, with death nearly befalling each of them. She thought about Cairren and how she endured prejudice because of their family's heritage, but she also endured a spurned would-be fiancée and a conniving brother-by-marriage. Allyson Elliot bolted when she learned she was to marry Ewan, the older Gordon twin. She faced traveling alone along the border rather than marrying the now-reformed rogue. He'd almost forced Arabella Johnstone to marry a man other than her now-husband, Lachlan Sutherland. The proposed suitor likely would have killed her. The king had also caused a rift between Laird Brodie Campbell and himself when he thought to make a point in Brodie's favor by offering a wager on Brodie's wife, Laurel Ross, and her devotion to Brodie.

"Well, I've been, and I've seen. Now I will return home with my bride. I accept and appreciate your detachment of men. I will not risk Caitlyn's safety on the road. We will leave in the morn."

"No." King Robert held up his hand and shook his head. "If it was only this morn that they pursued Lady Caitlyn, then they will expect you to leave tomorrow. You will wait another day, where you both have the protection of my men and being at court."

Alex looked askance as he fought not to point out that the attacks happened in the very keep the king alleged would keep them safe. If he didn't think traveling with the king's guard was a prudent idea, he would have asked Caitlyn to lead them out through the tunnels. But he wouldn't forsake a larger retinue because of the king's ludicrous comment.

"Your Majesty." Caitlyn waited for King Robert to turn his attention toward her. "It will appear questionable if my guards accompany me throughout the keep, but it will seem far more dubious if a royal guard traipses after me. However, Her Grace hasn't released me from her service. I cannot take shelter in our chamber, but neither am I comfortable moving around the keep on my own. I request she discharges me."

"So you might lock yourself away in a chamber with your husband." King Robert frowned.

"We are newlyweds." Alex wished yet again that he could cross his arms, but he was disinclined to release Caitlyn's hand. "My wife is safest in our chamber until we depart. I don't wish to confine Caitlyn, but I won't risk her life. Either she's accompanied by the Armstrong and Kennedy guards, or she remains sequestered."

"And what of you?" King Robert's lips flattened before pursing. Alex thought it looked tighter than a virgin's arse.

"I will ensure my wife isn't lonely." Alex couldn't keep the mirth from his voice as he gave Caitlyn's hand a brief squeeze.

"I may as well consent on the queen's behalf before you abscond with Lady Caitlyn. Again." King Robert shook his head in resignation. He couldn't blame either of them for fearing for their safety, nor could he begrudge them wanting time alone. He and Elizabeth had discussed the apparent rift between Alex and Caitlyn several times since Alex's arrival. They'd feared the couple wouldn't reconcile, and it saddened them. They'd silently rooted for them, not only because the alliance further secured the border, but they'd witnessed the budding relationship for years. It felt wholly unsatisfying if it hadn't worked out. "You will remain in seclusion tomorrow. Then you may depart the morn after."

"Thank you." Alex and Caitlyn spoke at the same time as he bowed, and she dipped into a graceful curtsy. Caitlyn prayed King Robert would soon dismiss them. Lingering only boded more trouble between Alex and him. She struggled to say only what she already had, her nerves frazzled from the long day. She wished for nothing more than a hot bath and retiring with Alex.

"Tend to Lady Caitlyn. She looks ready to drop." King Robert turned away from the couple, so Alex and Caitlyn hurried from the antechamber. They found both sets of guards waiting for them, eager to learn the outcome.

"The king will send a contingent of guards with us for the journey to Mangerton. But he insists we remain for another day. He argues it will give us time to put distance between the gallowglasses and us. I think it merely gives them more time to lie in wait."

"Gallowglasses, Alex?" David asked in disbelief. "Do you really think the Scotts can afford them?"

"I think they are desperate to accomplish what they didn't on the battlefield. They want me dead, and I'm certain they will come after Brice, if they haven't already. All the more reason I wish to return home." Alex nodded at Caitlyn's guards. "Now that Lady Caitlyn and I married, you would return to Dunure, but I'm asking that you travel with us. The more men we have, the better I will feel aboot Lady Caitlyn's safety. Once we're certain the road is safe for you to travel back to Kennedy land, you can return."

"We feel better aboot that too," Grant spoke up. The Kennedy guards appeared decidedly uncomfortable when Alex began speaking, but they noticeably relaxed when he suggested they continue to serve Caitlyn, at least until they arrived at Mangerton. Their loyalty and steadfastness moved Caitlyn.

"Thank you. I'm certain my parents will appreciate your dedication, and I'm grateful." Caitlyn smiled at the men she'd known her entire life. They weren't the only retinue she'd had while at court, but they were her favorite group. They were all experienced warriors, but they were also friends. She trusted them implicitly, just as her father did.

"Let us retire for the night." Alex wrapped his arm around Caitlyn's waist as the group moved through the passageways. The Armstrong and Kennedy guards formed a circle around the couple until they locked the door behind them.

EIGHTEEN

"Caity, it's going to be a longer route home than usual. We have to give the Scotts a wide berth because I'm certain they or these mercenaries are waiting for us. It also means coming closer to the border than I prefer to circle around to our home."

"'Our home.' I like that thought." Caitlyn wrapped her arms around Alex's waist and rested her head against his chest. Despite the turmoil they faced, nowhere felt better than in Alex's arms. She supposed it was both his massive frame and his iron will, but it was also the gentleness with which he held her. "Would that we could stay exactly like this."

"I wish the same, Caity. I'll do everything a mon can to keep you safe, but I feel best when I can shelter you in my embrace." Alex's arm pressed Caitlyn against him, neither wanting any space between them. He still held grave reservations that he could protect Caitlyn with only one arm to fight. He resolved to use his mind to do what his body couldn't. He'd been considering their route when David knocked. He'd considered many places someone might attack them. He plotted how they could alter their course if they suspected a threat. He was aware he had a canny sense for danger, and he intended to err on the side of extreme caution.

"I know you will, Alex. I've never doubted that, even when we were most at odds." Caitlyn leaned away as she offered him a soft smile. "While I always thought you and Cairren made a wonderful couple, I confess I was jealous. I envied how we all thought she'd found someone who'd love and protect her no matter what. I used to wish it were me you planned to cherish and guard."

"We thought ourselves in love." Alex brushed the back of his fingers against Caitlyn's cheek. "But I could never ignore how you drew me. I felt guilty because it split my feelings, but it was always different with you. It embarrassed me that I wanted to spend all my time with you when you still seemed so young. Cairren will always be a close friend, but I knew I couldn't marry her when I couldn't stop thinking of you when I…"

"When you what?" Caitlyn tilted her head as Alex's face flushed. He licked his lips before pressing them together. "When you what, Alex?"

"When I fantasized aboot being with a woman."

"You thought aboot me like that?" It was Caitlyn's turn to blush. "I did the same. Granted, I'm certain mine were less vivid than yours. You had the advantage of firsthand knowledge. But I felt wretched not being able to cease my dreams aboot the mon I believed my sister would marry."

"Back then, I had little knowledge. Since I assumed I would marry Cairren, it seemed wrong to venture to a tavern or take up with a servant. I would never humiliate her like that."

"You wouldn't." Caitlyn scowled. "Padraig never did aught, but he certainly humiliated her, nonetheless." She shook her head. "I don't want to think aboot that now."

"It took all the restraint I had and a good dose of discouragement from Daniel and Jamie to keep from murdering him." Alex's scowl matched Caitlyn's. It had pained Alex to arrive at the Munros' to discover how they treated Cairren, and to find out how neglectful her husband was at the time. It had also made him even more resolved to always show Caitlyn how much he valued her. He led her to the chair before the fire and sat, pulling her onto his lap. "Caity, I still feel horribly for what I said and did in the undercroft. That will haunt for the rest of my days. And despite that, you still came when I needed you."

"You hurt me beyond belief with what you said. I didn't think my heart could ever heal, and I definitely didn't think I wanted to lay eyes on you ever again. But when Grant knocked on my door and said someone had hurt you, it all fell away. All I could think aboot was getting to you as fast as I could. I *needed* to know you would be all right. You weren't an easy patient, but I started to understand you better. I made myself imagine what your life is like now. I never once pitied you." Caitlyn's voice took on a determined edge with her last sentence, but it softened once more. "I was sympathetic. My heart ached for you. It also made me more resolved to remain by your side, even if you only accepted me as a friend."

"I was fooling myself to think I could go through life without you. I thought I was doing the right thing. I thought I was being honorable, at least except in the undercroft. Caity, I'm better in so many ways with you by my side. I feel calmer and more self-assured. I feel like I have purpose again as your husband and even as my father's heir. I've slept better, and not only when there's light. I think that alone has improved my temperament. In the bleakest days, it was you who I wished was with me. My mother told me it was you I called out for."

"Alex, if I'd known, you must know I would have gone to Mangerton. The queen and court be damned. I couldn't have stayed away. I hadn't wanted to voice this, but I resent no one telling me."

"I told my parents and Brice not to. I wanted you —needed you—but I couldn't bear the thought that you would look at me with disgust. That you would remain with me because you thought me pathetic. I didn't give you enough credit. I should have known you wouldn't, that your feelings are more enduring. It was my disgust in myself and my self-pity."

"I can't blame you for feeling that way. Everything in your life changed. Every warrior and wife know it can happen, but it's altogether different when it does. I recognize people regard you differently, both your appearance and what they believe you can do. But they underestimate you, which angers me beyond belief."

Caitlyn scowled as she recalled the disrespectful, even vulgar, comments she'd heard about Alex since he arrived at court. But her face relaxed as she met his gaze once more.

"Alex, I've loved you unconditionally since I was three-and-ten. It won't change. You are still the singularly most desirable mon I have ever seen. I think the scar gives you even more of an edge of danger. I rather like it." Caitlyn waggled her eyebrows. "Even if you couldn't hold me, I still wouldn't let you go. I've admired you as a warrior, and I suppose that's why you became the mon that you are. But I never loved you because you're a warrior. Does that make sense?"

"It does. I'm sorry for how I acted when I arrived. It makes me ashamed. I won't take you for granted again, Caity. I love you too much to make the same mistake twice."

"And I love you too much to turn away from you just because life is hard. We pledged to remain true to one another for better *and* for worse." Caitlyn leaned toward Alex, their mouths melding together. It began as a light press as Caitlyn's body relaxed against Alex's. Her left hand cupped his neck as her right hand burrowed into his hair. Alex's long arms enabled him to lift his limp arm to rest on Caitlyn's hip while his right arm encircled her waist.

The kiss grew more passionate as their bodies brushed against one another. Their tongues dueled, caressing the inside of each other's mouth. Caitlyn sucked gently on Alex's tongue, eliciting a deep rumble from his chest. She shifted to allow her hands to work the doublet's buttons free. They pulled apart long enough for Caitlyn to help ease the garment off Alex's arms. She moved once again, gathering her skirts to her waist and straddling his lap. Her fingers skimmed over his chest and abdomen. Alex watched as lust and love gleamed in Caitlyn's eyes. Her right hand drifted toward his left arm, but she paused before she touched him. Their gazes met, Caitlyn asking silent permission. Alex nodded, his throat too tight to speak.

Caitlyn feathered her fingers over his scar, her tender touch a balm both to his injury and his soul. Alex never liked people noticing his scar, let alone touching it. Even his mother's touch wasn't as gentle as Caitlyn's. Any sort of contact would normally send excruciating pain coursing through his arm. But her fingertips barely grazed the surface as she ran them over his bicep and along his forearm. She skimmed them back up to his shoulder where she traced the livid, raised flesh. She wondered if he might have been better losing the arm altogether.

"Am I hurting you? Should I stop?"

"Please don't. I—I like it." It stunned Alex to realize that Caitlyn's touch actually made the injury feel better. He felt his arm relax, never realizing how tense it was. He'd always thought the dead weight of it pulling on his shoulder caused the unceasing pain. But as Caitlyn's touch soothed him, the discomfort eased. He closed his eyes and rested his head against the back of the chair. Caitlyn continued to stroke his arm while her other hand swept over his neck, shoulders, chest, and abdomen, over and over.

With his eyes closed, Alex's senses filled with Caitlyn's familiar fragrance, myrrh. It was a rarity in Scotland, but it was one of the few things Collette kept from her earlier life in France. Innes traded for it whenever he could, and both Caitlyn and Cairren favored the scent. The warm and sweet, slightly woodsy aroma reminded him of the days when he assumed he and Caitlyn would build a future together, with only blissful happiness surrounding them.

Curiosity prompted Alex to wiggle his fingers. Sensation shot down his arm like a bolt of lightning, and he nearly gave up. But when the initial shock wore off, he found there was movement independent from when he had to use his other hand to close his left hand around something. Caitlyn froze for a heartbeat, feeling the changing pressure on her hip. But she continued her ministrations, and it gave Alex confidence to keep trying. His fingers were stiff from being idle for so many months. They ached, but they moved. Growing braver, he focused on moving his wrist. It twitched but didn't bend. A moment of frustration flashed through him, but he moved his fingers once again. Taking a fortifying breath, he tried moving his arm. It twitched like his wrist, then fell to his side. He hadn't lifted it at all. He'd only made it feel more worthless.

"Alex." Caitlyn kissed the corner of his mouth. "You tried. Even if it didn't do what you wanted, you tried. Even if it's only ever your fingers, now you've found out you can do that. Mayhap more will come with time, and mayhap more won't. Either way, you don't seem to be in the pain you usually are."

"I'm not. I didn't realize how much tension I hold in it. I didn't think the muscles worked at all. I'm relaxed enough I could almost fall asleep." Alex's hand cupped the back of Caitlyn's head and guided her mouth to his. Before he kissed her, he whispered. "Though I won't until the wee hours of the morn."

Caitlyn sank against him once more. She'd felt Alex's body change from being as taut as a bowstring to a more pliant...rock. It still felt hard as a rock, Caitlyn realized, but Alex was calmer than he had been since she first sought him out in the Great Hall the day he arrived. She inched higher on his lap, feeling his rod brushing her mound. She rocked her hips, building friction between them. Between kisses, she panted, "No more clothes."

Despite the suggestion, neither hurried to break their contact until urgency had them yanking the garments off. Alex welcomed Caitlyn's help rather than resenting it. Wrapped around one another and kissing, they stumbled backward to the bed. Caitlyn slid backwards until her head reached the pillows, and Alex knelt between her legs.

"I believe you promised me dessert, *mo ghaol*." Alex's husky voice sent a shiver through Caitlyn that settled as an ache in her core. Remembering how his tongue felt against her heated flesh, eagerness turned almost to giddiness. But Alex was determined not to rush, drawing out their pleasure. He nipped at her inner thighs, kissing his way up her body one excruciatingly slow inch at a time. When he'd showered both legs with kisses, he nestled his face against the strip of smooth skin at their juncture. Alex relished the French tradition that he had only ever heard of but now had the pleasure of enjoying.

She lifted her pelvis to him, and he swept his tongue over her folds, making Caitlyn clutch the bedding as she moaned. Torn between closing her eyes and reveling in every sensation, and wanting to keep them open with fascination, they narrowed to slits. Her body felt heavy as it pressed against the mattress. Her breasts ached, urging her to squeeze and knead them as Alex dedicated his attention to sliding two fingers into her core as he drew her pearl from its shell. His teeth grazed the bundle of nerves, making her hips arch higher. Abandoning her right breast, her hand pressed his head closer. He obliged, increasing the speed and pressure as his fingers and tongue worked her toward a frenzy.

"Alex," she begged. "Ahh." A tightening low in Caitlyn's belly made her squirm as she tried to get closer. Alex continued working her nub and her slick channel until spasms tightened around his fingers. With more agility than he expected, he pushed himself onto his knees and then hovered his body over hers. She stroked his cock thrice before guiding him to her entrance. She grasped his buttocks and pushed as he thrusted of his own volition. Both paused as the feeling of joining was nearly as blissful as their climaxes. But it wasn't long before need overshadowed sentimentality. They moved together, heightening each other's arousal. Sweat beaded their skin, and the sounds of their lovemaking filled their chamber.

"More." Caitlyn begged as she used her feet to lever her hips to meet Alex's. He was happy to oblige Caitlyn, surging into her over and over with increasing force. "Yes."

Alex's heart thundered in his chest as he flexed his hips with more vigor than he ever had before. His need to be within Caitlyn, to pleasure her, to find release with her, consumed him so that he had a singular focus. The keep could have fallen down around his ears, and he wouldn't have cared until he felt Caitlyn climax again. He drove into her over and over, pushing her toward the headboard before gliding away. Her nails dug into his back, but always careful to avoid his wounded shoulder. Her knees gripped his hips as she encouraged him to give her all that he could.

"I'm going to explode, Caity. God damn, you feel good. I want my release, but I also never want this to end."

"Just keep going. I'm getting close. I need you." Caitlyn grasped his buttocks, enjoying the feel of the muscles flexing. Every movement brought her closer as lust for her husband overshadowed everything else. Friction against her nub had her head tilting back as she tensed and her core pulsated. Alex nipped where her neck and shoulder met as his essence poured forth. With the broadest grin she'd ever worn, Caitlyn teased, "See what you might have missed."

"Caity, you shall put me in an early grave. My heart will surely give out if it's always like this."

"Do you think it might be?"

"Mayhap we won't always want it so vigorous. But it's not only the ferocity of my need for you. It's how much my heart swells with love. God, Caity, I will never have enough time to love you for as long as I want."

"I intend to be a very auld woman with gray hair, and you shall be an auld mon with nearly no teeth, before I'm willing to let us go to our Maker. Then I shall track you down and drag you to my eternal bed." Caitlyn's mischievous smile told Alex that while their bodies might one day age, their attraction wouldn't.

"I don't understand why people think Heaven is the most desired place to go. I'm in no rush. I'd rather be right here with you, be it in a bed or walking hand-in-hand on our clan's land. This is more divine than any celestial court."

"Shh." Caitlyn stroked an ebony lock back from Alex's brow before kissing him. "You'd do well to never say that blasphemy where anyone else can hear. But I agree. I'm in no hurry, even if we will never age there. There will be no gray hair or missing teeth." Caitlyn winked. "But what we have now is what I want more than aught. I'm not convinced Heaven could be better."

"I found you in this life, and I will find you in the next." Alex filled his kiss with all the tenderness that was missing from their impassioned lovemaking. The balance between their urgency and their bliss surely symbolized their abiding love.

"I will always be with you in this life, and I will be with you in the next."

Alex eased to his side, neither enjoying the sensation of parting. Caitlyn nestled closer once they arranged the surrounding blankets. Her head rested on his right shoulder as he stroked her hair. He pressed a kiss to her forehead as they both drifted off to sleep.

Mo ghràidh, wake up." Alex kissed Caitlyn's temple as he tried to rouse her. She nuzzled closer and sighed, still content and asleep. "Caity."

"No. She's not here." Caitlyn grumbled when Alex's voice finally permeated her slumber.

"Caity, wake up. I think there's an alternative to staying here or going straight to Mangerton. If it's workable, we should leave soon."

Caitlyn cracked one eye open and spied no light coming from the window embrasure. The candles still lit from the night before burned low. The room was so dim, she could barely find Alex.

"Did you sleep?"

"Aye, like a bairn. But my mind came up with another reason to wake me. What if we travel to Dunure instead? We can visit your parents and announce our marriage properly. We can visit for as long as you wish. I'm certain Innes will send men with us to escort us to Mangerton."

Caitlyn sat up and twisted to gape at Alex before she burbled. "Do you think we could? I'd really like to see *Maman* and Papa again. It's been ages. I know they'll come to visit, but I'd really like to tell them in person that we married."

"No one will expect us to travel west rather than east. If we can travel far enough south without trouble and reach the road west, then it should be an easy ride. But we may need to travel overland to avoid encountering anyone. It'll make the ride more tiring for you and your mount."

"Goldie and I will manage," Caitlyn assured Alex, but she wondered how he would fare. He'd made strides by being able to use his left hand to hold his reins and made it easier to mount, but she doubted even a well-worn road could keep his arm from jostling. She couldn't imagine how riding across hill and dale would feel.

"It'll be misery." Alex felt there was no point in downplaying the truth since Caitlyn would know, anyway. "But I want to see Collette and Innes more, and I will endure the fires of hell to avoid endangering you."

"If you need to rest, give me a look or some sign. I'll ask you if we can stop. Let the men think I'm too fragile to travel long distances."

"Not your guards, nor mine, will believe that. They're accustomed to riding with you."

"But the king's men aren't. Your men and mine will understand and are likely to do the same thing as me before making you miserable. If you wish to save face before anyone, then they are the ones. No Armstrong or Kennedy will ever think less of you."

"I suspect you won't allow it." Alex sat up and bussed a kiss on her still-warm cheek.

"Absolutely not." Caitlyn crossed her arms and nodded, but she soon launched herself at Alex, who welcomed her ardent kiss.

They'd woken up twice in the middle of the night, but they both felt well rested despite not getting a full night's sleep. Alex realized he'd slept more than he usually did. It was still exceedingly early, so Alex wrapped his arm around Caitlyn as she guided his sword into her sheath. Alex watched her breasts sway as she moved over him. He couldn't imagine how any man didn't appreciate Caitlyn's innate beauty. Her golden-bronze skin shone in the little candlelight that flickered in the chamber. It was smoother than any satin he'd ever felt as she draped herself over his chest. A selfish part of him niggled that he appreciated he had no competition, since he suspected he would have fought to the death once King Robert announced her chosen suitor. If only they could abandon all responsibility and hide away somewhere warm where Caitlyn could remain bare all day and night. But he feared starving because he could never tear himself away long enough to hunt.

Their movements were slow and gentle, like they had been after their combustible coupling when they returned to their chamber. They relished the feeling of touching one another, pouring love into every kiss. When neither could last any longer and pleasure swept over them, they lay joined but still.

"What were you thinking aboot?"

"You." Alex glanced down at the top of Caitlyn's head. "I was thinking aboot how stunning you are. That if I could take you away somewhere where the sun always shone, I would do away with all your clothes, so I could gaze at you all day."

"You can stare at me all day even with my clothes on."

"Nowhere near as fun and definitely inconvenient." Alex's laughter vibrated his chest. "I will never get my fill of looking at you. I spent so many years wondering what you looked like, praying one day I would be the mon to discover it. My imagination was vivid, but it didn't come close."

"Outside our clan, you're the only mon Cairren and I have ever known who didn't look twice when he met us. Mayhap because we were still children, but even then, others shied away."

"That's because I'd gotten a bad sunburn that summer before I arrived to foster. I was jealous that you never got red or uncomfortable while my skin had been on fire before peeling. I thought you and Cairren were the lucky ones."

"I always wished my skin were as dark as *Maman's* and Cairren's. It wasn't until I arrived here that I appreciated being lighter."

"But that hasn't made it better."

"It's made it a little easier. I'm even lighter in winter, so it feels like people almost—never completely—but almost forget. Cairren didn't have that luxury."

"I don't think any Armstrong would look askance at you, or dare to speak against you, but that's something you cannot keep to yourself, Caity. Not ever. I need you to believe you can tell me. You'll be the lady of our clan one day, and I need to be certain people will respect your authority. But even more importantly to me, I want you to always be welcome in your home."

"I've been visiting Mangerton Tower and your clan for years. I loved that we traveled with you for the holidays. Sometimes it was difficult being away from our clan for some celebrations, and I loathed when you left without us—me—but I feel nearly as a part of your clan as I do mine. Your family feels like an extension of mine."

"That's how I feel aboot yours. Your parents welcomed me as a third child rather than merely a neighbor sent to train. I recognize I was more fortunate than most."

"That's why I didn't understand what to do with how I felt when I was younger. You stopped feeling like a brother, but then I thought you intended to become one in truth if you married Cairren. My thoughts were decidedly not fraternal."

"Nor were mine sororal. I think I've proven that. But if not, I'm happy to try again." Alex squeezed Caitlyn's bottom.

"We shall never leave this bed, or this keep if we keep talking aboot our feelings and what we'd like to feel." Caitlyn grumbled as she rolled away from Alex. She'd heard movement after they retired the night before and woken to find her maid slipping into the chamber with her packed satchel. They nodded to one another, both careful not to disturb Alex. It shocked Caitlyn that he slept through anyone entering or exiting the chamber, but it gladdened her that he finally slept soundly.

"Where did that come from?" Alex nudged his chin toward the bag Caitlyn rummaged through.

He'd pulled his breeks on while she pulled out stockings and a fresh chemise.

"Ellie brought it last night. What?"

Alex's face had darkened like a thundercloud. "I don't enjoy knowing someone entered our chamber, and I slept through it."

"I suspect that once you have a few more solid nights of sleep, you'll be as alert as you ever were. You know guards stand outside your door, so your mind must have been at ease."

Alex appeared skeptical, but he didn't press the issue. He finished dressing, and since it was Caitlyn, he no longer resented having someone help him. Once they'd finished, Alex even tying Caitlyn's laces at her waist, they met a combination of Armstrongs and Kennedys in the passageway. They made their way to the chapel, knowing the king was an early riser and preferred the first and second prayer services of the day. They arrived as the doors swung open, and King Robert's retinue of guards escorted him into the passageway.

"I hardly expected to catch sight of either of you." King Robert's surly greeting fazed neither Alex nor Caitlyn. They remained hopeful that he might agree to their change of plans. "Since the service is over and Terce isn't for another three hours, I suppose you seek my attention."

"Lady Caitlyn and I would like to travel to Dunure to visit her family and announce our marriage. This allows us to travel somewhere safe along a less-risky route."

"Do you still expect to travel with my guards?"

"I won't turn down the offer, if it still stands, Your Majesty." Alex still wanted the escort, but he would depart even with only six guards. If they could leave Stirling and the surrounding area without trouble, then he hoped they could have an uneventful journey the rest of the way.

"Men will travel with you as far as Glasgow." King Robert watched Alex, but the man's expression didn't falter.

"Thank you, Your Majesty. I feel better knowing that there will be more men with us. Hopefully, it will be a deterrent until we travel far enough from here that they no longer guess our direction." Alex bowed as Caitlyn curtsied. "How long do your men need? We will meet them in the bailey."

"Hoh, hoh. I didn't say you could leave sooner merely because you decide to change course. You will still depart tomorrow. The queen wishes to say her farewells, and I'm certain Lady Caitlyn hasn't seen to her belongings."

Caitlyn kept her face impassive, but it was clear he'd sent someone to snoop or someone to interview her maid. She appreciated neither of those possibilities. It made her suspect that's why Ellie brought the satchel when she did.

"My maid can manage, Your Majesty. She's from Stirling, so she won't travel with us. What we can't carry, I'm certain can travel on a wagon that Laird Armstrong sends."

"I expect you to join Queen Elizabeth for Terce." King Robert didn't relent, and it frustrated both Alex and Caitlyn.

"Your Majesty, is it safe for me to move around the keep when those men felt no compunction aboot following me during the light of day?"

"No more dangerous with your guards than you choosing to wind your way through the keep when the sun isn't even up." King Robert shot a pointed look at each member of their group. Caitlyn bit her tongue, knowing she would get nowhere arguing. She had to hope that the gallowglasses, if that's who they

221

were, didn't attempt to find her again. Turning his attention back to Alex, King Robert swept his eyes over Alex. "You will return to the lists today."

"Very well." Alex responded without hesitation. He didn't wish to go there; he wanted to climb back into bed with Caitlyn. But he understood the king's mind was unwavering, and he'd tested the man's good graces too many times already. With a nod, the Bruce and his guards left the others in the passageway.

"We have three hours until Terce. I can pack in that time. If I must remain with the other ladies, then I shall use them as a shield as much as any of you. No one will dare approach me in the keep with so many others around, especially if we are in the queen's company. I will make certain I'm never separated from the group." Caitlyn wrapped her arm through Alex's as the group made their way to the ladies'-in-waiting floor. Two men stationed themselves at the top of the stairs while pairs went to either end of the passageway. Alex waited outside Caitlyn's door. She'd forgotten entirely about her roommate until she held the door handle.

Caitlyn slipped inside the chamber and lit the candle on her bedside table. Moving as silently as she could, she opened her trunk then crossed the chamber to her armoire. She pulled out an armful of gowns, laying them on the bed before carefully folding each one and stowing them away in her chest. It didn't take her long since she'd always preferred a smaller wardrobe than most ladies. She kept aside three gowns that she intended to give to Blythe since they were nearly brand-new and had been an impulsive splurge during a trip into town. She knew Blythe liked them and would wear them, even if the hems had to be let out. She gathered her toilette items from the table with a looking glass. She rolled the vials and bottles in cheesecloth before tucking them into a burlap bag. Layering chemises and stockings on top of her fine gowns, she placed the bag inside. She'd kept her Kennedy plaid spread across the foot of her bed since she arrived. It was a rare occasion for her to wear it, but it had been a piece of home when she'd felt homesick. She placed that as the last layer before closing the lid.

Caitlyn glanced around the chamber and glanced at her roommate, who had stirred but had said nothing. She'd longed for the day when she could leave this space behind, either to return home or to marry Alex. For weeks, she'd feared she would leave it because the king ordered her to marry someone else. She'd sensed that decision had been coming, but it had made it no easier to learn of it. Now she glanced around one last time as she spun the ring on her left hand. A sense of rightness filled her, knowing she was leaving the chamber and the keep behind for the reason she wanted most: a future with Alex.

NINETEEN

A lex and Caitlyn passed the three hours before Terce by catching up on their sleep after one brief interlude. Caitlyn drew back the window hanging, and they left the bed curtains open. Alex was certain he slept peacefully from the extra light and Caitlyn's presence. He felt the tension he hadn't realized he carried in his back and shoulders release as he fell asleep. He woke refreshed, and his arm didn't ache for the first time in six months. Caitlyn's rosy cheeks when she woke stirred a tenderness in him that he didn't know he possessed. He'd been so singularly focused on her protection, and his assumed inability to provide it, that he'd lost sight of why he wanted to marry her. It was quiet moments like this when the rest of the world didn't exist. It was waking with her in his arms and feeling like he could face the world with a partner he trusted implicitly.

Caitlyn ran her fingers over Alex's beard, the prickliness still tickling even after all the kisses they'd shared in the past couple of days. He kept it well-trimmed, or at least had when he arrived. She'd taken scissors to it during his convalescence, but neither had done much in the days since he left his sickbed.

"You don't like it." Alex grinned as Caitlyn tugged.

"I don't mind it, but I miss seeing your handsome face."

Alex's expression darkened as he glanced away. Caitlyn pressed his cheek, but he refused to turn back to her. His arm throbbed when he realized that his left hand tried to curl around the bedding.

"Alex, I won't press if you truly aren't comfortable with it, but I've always preferred you clean shaven. I enjoy looking at *all* of you." Caitlyn's eyes glided over Alex's naked body, and she was certain to drool if she weren't careful.

"You haven't seen how bad it is."

"Do you intend to keep that from me forever?"

"You make it sound as though it were some great secret."

"It feels like you're hiding something. I know it's ridiculous and selfish of me to ask you to do something that you don't want. But I really miss seeing all of your face. I can't explain why, but I always found your chiseled jaw to be so appealing. I used to imagine stretching to kiss you and only being able to reach your jaw."

"You pictured that, did you?"

"Yes. I pictured kissing you in many ways, but for some reasons that's what I always thought of when I pictured us married. It seemed wifely." Caitlyn shrugged, ready to abandon the topic and feeling foolish for bringing it up.

"Will you help me?" Alex moved to the edge of the bed. "I need no more scars."

"Really?"

"How could I deny my bonnie bride her wifely privileges?" Alex felt no small amount of trepidation knowing he intended to expose his face. He couldn't imagine what he might do if he finally discovered his face made Caitlyn recoil. He wasn't eager to face the courtiers either, but this trip to court had done more to help him reclaim his old sense of self than even entering the lists at home. He was aware that had more to do with Caitlyn than anything else. He certainly would have preferred not to be attacked twice, but those events forced him to realize he wasn't as helpless as he believed.

"Mayhap I could just trim it really close to start with." Caitlyn followed Alex to the washstand. As she lathered the shaving cream, she wondered which ancient people created it. She started on the unmarred side, cautious not to nick Alex. When she struggled to reach, Alex smirked and drew her forward to straddle his lap. "You will leave here with only half your face shaved if you distract me."

"So I shouldn't do this?" Alex kneaded Caitlyn's breasts and ran his thumb over her nipples until they pebbled.

"If you don't want me to, then I won't." Caitlyn kept her voice low, but the nervousness rang like a church bell in their quiet chamber. Alex pressed a kiss to Caitlyn's lips, only getting a slight smear on her cheek.

"Caity, I would have told you no if I really didn't want to. I'm enjoying myself, not trying to distract you. If aught, I'm distracting myself."

Caitlyn nodded and brought the razor back to Alex's cheek, but hesitated. Their eyes locked, and she saw his encouragement. She worked efficiently as she scraped away months' worth of growth. When she finished, she leaned back and wiped away the remnants of the shaving cream. Her heart swelled as she finally laid eyes on the visage she'd fallen in love with nearly a decade ago and had known almost her entire life.

"By the saints, you are the most handsome mon I

have ever seen." Caitlyn grasped Alex's jaw in both hands and swooped in for a kiss that stole Alex's breath. The ferocity surprised him, but the relief that swept over him that Caitlyn still found him attractive nearly overcame him. She adjusted to take his lengthening rod into her core and rocked her hips before he wrapped his muscular arm around her, easily rising from the chair. They landed on the bed, and it wasn't long before the same fierceness that drove their first lovemaking in that bed returned. Caitlyn peppered kisses over Alex's face before returning to his lips. When his tongue slid past her lips, she sucked. Alex's responding growl made her giggle, but it was only a moment later that she moaned her release. Alex followed as his body went taut.

"Mayhap you should grow the beard back," Caitlyn teased. "Neither of us shall get aught done now that all I can stare at is your handsome face."

"I'm glad someone thinks that." Alex made to roll to his side but froze as anger then hurt flashed across Caitlyn's face. "What is it?"

"Do you wish other women would flirt with you still? Do you want to flirt with them?"

"Caity." Alex shook his head, realizing how his flippant comment sounded. "I need no one's attention but yours. I only fear how people will react. Even with the beard hiding half, it disgusted people. I'd hate to frighten children or make some lady swoon."

"You already make me swoon." Caitlyn laid the back of her hand over her forehead and closed her eyes, sighing. Alex nuzzled her neck, tickling her in a place he'd discovered the night before.

"I was flirtatious with other women, and we both know I was no virgin, but that was because we had no agreement between us. But once I started courting you in earnest, that ended. I haven't been with anyone since well before my injuries. I confess I tried because I just wanted to find someone I didn't appall. More fool was I for keeping it a secret or for not coming to visit you sooner."

"Even when you began paying me court, we never acknowledged it, and we made no pledges. I assumed naught changed for you."

"Everything changed, Caity. Were there still others in the beginning? Yes. But as you said, we made no pledges. I wasn't sure if you would accept me, and I didn't ask if your father had other plans. What I feel for you has never wavered."

"You know no other mon has kissed me, and I was obviously a virgin, but I flirted and considered other men. I didn't know if we had a future either, even though I prayed fervently that we would."

"Even if I hadn't been injured, I could never stray from you, Caitlyn." Alex's steadfast expression matched the seriousness of his promise. Caitlyn had never feared he might be unfaithful should they ever marry, but she appreciated the reassurance. Alex shifted to lie next to Caitlyn, tucking her beneath his chin, but they couldn't linger as the first bells for Terce rang. They hurried back into their clothes and rushed to the chapel.

They arrived as the last people slid into pews. Caitlyn couldn't join the other ladies without drawing attention to their late arrival, so she sat beside Alex. They held hands throughout the service, their shoulders pressing together any time Caitlyn had to fold her hands in prayer. Rather than listen to the service, Caitlyn reflected on all they discussed that morning. At the time, each subject had seemed rather minor, but when she considered how much closer she felt to Alex, she realized they'd been necessary. Each day spent together, each conversation they had, bound them more as a married couple. They shared things with one another that they could never tell anyone else.

Alex and Caitlyn left the chapel before the congregation loitered in the narthex. With a brief kiss they parted ways, Caitlyn headed to the queen's solar, and Alex headed to the lists with their guards.

"They suit each other." Margaret Hay turned up her nose as Caitlyn and Alex walked past the ladies' tables on their way to their own. They'd arrived early to the evening meal, hoping to avoid undue notice, but the queen sent her entourage ahead of her. The Great Hall wasn't full, but Margaret's voice intentionally carried.

"They should hide themselves like lepers." Sarah Anne's lip curled in disgust. "Shame he couldn't do any better these days. He was once so handsome that I'd chosen him to marry. Now he's stuck with that brown-skinned foreigner."

Caitlyn wanted nothing more than to snatch Sarah Anne's hair and drive her face into the table. She cared not that Sarah Anne called her a foreigner since everyone was aware it was ridiculous. She'd traveled no farther from home than a visit to her sister's home in the Highlands. She'd been born and raised at Dunure along the western Lowlands' sea coast, and had never been to her mother's French homeland. But it was Sarah Anne's comments about Alex that riled her. Whether the other lady-in-waiting set her sights on Alex or not, she was confident he had no desire to marry her. It was the implications of her comments about Caitlyn that made her want to commit violence against her peer.

"Sarah Anne, how I'd hoped to wish you well upon your betrothal. But that won't be possible since

I will have already left with my husband. Hopefully, you won't have to wait that much longer." Caitlyn offered what she hoped appeared like a sincere smile, knowing it only added insult to injury. She squeezed Alex's arm, around which hers was curled, and they moved forward. She lowered her voice. "I know I shouldn't let her goad me."

"She's lucky she's a woman. She would be dead already if she weren't."

"Neither of us can go around killing anyone who speaks ill of us. That would leave very few people."

"Do you think he'll share her with his brother? I heard they trade those harem women back and forth. I suppose she won't care if he has a leman since she'll be busy elsewhere." A man's voice drifted to them. "Mayhap he'd share her before they leave."

Caitlyn swallowed her scream as a knife sailed through the air and landed in the table beside the man's hand after knocking his mug into his lap. She snapped her eyes to Alex and nearly took a step back.

"My ears still work, you bluidy bastard. Do not underestimate me. Others have, and they haven't lived. Speak aboot my wife so disrespectfully, and I will lay you in the ground." Alex's voice boomed over the crowd as everyone turned to gawk. "Kerr, you shall make a powerful enemy. The Armstrongs have left you and the Elliots to handle your own differences, but you'd do well to remember we are allies. We already know we fight well together. Would you like to see?"

"But she's just—" The Kerr delegate's mouth hung open as another blade landed embedded in the table, except this time it landed in the narrow space between his fingers.

"I have dirks you can't even spy." Alex left Caitlyn's side and retrieved his knives as the men sitting with the Kerrs watched in shock. He slid them back into their sheaths before leaning forward. "I do not share. Nor do I get along well with others."

Alex held out his hand to Caitlyn, who remained silent, but she didn't bother to hide the pride that shone from her eyes as she beamed at Alex. She glanced down at the frightened man and shrugged. They settled at a table with their guards, Alex ensuring neither he nor Caitlyn had their backs to any doors. After the blatant insults, he trusted few.

"Lady Caitlyn?" Devlin raised a brow as his gaze swept over the diners.

"All is well enough. No one said aught I haven't heard before. But I won't lie; it's nice having a husband to defend me. You, Duncan, and Grant have always served me well, and I've always felt safe with you when we leave the keep. But we all know it isn't the same."

"I'd say you made a fair impression." Stephen raised his mug. "Between the lists today and the dirks now, I don't think anyone will be so foolish as that eejit."

Caitlyn glanced at Alex before looking at the guards. She felt excluded, not knowing what happened in the lists. Alex kissed her temple before explaining. "Callum Sinclair is here on behalf of his father. He's apparently been in a foul mood since he arrived because his wife is expecting. However, she's not as far along as her three sisters-by-marriage, who are too close to their confinement for their husbands to travel."

"Oh." Caitlyn's eyes widened as she twisted to find the Sinclair delegation. It was no secret that the four Sinclair brothers were among the best warriors in the Highlands, if not the country. It was also well known that the husbands and wives were fiercely protective of one another. Ceit, the wife of Tavish, the third Sinclair brother, had once been a spy for the

Scottish crown. Caitlyn understood the reason for Callum's foul temper was being so many days' ride from home. She turned back to Alex.

"He and I have always gotten along well, so he welcomed me when I entered the lists. He didn't even look twice at my scar or my arm. He merely raised his sword in invitation. He didn't go easy on me, but when he realized that I'm not such a cripple, he unleashed his foul mood. I knocked him on his arse a few times, which didn't improve his temper." Alex shrugged his right shoulder. His left arm pained him from bashing Callum in the arm with his targe, but he felt better than he had in ages.

"He's lucky he came out in one piece. I don't think Callum expected anyone to be as strong as him." Stephen grinned. "We are several coin richer, so our thanks, Alex."

"You wagered on me?"

"And won a small fortune." Duncan chuckled. "We should take you on the tourney circuit."

"You will not." Caitlyn scowled. The men grew contrite, thinking she feared for Alex. "We are newly married, and I refuse to let him leave for that long. And I don't want our marriage bed to be on the ground."

Seven faces stared at Caitlyn as she playfully harrumphed. Alex was certain he was blushing. He hadn't expected Caitlyn ever to be so blunt about their coupling. It was clear the other men hadn't either.

"What? I'm married now. It's not like none of us here doesn't know what happens. You needn't protect my ears." Caitlyn grinned. "Eat up. We have a long day in the saddle tomorrow. I don't want to stop because your bellies are rumbling and spooking the horses."

As the group ate, Caitlyn and Alex kept up with

the lively conversation, but they both sensed the stares and heard the ongoing insults. They forewent the dancing and retired before either of them got into a fight, either with their fists or their words. Caitlyn tried to hide how much the degrading comments about her skin and heritage bothered her, but they were some of the worst she'd heard since arriving at court. She understood it upset Alex and made him anxious. They slipped into bed and held one another, neither wanting to discuss the meal, but both taking comfort from being together.

TWENTY

A lex stood beside Caitlyn as King Robert's royal guards turned back northeast, making their way to Stirling Castle. They'd spent two uneventful days in the saddle until they reached Glasgow, where the couple spent the night in an inn and the men bedded down in the tavern or stables. Once the entourage disappeared, Alex, Caitlyn, and their six guards set off, continuing their course to Dunure. They'd seen few people traveling, so Alex thought they might be fortunate. It was approaching late autumn, and while there had been no more severe storms, the weather threatened an early winter. If the weather deterred others but held for them, they would reach Dunure in two days.

The sun was barely over the horizon as the group chewed on dried beef and fresh oatcakes the tavern owner's wife gave them. Caitlyn wasn't eager for another night sleeping outdoors. While she remained warm with Alex curled around her, she was aware he barely slept, and he woke with a sore arm from the cold. She glanced at him as the men moved into formation with Alex at the lead and her in the middle. She recognized Alex's discomfort with the position, still thinking he wasn't adequate to defend her or lead the men. But none of the guards had moved to take the position, instead waiting for Alex. Caitlyn said nothing, but she observed Alex grew pensive and withdrawn the longer they traveled.

When they stopped at midday, Alex nodded toward David to accompany Caitlyn into the trees, so she could have a moment of privacy. She smiled but shook her head. She cocked an eyebrow and tilted her head when her eyes met Alex's. He scowled but followed her. She ducked around a bush but was soon shaking out her skirts as she peered past Alex. The men watered the horses and stood chatting. Certain they were close enough to call for help but far enough not to be overheard, Caitlyn backed Alex against a broad tree trunk and tugged at his doublet. He obliged without hesitation. They'd stolen a few quick kisses while the royal guards accompanied them, and they'd kissed beneath the blankets on their bedrolls, but none compared to the one they shared now.

Caitlyn was starved for Alex's touch, and she longed to run her hands over him. Alex's hand cradled her skull as she slid her arms around his neck. The kiss drew on, passion building to a near-roaring fire. With one hand tunneled in Alex's hair, Caitlyn's other hand skimmed down his back until she clutched his chiseled buttocks. She moaned as he shifted, and the muscles bunched.

"Caity," Alex breathed. "You're too much." His grin, when he pulled away, showed his comment wasn't a complaint. "How am I supposed to walk back to our men, and mount my horse, with this raging cockstand?"

"Mayhap I can ease that." Caitlyn's hand moved to his groin and stroked his rod. Alex caught her wrist in a light hold.

"Do that once or twice more, and I shall be just as embarrassed when I leave a stain."

Caitlyn pretended to pout. "We spent the night alone, and that should hold me over, but it only made me want you more." She stretched to kiss Alex's jaw where the scar ended at the bone. He'd flinched the first few times she'd done it, but he remembered kissing his jaw was something she'd once dreamed of as a wifely privilege. He sensed it contented her, and he enjoyed the affection. "If only we rode Pegasus, and our mounts could fly as the birds do. We would be home before this eve."

"Mon was meant to be on the ground and not soar so high. I would hate for the sun to scorch us like Icarus."

"I'd take my chances on Pegasus to be in bed with you tonight." Caitlyn gave Alex's backside an affectionate pat before they rejoined the men. As Alex mounted, he froze. Something made him uneasy. Swinging into the saddle, he used the height to improve his view. As he swept his gaze over the surrounding area, nothing appeared out of place. The animals were neither overly excited nor eerily quiet. He spotted no metal glinting in the sun between the leaves. The ground didn't vibrate with galloping hooves. Despite everything seeming normal, his senses warned something was amiss.

"Caity, no matter what, you remain in the center. There is nowhere near here that's safe for you to hide. Trust that we will keep you safe." Alex shifted in his saddle, turning toward Caitlyn, but his eyes continued to roam. Keeping his voice low, he spoke to the men. "Someone is there, but I can't find them."

"Aye." Grant nodded as he and Devlin moved their steeds closer to Caitlyn's. Goldie tolerated the Armstrongs' horses but was far better behaved around the horses with which she was acquainted. Alex wrapped his left fingers around the reins before drawing his sword and resting it across his lap. The other men followed suit before they spurred their mounts. Alex couldn't shake the trepidation, even as they put distance between them and the glen where they'd rested.

"Do you sense it too?" Caitlyn whispered to Devlin, who only nodded. He and the other men were on edge, making her wonder if they feared a warband rather than mere highwaymen. Even as an hour bled into two, then three, the men still hadn't relaxed.

Alex glanced back at Caitlyn. "Ride!" He spurred Strong, whipping his destrier around and leading them on a mad dash away from the hill they approached. He heard the thunder of mounted attackers streaming over the rise, but he didn't dare look back, worried about scaring Caitlyn more. They barreled down the road before veering sharply to the left and racing overland. Now the attackers were in Alex's peripheral vision, and he could tell their pursuers vastly outnumbered them. There was at least a score, and he was certain they were gallowglasses. "Keep Caity in the center."

As their foe teemed down the hillside, it was his nightmares come to life. It was reminiscent of his battle against the Scotts. But it was his nightmares he remembered as Caitlyn became caught in the middle. Try as they might, they couldn't outrun the larger force. Alex swung his sword, thrusting and hacking at anyone who came near. He heard cries of pain, but they were all masculine. He prayed none were from their men, for his friends' sake and for Caitlyn's safety.

"Armstrong, come with us without a fuss, and your lady lives." A booming voice sounded from behind Alex. He twisted to glance back, taking in the horrifying scene. Grant held his arm as blood poured between his fingers. Devlin's chest moved, but he lay unconscious on the ground. And a mercenary held his sword to Caitlyn's throat.

"How can I be sure you won't kill her anyway?"

"You don't. But they did not hire us to kill anyone but you. If your men suffer, so what?" The man shrugged. "They're meant to fight. But we aren't interested in involving the Kennedys. Our employers would prefer we didn't."

"The Scotts." Alex narrowed his eyes as he recognized the man who held Caitlyn hostage. He'd been part of the second wave in the meadow when they'd gone riding from Stirling.

"We're aware your wife's family hasn't learned of your marriage yet. She's free to go, but she will be a widow before she arrives home."

Alex shifted his attention to Caitlyn when he noticed her arm moved. Her hand slid toward her pocket where she kept her hidden knife. Their gazes locked, and Alex prayed she understood his silent warning not to draw a weapon on a battle-hardened man twice her size. Alex returned his focus to the gallowglass leader and nodded. Moving slowly, he dismounted from Strong and tossed his sword away from him. The moment he did, the mercenary released his hold on Caitlyn, who didn't wait to maneuver her horse away. Men rushed forward and grabbed Alex.

"His arm!" Caitlyn cried out in anguish as she watched their enemy manhandle Alex and how it tested his stoicism.

"Caity, go home. Now." Alex loathed each word that left his mouth, but he would do anything to get Caitlyn away from the mercenaries. He sensed it tempted her to argue, but she must have understood his meaning. They were closer to Dunure than Mangerton Tower. From where they were, she estimated it taking them six days to reach Mangerton, but about four days to reach the Scotts' keep at Buccleuch. It took the same time to reach Redheugh Tower and the Elliots.

Her mind racing, Caitlyn nodded to Alex and mouthed, "I love you." Alex returned the sentiment before turning his attention to the guards still tasked with protecting Caitlyn. Devlin was back on his feet, swaying as he reached for the reins. Grant continued to bleed, but it had slowed. He prayed the men were hale enough to protect Caitlyn the rest of the way. Once Devlin mounted, Caitlyn watched Alex as they left the clearing where mercenaries restrained her husband. She wanted desperately to believe in his survival, but her mind was already preparing her for the reality that there was little likelihood. As the tidal wave of grief threatened to pull her under, rage unlike any she'd imagined she could possess pushed back the pain.

"Stop."

"Lady Caitlyn—" Stephen began.

"I said 'stop.' You can, or you can carry on without me." Caitlyn looked back, but nothing remained visible from where the gallowglasses attacked them. The men continued to encircle her. "Grant, ride to Dunure. You need tending, and it's closer than Mangerton or the Hermitage. Which of you is the fastest?" Caitlyn stared at David, Mitcham, and Stephen.

"I am," Mitcham spoke up.

"Ride for Mangerton. Get Brice and the laird. The rest of us ride to Redheugh."

"Nay, my lady," came a rumble of deep voices.

"We go to Dunure," David decided.

"You may go where you wish then. But I am

239

going to Redheugh. I am not riding farther from my husband, and I don't trust that there aren't men along this route waiting for all of us. They are less likely to go after one mon, especially one who poses little threat. Grant can move off the road and hide easier than seven of us. I'm not so foolhardy as to think I can ride to Mangerton Tower or Buccleuch without facing more threats. If not Redheugh, then the Hermitage. Robert Bruce will allow us to rest, and he will send for Angus and his men. Robert will be livid that the Scotts disobeyed his father, and he won't be thrilled to have another battle so close to his home. He will side with us."

Caitlyn's certainty made the men pause. They each knew they could easily overpower her and force her to ride with one of them. They also knew someone needed to ride for Mangerton, and rallying the Elliots and Robert Bruce, the king's illegitimate son, was a wise plan.

"If you take me to Dunure, my father will make me stay. He'll do it to protect me, but I'm an Armstrong now. I need to get to Mangerton more than I do Dunure. And it they kill my husband, I—I—need to see him before they bury him. I—I—can't do that from Dunure. I—" Caitlyn choked as she struggled not to sob as she considered the next time she saw Alex might be when the Scotts dumped his dead body on Armstrong land.

"Two lairds and Alex are likely to kill us." David frowned as he exchanged glances with the other men. "Grant, can you make it?"

"Aye. It bled like a stuck pig, but it's not that deep. If I douse it with whisky and try to get it clean, I'll survive to Dunure." Grant twisted his arm and grimaced, but he inspected his wound again. Duncan reached over and ripped Grant's shredded sleeve from his arm and tied it as a tourniquet.

"Thank you," Caitlyn whispered, her voice rasping as she forced forth the words. She reached her hand to Grant, squeezing it before he backed his horse from the circle and set off toward Dunure.

"Lady Caitlyn?" David shifted uneasily in his saddle. He glanced at Mitcham and Stephen. "Do you think less… Do you believe we…"

"Do I believe you should have tried harder to defend Alex?" Caitlyn guessed the man's question. The three Armstrong guards nodded. "No. I don't. I wish you could have, but Alex wouldn't forgive you if you had. To fight for him meant leaving me unguarded. That's unacceptable to him. He was more likely to die in that field than to leave it alive even before we rode out."

"Lady Caitlyn," Devlin spoke up. "We did the best we—"

"I know. I trust all of you with my life and Alex's. There was a score to seven. They were going to overwhelm us with me there. If I hadn't been…" Caitlyn swallowed the lump in her throat. "It would have been different. You could have really fought. You did what Alex wanted and what you've been trained to do. For that, I am more grateful than I have the words to express."

"Mitcham, head home." David clamped his friend on the shoulder and squeezed. "Keep yourself alive, cousin."

It surprised Caitlyn to learn the men were family. She'd met all three of Alex's guards before, but she'd never known their connection.

"Do the same." Mitcham nodded before he left the group. He intended to travel overland rather than sticking to the roads.

"I don't know why the gallowglasses aren't interested in me, but we can't be sure the mon spoke the truth. None of them will expect me to ride to Redheugh. I won't believe Alex is dead until I see it for myself. The Elliots are our fastest chance for getting him back." Caitlyn remained in the center of the four remaining warriors as they continued south.

Alex feared his teeth cracking as he clenched them, pain blurring his vision with each of Strong's steps. The gallowglasses allowed him to ride his own horse. Realizing that his left arm posed no threat, they only tied the right to his saddle. He recognized it as silent mockery, not ambivalence. Unable to move it to rest in his lap, it swung lifeless at his side. Each motion tugged at the damaged sinews that barely connected his shoulder and arm.

The battle ended before it began, leaving Alex to listen to his opponents' goading and gloating. They taunted him for surrendering, but he would have stripped naked and jumped into a pit of asps if it meant Caitlyn got away unharmed. Only the leader of the group seemed to recognize Alex's reasons. A silent respect passed between them, and Alex wondered if the man had a family at some point. Comments about being a cripple buzzed around him, coupled with insults about his cowardice. He swallowed his tongue and forced his temper to remain in check.

Until Alex learned where they were taking him, and for what purpose, he planned to remain silent. He wondered if they headed to the Scotts' keep or somewhere else. If they tasked the gallowglasses to murder him, he would already be dead. It meant the Scotts wanted him alive, either to torture or to kill. He'd endured more pain over the past half-year than any man should, so he doubted the Scotts would reap the entertainment they intended by torturing him.

"Armstrong." The mercenary leader approached Alex as they pulled their horses to a halt near a stream. The man untied Alex's hand before drawing a dirk and watching Alex climb down. "You fight like a caged animal, even with a wounded arm. If you weren't an heir, I would hire you."

Alex swept his gaze over the man, uncertain what to make of the compliment. "What're you called?"

"Henry." Both men knew he would give no clan name, so Alex accepted what the man shared.

"I'm curious aboot how much the Scotts spent to have more than a score of warriors chase after one mon."

"We always travel in packs." Henry shrugged as he glanced around at his men. "You're worth a hundred pieces of silver. Five apiece." Henry jerked his chin toward the men standing close enough.

"Why hire you? The Scotts had men at Stirling while I was there. They attacked me in the keep."

"And didn't kill you." Henry grinned. "One bled to death, apparently. And the other can't move his arm. Fitting, I would say."

"From what I learned, they already intended to hire you, even before I had to defend myself."

"The Scott had no faith in them. He was right not to."

"Yet you keep me alive when they tried to kill me."

"He doesn't trust us." Henry shrugged. "He wants to enjoy you dying at their hands."

"Wonderful." Alex scowled as he led his horse to the stream for his turn to drink. Henry followed him, someone else tending to his horse. Alex cupped water in his hand and drank from it before rinsing his face.

"You threw down your sword, and we've stripped you of your knives. I will not tie your hand."

Alex regarded Henry in confusion. The mercenary fought and killed as an occupation. The man had to realize Alex had other knives hidden that they hadn't found in his boot and at his waist. Henry stared pointedly at Alex's arm.

"Even if you killed one, maybe two, of my men, we would easily overpower you before you could get away. You don't strike me as the type ready to die now that I no longer have hold of your wife." Henry leaned back as Alex bared his teeth like a rabid dog at the reminder that Henry held a sword to Caitlyn's throat. "I also don't need you to pass out and your horse drag you. Do what you must with your arm to make it bearable."

"Why the mercy?"

"Like I said, the Scotts want you alive, and I don't need your arse dragged behind your mount."

Alex doubted the explanation's simplicity. He had nearly a sennight's ride ahead of him, so he held little confidence about remaining unscathed until he reached the Scotts. While Henry might afford him some decency, he held little hope for the other men. Henry wouldn't be his nursemaid. If the men beat and battered him a bit, Alex didn't expect Henry to speak up. The mercenary leader would only speak up if the damage done threatened their payment. But Alex wouldn't turn down the reprieve offered. When he mounted Strong again, he wrapped his left hand around the reins and wrapped his right hand over that. It kept his lame arm from jostling with each step. Night couldn't come soon enough as they trudged along.

"Lady Caitlyn, we cannot keep pushing the horses as we are. We will run them into the ground." Devlin stood beside Caitlyn as their horses drank from a loch. They faced south, and Caitlyn wished she could see all the way to the Hermitage. She wished once more that there was a way to soar through the air and travel faster than their mounts could carry them. They'd traveled past sunset for three days, and Caitlyn wanted to insist they ride through the night, but her common sense told her she would only endanger man and beast.

"I know, Devlin. But what would you have me do? Take a leisurely ride? They have my husband, Clan Armstrong's heir. This is no minor event. God willing, and not soon, I will one day be Lady Armstrong. My duty is to my husband and my new clan. We shall ease the pace for the horses' sake, but not by much."

"Thank you, my lady. If they can have another quarter hour, we can safely be off."

Caitlyn nodded, but her focus remained looking toward their southern route. She had slept only when her body could no longer fight its need for rest. She woke before everyone else, nightmares filling the few

245

hours of rest she found. She wondered if she would experience an overwhelming sense of grief if the gallowglasses killed Alex. As the thought tried to take root, she threw it aside, adopting an abiding optimism that he would survive.

Mounted once more, Caitlyn and the four guards carried on. The day felt much like the last ones: interminable. Caitlyn was sore and weary, unused to riding so hard and for so long. But she reminded herself that her discomfort could only be a small measure compared to Alex's. His stoicism fortified her, doing what she could to make him proud. The long hours gave her time to ruminate about their life once reunited. Tavin and Coira were still in fine health, so Caitlyn doubted she would be inheriting the title of lady of the keep soon. Nor did she put much store in Alex becoming laird within the next few years. She prayed Alex's parents, and hers, lived long enough to enjoy grandchildren. That thought made her wonder if that time might be approaching.

Caitlyn had wondered over the years if wishing to marry and have children was selfish of her. No one could anticipate whether they might take after their father, or if they might have darker skin like Caitlyn's. She feared the ostracism they might face. When she imagined marrying Alex, she hadn't feared for her children among the Armstrongs. It was when they inevitably faced the rest of the world, when a son one day became laird, that she feared her heritage sentencing them to emotional and physical hardship.

Caitlyn's clan had been hesitant to welcome Collette when Innes returned from being a hired sword in France and had a foreign wife on his arm. He wasn't high in line to inherit the lairdship and had planned to make his life in the south of France. But when his father and brothers died, it forced him to return to Scotland. While Collette never faced the extreme bigotry Cairren had, mostly because Innes had been supportive and protective from the start, it hadn't been easy.

However, by the time Collette gave birth to both daughters, Clan Kennedy thought of her as much a part of the kinship as they would have had she been born there. Few took interest in Caitlyn and Cairren appearing different from the other children and young adults. There were other children close in age to the laird's daughters. But none were nobility, none were being trained for a life of leadership and service. Except for Alex. From the moment he arrived at Dunure to foster, Alex gravitated toward the Kennedy sisters. Never once had Alex a cruel word to say about the girls looking different. Caitlyn understood, even before Cairren went to court, that others didn't share the sentiments the Kennedys felt toward the laird's family.

As she and her guards charged toward the Hermitage, she once more wondered if she would cause Alex and their unborn children undue hardship by wanting a family of her own. She didn't regret marrying Alex for her own sake of happiness, but she had pangs of regret for marrying at all when she couldn't ensure a safe and welcoming world for her future children. As deep despondency threatened to take hold, Alex's voice rang in her mind.

Caity, you think such nonsense. Should I not have children because I have a lame arm? I thought I shouldn't, but you would never agree. Why should I agree that we shouldn't have children because they might resemble you? Can't you imagine how handsome our sons will be, and how beautiful our daughters will be? I pray our children resemble their mama exactly.

Alex and Caitlyn discussed their future family while they'd been tucked away in their chambers. They'd shared their fears for the future as well as their hopes. Alex had been adamant that their future held children and happiness. After he'd nearly denied them both that opportunity, he welcomed the thought of creating life with Caitlyn. He swore to arrange no marriages for their daughters, promising the freedom for them to choose their mates to ensure their safety and happiness. He was certain their sons would be braw warriors who men would fear for their sword wielding prowess not any difference in skin. Caitlyn hadn't been so certain, but Alex's conviction eased her fears.

As a fourth and fifth day passed in the saddle, at a pace much slower than she wanted, Caitlyn resolved to face whatever the future held, be it children who resembled her, neighbors who underestimated Alex, or widowhood. She didn't wish for any of those, but she steeled herself for them. When the Hermitage finally came into view, and they decided to stop there rather than push on to Redheugh Tower, her fears and anger had settled into a low simmer. She felt composed now when she'd come close to falling apart several times during the journey. David called out their arrival to the castle's guards, and they clattered into the bailey. She dismounted before the others drew to a stop.

"Where's Laird Bruce?" Caitlyn demanded of the first person she encountered. "It's urgent."

"Who rides into my home and demands to see me?" Robert Bruce, illegitimate son to the king, appearing remarkably like his father, tall and ruddy with russet hair. There was no denying his paternity.

"Laird Bruce, I'm Lady Caitlyn Armstrong. I've come seeking shelter and help." Caitlyn dipped into a curtsy as Robert bent over her hand.

"What help do you request?" Robert's wariness rang in the quiet bailey, nearly everyone staring at the newcomers.

"The Scotts have Alex." Caitlyn kept her voice for Robert's ears only. "They hired gallowglasses, who took him while we rode to Dunure. They injured one of my guards only a day from my parents' home. He rode on to summon my father and my clan of birth. One of Alex's guards rides for Mangerton. I didn't trust the road was safe for all of us to travel to Dunure, and I came to seek your and the Elliots' support."

"You want four clans to ride on the Scotts?"

"I want holy fire and brimstone to rain down on every Scott's head and scorch the land upon which they stand." Caitlyn snapped before catching herself. She supposed she wasn't as composed as she'd believed. "But what I ask for is help to free my husband. He is with them because he saved my life over his. Now it is my turn to save him. I may not swing a sword, but I can ask those who do to help."

"You intend to have the king's son take sides in a tiff between neighbors." Robert's statement rang in the air, a warning edge to it.

"The king already took sides when he ordered the Scotts to cease their incursion. You merely carry out your father's orders. He is your liege."

"You are quite outspoken, Lady Caitlyn." Robert studied the guards who stood at a discreet distance but were clearly loyal to Caitlyn. "I suspect you get that from your father. Though the temper surely comes from your mother."

"Imagine what that combination bodes." Caitlyn raised her chin mulishly, daring Robert to deny her request after pointing out the Scotts ignored his father's orders. "If you cannot lend your arm, then I ask that you send a rider to Redheugh. My men deserve a night's rest, not another day on the road. But I will send one if I must."

"And you think to have everyone rally at my keep." Robert scowled and crossed his arms.

"They need not step foot in your bailey. They can meet at the battlefield you watched as the Scotts attacked the Armstrongs and the Elliots."

"You must think me able to see for miles."

"From that battlement, I'm certain you can." Caitlyn shifted her gaze to the highest point on the keep's northeastern wall.

"Be that as it may, I want you to understand I didn't simply stand by as the Scotts tried to slaughter your new clan and its allies." Robert released his arms, and his voice softened. "You can imagine the position I'm in among my neighbors and with my father."

"I can, and I sympathize. But you have the power to help end this."

"More so than you realize. Come inside, Lady Caitlyn. You are not my only guest."

Caitlyn's brow furrowed as she shot a glance at her guards. They'd relinquished their swords while Caitlyn and Robert spoke, but she was certain they still carried knives. They followed her into the Great Hall and nearly tripped over her when she halted.

"You bluidy bastard." Caitlyn's expression could only be described as menacing as Robert stepped onto the dais beside Laird Abraham Scott. Neither man was sure who she addressed. She knew she spoke to them both. "You play me for a fool while you sup with my enemy. My enemy sits, gorging his face while his men take my husband to his death."

"Who are you?" Laird Scott asked around a mouthful of food.

"Lady Caitlyn Armstrong." Caitlyn watched as Abraham dropped the lamb chop he'd been about to gnaw on, and his face took on a pasty shade. "Until a few days ago, I was Lady Caitlyn Kennedy. Imagine our surprise when your gallowglasses attacked us only a day from Dunure. Imagine how easily one of my guards rode to tell my father that you delayed our surprise arrival. Imagine in two days' time when Laird Armstrong realizes his heir has been kidnapped and his only daughter-by-marriage was held with a sword to her throat. I imagine you're not long for this life because if I don't kill you, at least three lairds will line up to take their turn turning your arse over a spit."

"You screech like a harpy over something I know naught aboot." Abraham licked his fingers and rose. Caitlyn sensed Robert's unease as the towering man leaned toward where Caitlyn now stood before the dais. "Your husband had best not be on my land, or I will have him killed."

"And that is how you shall justify it. You have men drag him there and keep him alive long enough to have the satisfaction of being a murderer. You sweat now because your soul is already touching the fires of hell."

"I may be a warrior and more mon than your bonnie little head could imagine, but I am no murderer."

"No. You hire others to do so, so only the grease you lick from your fingers soils them."

"You mother failed to teach you manners, lass," Laird Scott spat.

"My mother taught me to accept no address but Lady Caitlyn or my lady. You may mock me, and I may insult you, but your clan will perish once the Kennedys, Armstrongs, and Elliots rain down on them. Your gallowglasses cannot defeat them all. And I shall pish on your grave myself." Caitlyn would not back down.

"Vulgar bitch." Abraham grunted as he sneered.

"Give me back my husband, and you might find me more reasonable."

"I do not have your husband."

"Your gallowglasses do. But he will be at Buccleuch within the next two days."

"I don't believe you."

"Then ride home and find out. You'd do well to prepare your women and children to be widows and orphans."

"Laird Scott has been my guest for the past sennight. He arrived before this alleged attack by gallowglasses."

"There is naught alleged. The king knows since *his*," Caitlyn hissed at Abraham, "mercenaries chased us while we were on a morning ride a fortnight ago. The king knows these men chased me through Stirling Castle."

Abraham sat down abruptly and squeezed his brow. "I shall kill my son." The beleaguered laird scowled but nodded his head as he looked at Caitlyn. "I did not hire or fund anyone to attack any Armstrong, certainly not the clan's heir. I cannot say Sully is that judicious, especially as my tánaiste who leads in my absence."

"Your absence? I told you this began well before we left Stirling. Guards overheard your delegates discussing needing more coin to pay these men."

"Christopher, Collin." Abraham's booming voice rang through the Great Hall. "Now."

Two men Caitlyn recognized from court approached. Neither appeared fearful or repentant. Caitlyn saw red as they came to stand next to her. Shifting to put a wall at her back, she stood so she could watch either man's face while not losing sight of Robert or Abraham.

"Which of you started the fight?" Caitlyn's voice hissed as she demanded an answer.

"There was no fight." Christopher smirked.

"Are you the one who can't move his arm after my husband's blade landed in your shoulder?" Caitlyn studied the two men before pointing to the one on the left. "You. I can see it. You will live now like my husband does. Mayhap you regret your choice to attack a mon you consider useless. Where is the third mon? Did he really bleed to death from my husband's blade?"

"Attack?" Abraham demanded. He glowered at his men. "You said highwaymen set upon you."

Caitlyn snorted with mockery. "My husband has no need to turn highwayman. But he needed to defend himself when they cornered him in a passageway and beat him. They underestimated Alex's will and his strength. He maimed one and sliced through another. It shocks me to find even two alive."

"It surprised us that your husband survived. Though back then he was only your lover."

"You think to insult me. You think to outwit my husband. You think to defeat us. All you have done is cause a feud that will probably last generations. You will find your land surrounded by our allies who will eagerly chop up your territory. Is that what your laird sent you to do?"

"I sent them to make peace and pay recompense to the crown, the Armstrongs, and the Elliots. I did not sanction an attack in the keep or hiring mercenaries." Abraham continued to glare at his men, who finally appeared ill at ease. "Lady Caitlyn speaks the truth. You and my son have likely created a feud that will last generations. What had been a gory squabble shall likely end up costing us our land and our lives. I hereby banish you. Ride out and never return to Scott territory. You have one hour before I send men after you. You'd best get lost among the hills and the trees if you wish to live."

The deadly calm in Abraham's voice contrasted with the loud bluster Caitlyn had heard since she arrived. She was confident the laird finally took seriously the imminent threat to his clan's existence. She watched as the two disgraced and disowned Scotts practically ran from the Great Hall. She shifted her eyes to David and Stephen before nodding and darting her gaze to the doors. If Robert refused to send men to rally the Elliots, she would. She trusted not that Laird Scott intended to hurry to protect Alex. She pointed out as much.

"You send your men away, but you send no men to stop your son."

"He is a fool, but he is not so stupid as to kill Alex while I am away. Ambitious eejit will wait until I am home but will not tell me he has Alex. He will spin a tale to blame Alex and claim he killed your husband to protect his laird."

"How do you know? It sounds like you've discussed this before."

"We have, and I refused. After the losses we suffered the last time we faced the Armstrongs and Elliots, we are not in a position to have half the Lowlands ride on us."

"And yet, that is what shall happen." Caitlyn considered whether she should press the threat that the Moffats and Croziers were likely to join as allies to the Armstrongs. Instead, she stared at Robert. The Bruces were one of the Kennedys' closest allies. Between their alliance with the clan at large and Robert's relationship to the king who'd already told the Scotts to desist, there was little chance Robert could abstain from the fight. Her eyes bored into Robert.

"Laird Scott, you are being called home, I see. I wish you safe travels." Robert kept his eyes locked with Caitlyn as he bid his guest leave with haste.

Caitlyn dipped her chin an inch. Abraham frowned, but nodded.

"It is only midday. My men and I can put several hours' distance from here." Abraham lumbered to his feet, seeming to have aged since Caitlyn arrived. She didn't envy the man his position, but neither did she feel sympathy for him being unable to keep a tighter rein on his son. When she glanced back at her guards, she noticed Stephen had slipped away. She prayed he'd already retrieved his horse and could ride the couple hours to Redheugh. If Angus's father accepted the call, the Elliots could arrive by nightfall, and her father could arrive as soon as the next day. Once Abraham left the dais, Caitlyn accepted Robert's invitation to join him.

"It is only because I'm certain you fear my father that I trust aught you put before me. I'm aware you resent my arrival, and you disapprove of me antagonizing the Scott."

"It wasn't wise. I will say that." Robert poured wine into his own chalice and drank from it before filling Caitlyn's. She nodded her thanks for the beverage and his reassurance that no one poisoned it. "You've surely got a pair of ox's bollocks beneath those skirts."

Caitlyn remained quiet. Robert released an aggrieved sigh before once more serving himself first, then placing food on a trencher before Caitlyn, proving the food was untampered. She accepted the offering graciously and ate, famished from her journey. Her guards found places at the table below the dais.

"I notice you've lost one of your men," Robert mused.

"I doubt he's lost."

"Already on the way to Redheugh?"

"I didn't see you send anyone."

"I don't know who I'd rather not see: Angus or Graeme. They can be as foul-tempered as one another."

"I can think of a mon who will be in a fouler temper than even Tavin."

"Aye. My father will have an apoplexy. I will dispatch a mon to court in the morning."

"Thank you." Caitlyn relaxed at the sincerity in Robert's voice.

"I would not have hosted Laird Scott had I known you and Alex married, or that his son was wreaking havoc."

"I believe you. Though I think you could have extended the courtesy of warning me rather amusing yourself with my shock and anger." Caitlyn looked pointedly at Robert, who regretted meeting her gaze.

"I suppose that didn't set a very conciliatory tone."

"It did not." Caitlyn swallowed her wine. "Robert, I'm aware you hold the Hermitage in trust for the king, but it is still on Elliot land. They will come."

"As they should. And I sent someone, my lady. Before we entered the Great Hall. You may not have seen it, but my second-in-command understood my silent order."

Caitlyn opened her mouth to thank Robert again when a commotion stole her attention. The doors to the Great Hall swung open and Innes Kennedy stormed in. "Papa!"

Caitlyn dashed from the dais and flew into her father's arms, finally feeling safe after days of terror. Innes clung to his daughter, relieved to watch her running and knowing she was unharmed. It had shocked everyone to find a wounded Grant charging into the bailey and calling out that Innes raise their standard. He'd tumbled from his horse and explained everything with halting words before passing out. Innes and his men set off that night. He would have set off that moment if it hadn't taken nearly an hour to convince Collette that she couldn't ride out with him. He'd never met a woman more fiercely protective of her children, though he assumed others existed.

"Caity." Innes breathed a sigh of relief as the familiar scent of myrrh wafted to him, reminding him of when three women once filled his keep with the woodsy scent. With only Collette there to wear the perfume, it only permeated their chamber. "Caity, what happened? Grant said gallowglasses attacked you and Alex while you rode to Dunure. He said the men took Alex but left you."

"Papa," Caitlyn pulled back, "did Grant tell you Alex and I married? We were riding home to tell you and *Maman*. I'm sorry you found out that way."

"He did. You know your mama and I would have liked to be at your wedding, but it relieved us you and Alex finally married. Tavin sent a missive aboot a moon ago, right after Alex left for court, explaining everything that happened. He warned Alex might never ask for your hand, but that it was Coira's and his fervent prayer that Alex would. It became your mama's and mine too. It would have shocked and pained us more if you hadn't married."

"When this is over, mayhap Alex and I can still come to Dunure. Or mayhap you and *Maman* can feast with us at Mangerton Tower."

"There is naught we could want more."

"There is one more thing. Do you think Cairren could come?"

"If Padraig can keep her from getting with child long enough to agree it's safe for her and the weans to travel, then, aye. She will come."

"Laird Kennedy, please join us for the rest of the

midday meal. You must be famished." Robert offered the pair seats and ordered more food served. Innes sat with his arm around his daughter's shoulder, both as a comfort and as a warning to anyone who thought to endanger her. He trusted Robert Bruce and his clan, but he trusted few connected to the royal clan if they weren't already acquainted. A threat to Robert could lurk within the walls, and that put Caitlyn at risk as well. It relieved him to discover Caitlyn was no longer on the road, but it made him uneasy that this was the keep where she found shelter.

"Caity, I sleep inside your door." Innes whispered as he reached for a heel of bread.

"I understand, Papa," Caitlyn murmured from behind her chalice. Collette, Cairren, and Caitlyn had always shared a chamber when they stayed at inns or with clans Innes didn't entirely trust. He'd slept with his sword in his lap inside their chamber. Hosts always offered rooms to Collette and him, to which they retired and appeared to rise, but the family slept together. It was a silent admission that the ladies were different, and that posed an inherent danger.

Caitlyn looked up as the Great Hall's doors opened once more and her father's cousin, Daniel, and his son, Jamie, entered. Caitlyn beamed as she offered a small wave to her other family members. The men joined them on the dais since Daniel was Innes's head of the guard, and Jamie—as the closest male relative of an ideal age to be an heir—was Innes's tánaiste.

"Caity, are you well?" Jamie scanned the crowd as he kissed his cousin's cheek. He and his father were among the men who traveled to Foulis after Cairren married. They'd delivered Cairren's dowry and stayed on to visit. Alex had accompanied them, and it infuriated the men to discover how the Munros treated Cairren. Daniel and Jamie had always been protective of Caitlyn as family and as their duty, but they'd become more so after their visit to Foulis. They accepted the years had improved Cairren's situation, and they accepted she was happy with her husband and clan. But the two men were still wary for Caitlyn.

"I will be better when it's my husband kissing my cheek and not your prickly whiskers." Caitlyn half-jested.

Jamie ran his hand over his beard. "My Kayla likes my whiskers. She says they tickle."

Daniel clapped his hand on his son's shoulder and squeezed until the younger man nearly folded. Caitlyn giggled, surprised to hear the sound when the situation remained so grave. She winked at Jamie, understanding what she was certain Innes and Daniel hoped she didn't. With another clap on the back that rattled his heart, Jamie sat beside his father.

The meal progressed with little more jocularity as the men planned with Robert. By morning, the only thing left was to wait for the Elliots to arrive. Caitlyn argued that she should not remain at the Hermitage. Either she rode with the men, or someone took her to Mangerton. She argued once the fight was through, they would take Alex home, in whatever state they found him. She would either ride back with him or be waiting at their home, not waiting for someone to retrieve her. The men relented and agreed she could ride with them, but they intended to keep her far from any battlefield. Caitlyn wished for them to ride up to Buccleuch, run Sully through, then ride out with no battle fought. She was aware there was little chance for it to be so simple. She prepared herself to witness her first battle.

TWENTY-TWO

A lex grunted once more as jarring pain shot through his arm into his shoulder, causing the knot in his belly to clench. He sat atop Strong as the horse trudged through the mud. It had rained incessantly for two days; fortunately, it hadn't been a thunderstorm. Alex pushed his sopping hair from his eyes as he watched the road ahead, trying to steer Strong from any divots that might cause the horse to go lame. The inclement weather slowed their progress, which was the only blessing in Alex's misery. He knew not if the rain spread as far southwest as Dunure or southeast to Mangerton. He was certain one of his men left Caitlyn's side and rode for home. He loathed that Caitlyn was down two guards, since Grant couldn't lend much help to another attack, but he knew his father and Brice needed informing.

"You seem to have God on your side." Henry held back and allowed the other men to ride past as he moved beside Alex. "This weather will slow us long enough for your family to learn of your abduction. Mayhap they will arrive at Buccleuch in time to claim your body before the Scott puts your head on a pike."

"He is an eejit, but not so foolish as to boast

when he murders me. He may kill me, but he will claim I crossed onto his land and met with an accident. Aught else will bring the Kennedys, the Moffats, the Elliots, and the Croziers to his door. With the Kennedys will come the Bruces, especially once both Roberts learn of the Scotts' further perfidy."

"You are an arrogant mon for one who rides to his death."

"Though you explained it already, I still say, if the Scotts wanted me dead, you would have killed me. Sully may be a sick bastard and may want me to die by his hand, but he knows he risks much by doing so. It benefits him if hired men killed me and then disappeared. There is something else he wants."

Henry glanced around before leaning close to Alex. "He wishes to defend his father from your nefarious attack."

"Nefarious attack?" Alex's brow furrowed, but then understanding dawned. "He will claim I came to murder Laird Scott, and he had to kill me to stop me. He will seem like a hero. It will endear him even more to his people, but it will silently say Laird Scott cannot defend himself. Sully wants the lairdship without further wait, but he knows he can't commit patricide."

"I said no such thing." But Henry's astute gaze told Alex he'd guessed Sully's plot. He still didn't understand why Henry showed him any mercy or offered him any insights. "I confuse you, and rightly so. Before I became a mercenary, I had a family. I was a second son and newly married when a rival clan attacked while my wife and I returned from visiting her family. They slew her before my eyes. I was wounded and unable to ride. I wouldn't leave her side, anyway. That clan arrived at my home and killed my mother and sister before my father and brother's eyes. The destruction nearly impoverished us. With no wife to

261

keep me home, I hired out my sword arm. My earnings go back to my clan. But I will never make war on women. I will never force a mon to watch his wife die. Even mercenaries have limits."

Henry's humanity and truthfulness left Alex speechless. As he thought about Henry's tale, even more shock ran through his mind. "You're Henry MacSween. Everyone swears you're dead. No wonder you sound like a diluted Highlander."

Henry's eyes narrowed as he gave a jerky nod. "No one has called me that in nearly a score of years. But, aye, that's who I once was. I left Argyll in mourning, and I only look back when I have an assignment there. The rest of the time I live in Ireland or travel."

"I remember hearing the tale when I was a child. I—" Alex paused, unsure what he intended to say. He settled for, "thank you for sparing Caitlyn. But you attacked us once before when she was with us, and you chased her in the keep."

"You killed the mon who originally led this mission. I did not assume the leader's position until *after* some of these men foolishly chased Lady Caitlyn. I took control when I learned of it. They could have had us all swinging from the gallows. I haven't survived this long to die from a botched game of hide-and-seek. We have been together," Henry nudged his chin toward the men ahead of them, "long enough that they accept I won't kill a woman. Now that I lead, they understand that isn't an option. There isn't much else I won't do, but I forbid women and children to me and to them."

"That explains not harming my wife, but why not roughen me up more than the men have?" Alex sported a blackened eye and sore ribs, but they hadn't beaten him as he expected. "If I am the only target, then why such a large force for one mon?"

"We rarely travel in small groups. We are more of a trained army than we are a loose band of cutthroats."

"All the more reason to ask why?"

Henry gritted his teeth and shook his head. "The former leader was a MacCabe."

"Bluidy hell. Sully's wife is a Hebridean. Was she a MacCabe? Did he hire his wife's cousin or some such?"

"His brother-by-marriage. Slaying him will not do you any favors."

"Apparently, breathing doesn't either. Surely your family no longer needs the coin after so many years of being a hired sword."

"Had your father-by-marriage not been called back to be laird, there's a fair chance he'd still be a mercenary in France."

"Hardly," Alex snorted. "He loves his wife too much to make her endure that way of life. He leaves her side when he must, and he's as fierce as I'm sure he was then. But he has no wish to leave her for months on end."

"Fair. But what life do I have to go back to after six-and-ten years as a mercenary? Only shame awaits my clan if I make a home among them. It's one thing to send them coin with only my brother knowing. It's entirely another for them to welcome a murderer under their roof. I chose this life when I thought I didn't have one to look forward to. I keep this life because it's what I know, and it's the only way I can continue to serve my clan. I have no need for the wealth I own, but my people need roofs over their heads and food in their bellies."

The two men fell quiet, and Alex felt a peculiar sense of respect for the man who spent his days roaming the British Isles to kill one target after another. Alex was grateful for the warped sense of honor that protected Caitlyn, so he didn't question it. He appreciated still being alive. Each day he drew another breath gave him hope to return to Caitlyn. He pressed his lips together to hide his smile. As much as he didn't want to accept it, he suspected Caitlyn hadn't ridden to Dunure. He didn't think the guards would agree to Mangerton, since it posed too great a threat to travel that close to Scott territory. He deduced she likely went to the Hermitage. He expected the Kennedys, Elliots, Bruces, and his own clan to rally there. He only prayed the weather allowed them to make more progress than he and his captors were.

"This blummin' rain is slowing us to a near halt." Angus Elliot griped. He'd ordered his men to gather their supplies and mount as soon as the Bruce messenger arrived. He'd hurried the men when Stephen arrived. His younger brother Graeme remained behind as tánaiste and clan leader in Angus's absence. He'd rallied three score men to ride for the Hermitage, arriving in the dark. It surprised him to find Innes there, but it gladdened him to find another ally. He, Innes, and Robert discussed their plan in Robert's solar while Caitlyn sat silently listening. He'd expected her to chime in, but she'd remained quiet and solemn. Now he respected her even more as her horse trod not far behind his. She hadn't complained once and had kept up while the weather remained fair.

"It will slow them too. And we ride into rain they've likely suffered for a couple days. We may be slow, but I suspect we're catching up." Caitlyn spoke for the first time that day. She was bundled beneath her own plaid and her father's, leaving him trying not to shiver in just his doublet. He'd adopted a fatherly tone that warned Caitlyn to cease arguing when she tried to turn down his offer. She adjusted the layers to speak, but soon covered most of her face to shield her from the wind and icy raindrops.

"Caitlyn is right." Innes spoke from beside Caitlyn. He pointed to shapes in the distance. "That must be them."

"They're still far enough ahead of us to make it to Buccleuch in another hour or two. We won't catch them before they're within the gates." Robert shook his head, water flicking from his russet locks. "At least we aren't far behind." He glanced at Abraham, who they'd caught up to the day they set off. The laird hadn't hurried home as he should. He'd ridden out but made camp only a few hours away from the Hermitage. The combined Kennedy, Bruce, and Elliot forces caught up to them the next afternoon. The Armstrongs met them the following day.

"If their scouts haven't spied us yet, they will soon," Tavin noted. He and Brice rode side-by-side at the front. The father and son spoke little after greeting Caitlyn with embraces that nearly swallowed her whole. They'd shaken hands and clapped backs with Innes to celebrate their clans finally being allied by marriage. However, they sobered once they were in the saddle again. Caitlyn knew the men well, but she had never seen them prepared to ride into battle. The fury that simmered within her father-by-marriage and brother-by-marriage was like a poker heating over a flame. Anyone who came too near was likely to be singed. She suspected they shared her desire to burn Buccleuch to the ground and crush the Scotts beneath their heels. The difference was the Armstrong men had the might to do just that.

"Lady Caitlyn, there is a copse of trees about

three miles from Buccleuch," Brice interjected. "You will wait there with a dozen Armstrongs."

Caitlyn glanced at her father, unprepared to receive orders from someone other than Innes. She supposed that was her welcome to Clan Armstrong. She nodded, knowing she belonged nowhere near the ensuing battle. Either Alex would ride out of the battle and find her there, or someone would come to guide her to the keep.

The massive warband made slow progress until it was nearly too dark to see. The cloud cover blocked the sun, and Caitlyn wondered if this portended a repeat of the last battle the Armstrongs and Elliots fought against the Scotts. She strained to catch any movement in front of them. She supposed if they spotted the mercenaries holding Alex captive, they must have seen the veritable army of men riding after them.

"Will they stop if it grows darker?" Caitlyn asked anyone who might answer.

"If the rain worsens, and it remains this dark, then it's likely," Tavin called back over his shoulder. "But we will have to stop, too."

Caitlyn held her tongue against demanding they continue and use the weather to catch the gallowglasses and free Alex. She had faith Tavin wouldn't relent in his pursuit to free his son. If they stopped, it was because Tavin believed it was better for their mission. She trusted him to only do what was best for Alex in the long run.

Another hour's ride across a boggy meadow forced the army to stop for the night. The horses could barely continue, having strained against the mud trying to suck their hooves deeper with each step.

Wrapped in three plaids, two Kennedys and a spare Armstrong, Caitlyn huddled beside her father, who wrapped his brawny arm around her shoulders and drew her closer. She rested her head on his shoulder as she had countless times since childhood. His warmth seeped into her, giving her a sense of calm and reassurance. If she couldn't sit beside Alex, her father was the next best thing.

"Caity, we'll get to him. We've already joined Laird Scott." Innes's description was an understatement. While they'd caught up to the Scotts and supposedly joined them for the ride to their home, everyone understood they'd captured the laird. The leaders of the veritable army already decided to send a scout ahead if they couldn't overtake the gallowglasses and warn Sully that his father didn't ride alone. They planned to trade Alex for Abraham. "Sully may be impatient to become laird, but pride dictates he try to rescue his father. He won't appear weak before his clan and merely accept us getting the better of him and his people."

"What if we can't get a mon there soon enough?"

"We will, Caity. Have faith."

Caitlyn was desperate to believe her father, and she'd held onto her hope with a death grip. But the weather and the days on the road made her question whether God heard her prayers. Perhaps he did but wasn't listening. Caitlyn wasn't sure what to think. She closed her eyes and drifted to sleep, but as with the previous nights, nightmares filled her slumber. She woke feeling emotionally drained and physically exhausted. She hauled herself into the saddle once again. The rain cleared overnight, and the sun fought to peek around the clouds. As they rode away from their camp, a beam of sunlight appeared between the clouds, casting gold, pink, and blue hues toward the ground.

There's God.

Caitlyn inhaled deeply with her eyes closed. When she opened them, a sense of calm finally returned for the first time in days. As though to make a point, the sunlight shone on the moving dots on the horizon. Caitlyn squinted and realized the distance between her party and the gallowglasses had lessened. They were approaching her attackers' camp rather than following riders. As the space between them grew smaller, she watched in frustration as the men they pursued mounted and raced ahead of them. They no longer had an advantage, and the distance once more grew.

Alex surveyed the surrounding area as they broke camp. Henry rushed into the camp and ordered everyone to mount, whether or not they had covered their campfire rings. Alex and the men mounted with haste as Henry warned that their pursuers grew closer. He wondered aloud who still followed them. The distance and gloom kept Alex from recognizing any standards, but he suspected from the size, at least three, if not four, clans rallied to retrieve him. It had given him hope when despair threatened. After Henry's explanation, he'd felt less panicked. His thoughts turned from trying to escape and likely dying to remaining alive once he was in Sully's clutches. He planned to bide what time he had with his enemy, knowing someone sought his freedom.

As the hours passed, Alex sensed his rescuers made steady progress, despite the pace Henry set. The road divided a densely packed forest. Remaining alert to any new threat, Alex was certain he noticed movement in the woods far too large to be a wolf. Keeping his head forward, his eyes darted to his right. Whoever rode past was too far into the close-standing trunks for him to make out more than a shadow. As a single rider, despite weaving among the trees, the person moved faster than the gallowglasses and him. He was certain it was a scout sent ahead to inform Sully that he had few remaining options. Alex hoped the secret rider delivered his message before any of the men Alex rode with spied him.

When Buccleuch came into view, the only thing that relaxed was Alex's left arm. After days of pain-jarring riding and the continuous damp air, it ached more than the few times he'd used it to ram opponents in fights. All he wanted was a scalding hot bath and Caitlyn's ministrations, but he expected to find his accommodations in the dungeon. Villagers lurked in their doorways, terrified of the mercenary horde riding along their lanes. It was clear they were unused to such men, so it reassured Alex that hiring gallowglasses wasn't already a customary practice for the Scotts. These people had never seen the likes of these hired killers.

"Alexander Armstrong." Sully Scott awaited them in the bailey with a woman and David standing beside him. "Not only do I have an Armstrong miscreant spy in our midst, I have the laird's very own heir. You violated the king's orders and stepped foot on my land."

"You never were a bright one. Did you finally kill your father? Because last I checked, this was still his land and his keep. I suppose your messengers failed to relay the correct message. King Robert was extremely specific that if *you* caused more trouble, your clan's land is forfeit. I believe Angus and my father are on their way to claim the deeds."

"Your spy said something similar. Your father and Angus don't ride alone. Kennedys accompany them. I hear one is finer than the rest. It's been ages since I've seen Caitlyn."

Alex fought not to dart his glance to David, angered that his trusted guard shared that Caitlyn was approaching. He was even angrier that no one tucked her safely at Dunure, or at the very least kept her at the Hermitage if she went there.

"Didn't know that, huh?" Sully crowed. "Fear not. It wasn't your trusted messenger. He wasn't the first to arrive with news. I pay well to remain informed."

Alex shifted his gaze enough to focus on the woman who stood beside Sully. Kenzie MacCabe was born in the Hebrides and raised there until she married Sully and moved to the mainland. The Scotts intended the marriage to gain them more access to the seas and trade. They'd underestimated the distance to ship goods from the border to the western isles. They'd also overestimated the Hebrideans' willingness to partner with mainlanders. It was no secret that Sully was enamored with his wife, despite the useless alliance. As Alex watched them, he was certain Kenzie didn't return his sentiments. But their marriage had finally been useful for more than siring a passel of children. Her connections afforded Sully the opportunity to hire the gallowglasses.

Alex watched as Kenzie scanned the men amassed in the bailey. "He's not coming, my lady." His voice held a note of regret when he recognized her fear as she searched for her brother and couldn't find him. When she heard Alex's words, she wrapped her arm around her swollen belly and stared at Alex. "His occupation got the better of him."

"Is that a vague way of saying you killed my brother-by-marriage?" Sully demanded.

"It's a vague way of saying I defended myself better than he attacked," Alex countered. Sully snorted until David cleared his throat. Henry approached and bowed to Kenzie, barely sparing Sully a glance.

"Your brother was a fine leader but an impetuous mon." Henry said no more as Kenzie nodded. She assessed Alex, taking in the scar on his face, his lame arm, and the empty scabbard at his back. He expected her to weep or launch into an angry tirade, but she merely nodded again.

"We each have a path. Some get to choose, and he did." Kenzie turned her head to stare at Sully, and it was the first sign of anger Alex witnessed. If she grieved her brother's loss, it was clear she blamed Sully and not Alex.

"Sully, you forgot to mention that your clan travels with mine and our allies. Your father accompanies them." David locked gazes with Alex as he spoke. "I imagine he is eager to return home but may be delayed."

That's not what I expected. Where was the auld coot and how did he wind up with at least Innes and Angus? Whoever rode for Mangerton—Mitcham, most likely—must have nearly ridden his mount into the ground. That doesn't explain how Da could already be here.

"It sounds like a trade." Alex's voice boomed through the bailey, ensuring everyone heard that Laird Scott was a hostage, and Sully's choices decided his father's and his clan's fate. Sully's expression took Alex aback as whispers buzzed around them. He seemed unconcerned for his father's well-being and freedom. It made Alex wonder if Sully held no qualms about letting his father die despite his clan knowing he was the one with the choice. Alex's memory flashed to the happier dreams he'd had, where he and Caitlyn had children and led their clan. He'd imagined tension with the Scotts remaining, but he'd never pictured Sully overthrowing his father.

Alex watched as Kenzie slipped away from her husband's side. Sully didn't notice, but he was certain Henry had. Something about their dynamic struck Alex as odd. Henry had given him no impression that he wanted to be involved with another woman after losing his wife. He supposed the mercenary sought release where he wished, but Kenzie wasn't the type to dally with.

Henry muttered, "Cousin."

The MacSweens and MacCabes have been thick as thieves for generations. I should have guessed. Though Henry could have told me I killed his own kin.

Alex thought he'd understood Henry, but the man remained an enigma. Rather than focus on Henry, Alex kept his attention on Sully, wondering when the power-hungry tánaiste planned to throw him in the dungeon. Sully assessed him, a wicked gleam in his eyes. When his eyes shifted to his left, Alex followed his gaze. They'd set up stocks near the well in the center of the bailey. Alex barely kept from flinching. Having his left arm trapped in the restraint for hours would create an agony that made him wish he already burned in the fires of hell.

"Pay up, Scott. You contracted my men and me to fight a battle for you. We leave before your neighbors arrive." Henry placed his hands on his hips and tapped his foot against the bottom step, his impatience feigned, but his demand clear.

"I shall have to get the coin for you." When Sully made no move, Henry ascended three steps.

"I will monitor your captive while you fetch my money." Henry's offer held no gallantry. It was a command.

"It will take me a day or two."

"Unacceptable. You expected us sooner, so you should have the money waiting. This makes me believe you never intended to pay. Did you demand

272

MacCabe take this job because you've gained naught by marrying his sister?"

Sully remained silent. It made it clear Henry surmised the situation accurately. Men behind them grumbled, threats traveling to Alex's ears. While Henry had seemed almost magnanimous to Alex, he grew openly hostile as he continued up the steps. Scott guardsmen rushed forward, but Henry held his hands up by his shoulders. This unassuming posture fooled no one. A killer for hire would be quick to draw a weapon, likely from some place no one guessed.

"You are an incredibly lucky mon to marry my cousin. Not only has she always been too good for you, but it's kinship that keeps you breathing. My men and I expect to be paid the amount *I* demand. If you do not, we will take what we believe is fair. If that includes several lives, we will still sleep fine. If you do not pay, then I have no reason to hand over a prisoner. I will watch him walk free through your gates. It wouldn't surprise me if the Armstrongs didn't hire us next. I already know my way around your keep."

"You would leave your cousin a widow?" Sully mocked.

Henry shrugged one shoulder. "I doubt she'd miss you much."

"My wife adores me," Sully snapped before realizing how peevish he sounded. "I'll get you your money. I need a few hours."

"To convince your clan council to pay for this unsanctioned attack?" Alex chimed in. "Whatever will they say when you bleed your coffers dry from paying mercenaries and paying recompense to not one, but now three clans? You involved the Kennedys when these men pursued my wife and me."

"Take him to the stocks," Sully ordered, ignoring

273

Alex's comments. Alex didn't fight the men dragging him away. He gritted his teeth against the pain when they yanked his arm to rest in the hollowed space. But he laughed when the Scotts tried to shame and humiliate him. He shook his head as though he pitied their foolishness. He planned to bide his time if he had to. Then he plotted to kill Sully Scott for even speaking Caitlyn's name, let alone endangering her.

TWENTY-THREE

Caitlyn paced as another night of waiting to reunite with Alex descended on her with a crushing weight. David hadn't returned, so now the Scotts locked two Armstrong men within Buccleuch. Abraham sent one of his men to inform Sully that he wished for his son to release Alex so the laird could enter his home, but no one returned. Caitlyn remained within the camp circle but walked the edge as she tried to keep her racing thoughts from overwhelming her.

"Lady Caitlyn."

Caitlyn spun around, her skirts swishing at her ankles when a woman called out to her. Caitlyn peered through the trees but spied no one until a murky shadow materialized and stepped into the light. Caitlyn drew back at the sight of the pregnant woman who ducked back behind a trunk. Caitlyn scanned the men in camp and found her father talking to Brice and Tavin. She went nowhere where she couldn't see them because she knew they couldn't see her.

"Who are you?"

"Lady Kenzie Scott."

Caitlyn's face shuttered as she struggled to remain calm as a fresh wave of anger roiled through her. She trusted the woman not at all if she was a Scott. "Why are you here?"

"Because ma husband will kill yers and blame it all on him."

"Why do you care? Wouldn't it help your husband to have mine dead?"

"Most likely, but Sully will get us all killed. I have ma bairn and weans to think aboot. We willna survive three clans attacking or a besiegement. Alex needs to leave, and Laird Scott needs to return."

"I already know this, so why make the risky trek here to tell me? I assume you came alone."

Kenzie shook her head, and David emerged from the shadows. "I led us out of a tunnel, and yer guard led me here."

"Lady Caitlyn, I'm certain we came alone. I watched Lady Kenzie with her children. She wouldn't risk her life or her weans if she weren't certain she had to." David eased away from the tree and made to return to camp.

"Wait!" Kenzie hissed. "I willna help ye if anyone learns I'm here. I'll lead ye back and help ye get yer husband out. Anyone larger than ye will be questionable. Nay one will pay attention to a woman."

"Why should I let you have the Armstrong's heir and the Kennedy laird's daughter?"

"Because ye are as desperate to free yer husband as I am to keep ma children safe."

"You ask me to trust you a great deal when it's clear we have the forces to overrun you. My father and father-by-marriage do not make war on women. They will spare you and your weans."

"It's Sully I dinna trust. I fear he will use me or one of the weans to force yer clans to retreat. I willna put it past him to kill me. He may love me in his own

276

perverted way, but he loves becoming laird far more."

"I'm not leaving without telling my father, and he'll never agree. I won't do that to him, just run off."

"I understand. Bring one or two guards, but they can only come to the wall. I canna let them in. It defeats the purpose."

Caitlyn considered what Kenzie offered. It was ridiculous to trust her, but she couldn't ignore the chance to rescue Alex without bloodshed. She considered who else could go with her. She wanted it to be Brice, but she couldn't ask Tavin to have both his sons captured.

"What will Laird Scott think when I don't bed down soon?" Caitlyn wondered what role the laird played in Kenzie's fears. When the pregnant woman stepped further into the shadows, Caitlyn had her answer. She feared her father-by-marriage. It made Caitlyn appreciate Kenzie's risk taking more. "Let me speak to my father. It may take a moment to convince him. Would you speak to him?"

Kenzie stared past Caitlyn's shoulders for a long moment before she nodded. Caitlyn cast her a long stare before turning away and picking her way through camp until she reached her father's side. Tavin and Brice greeted her but turned away to check on the Armstrongs assigned to their portion of the watch.

"Papa, I need you to come with me, but I can't explain until I'm certain no one can hear." Caitlyn spoke in rapid French, knowing none of the guardsmen understood, but Tavin, Brice, Angus, and Robert could. All four men were educated and spoke multiple languages, as Innes did even before meeting Collette. They stepped away from the fires and into the shadows. Innes drew his sword but held the tip

277

toward the ground. "Papa, Kenzie Scott is waiting in the trees with David. She snuck him out and can sneak me in to get Alex. She's terrified that, even if you and the other leaders won't harm her and her children, Sully will. She knows the clan won't easily survive an attack or a besiegement. She fears Sully will pray on your unwillingness to let a woman suffer, then he will blame you if you don't relent and will kill Kenzie or their weans."

"Sick bastard."

"Aye. And from what I can tell, she fears the laird too. It's clear she doesn't trust him. She believes Sully will let his father die because this makes it more convenient for him to become laird. She said David and one other guard can come with me to the walls. There's a tunnel she can lead me through. She believes I'll be less noticeable than any warrior."

"She is right aboot that. I don't like it, Caity. I don't trust her."

"I wouldn't either if she weren't pregnant."

"She's carrying a bairn and slipped this far from the keep, helping us when she fears a mon in this very camp?" Innes peered toward the trees, straining to find anyone in the dark. "She's brave or stupid, but she and her bairn are likely to wind up dead."

"She knows, but she took the risk to save her other children."

"I'm coming then."

"What aboot the others? They'll notice if you and I disappear."

"Go to Kenzie. I must tell Tavin and Brice. If anyone else asks, they'll say you had need of more privacy for a womanly matter. No one will question that." Innes grinned. With a wife and two daughters, inevitably he faced "womanly matters," and he knew it made other men uncomfortable. No one would gainsay him, Tavin, or Brice.

"What aboot Angus and Robert?"

"Tavin will tell them if they must. Go on now. I'll follow in a moment."

"Straight ahead, then aboot ten paces to the left." Caitlyn squeezed her father's forearm before slipping back into the darkness. Innes rushed to explain the development to his new family-by-marriage. Brice demanded to go, but Innes pointed out what Caitlyn already realized: Tavin couldn't risk losing both his sons inside Buccleuch. With his sword near his waist, Innes crept to the trees and found Caitlyn standing with Kenzie and David.

"The tunnel comes out close to the keep's southern wall, which abuts the loch. I can get Lady Caitlyn in through there, and ye can hide near the wall. The shadows make it difficult to see, even from the battlements. We rely on the loch being our primary defense for that side." Kenzie drew back her cape and held up her chatelaine's keyring. There was one key on a separate loop. "He's in the stocks nae the dungeon."

Caitlyn's heart sank when she imagined the pain Alex must be enduring. At least in a dungeon, they might not have chained him within a cell. She nodded as Kenzie continued to explain that despite its central location, the storage buildings and bailey wall cast it in a shadow. She intended to take food to Alex, arguing that they might still exchange him for Abraham, so he needed to be in decent condition. She planned to unlock the stocks but leave the bailey before Alex escaped. He was to wait at least ten minutes, so people were less likely to blame Kenzie. Caitlyn's part was to help Alex from the stocks if he needed it before leading him to the tunnel. Kenzie would already be there to guide them back out.

"There is something ye must ken before I take ye. Something that I canna change and is indirectly ma fault, by nay choice of ma own." Innes and David froze, but Caitlyn nodded encouragement. "I didna want to marry Sully, but our fathers decided for us. I was a MacCabe before I married into the Scotts." Kenzie glanced at David, who already guessed what she would reveal once she said her former clan's name. She looked at Innes and lowered her chin, ashamed. "Ma brother died at Alex's hand because he led the gallowglass men who attacked. Ma cousin leads them now, and he is the one who brought Alex to us."

Caitlyn shot David a warning glare as he opened his mouth. She feared he might add that the man also held a sword to her throat. It wasn't the time to enrage her father. She shook her head once, and David closed his mouth. With no more to confess, Kenzie led them through the trees, across a strip of tall meadow grass to what appeared like a berm. On the far side was a bush she pushed aside to reveal a door. She pointed to where Innes and David could approach without being seen. Then she disappeared into the tunnel, forcing Caitlyn to follow her. When the door closed behind them, pitch black shrouded the women. Kenzie reached back and took Caitlyn's hand, leading her into the dark abyss.

Caitlyn knew her way through the tunnels at Stirling Castle, but Laurel was the one to teach her the routes, and Caitlyn trusted Laurel. As Kenzie guided her, Caitlyn prayed she hadn't misplaced her faith in this stranger. The tunnel seemed to go on for miles, but it was only minutes before Kenzie stopped, and Caitlyn bumped into her.

"Ye must remain silent. The tunnel opens near the kitchens," Kenzie whispered in the pitch black. Caitlyn couldn't even see six inches in front of her to where Kenzie stood. The pregnant woman eased open the door a crack, placing one eye to the sliver of light. She tugged the door closed with a soft snap. "Sully."

Caitlyn's heart accelerated, already racing to the point of pain. She waited for the irate warrior to yank the door open and drag both women out by the hair. When nothing happened, but Sully's muted voice drifted to them, Kenzie pressed against the door again. The crack was only wide enough for sound to filter in. Opening the door another inch and looking through the narrow space, Kenzie watched her husband taunt Alex. She shifted as Caitlyn ducked beneath her to squat and watch too.

"I should have killed you the first time. I shouldn't have trusted any of my men to do the job. That arm should have laid beside your dead body. It should have fallen and left you to bleed to death." Sully sneered as he spat onto Alex's limp hand.

"And yet I survived. It must be so galling that you keep trying to kill me, yet I persist in living. How does it feel to fail so often? I wouldn't know."

"You fucking piece of shite." Sully raised his foot to kick Alex in the groin, but he had enough freedom to turn his hip toward Sully instead. He swept his leg out, connecting with the outside of Sully's ankle. Off balance from standing on one leg, Sully dropped to the ground. Alex said nothing but raised his eyebrows, mocking Sully. "Mayhap I shall finish the job now."

"And mayhap my father and our allies will raze every village on your land, then burn your keep to the ground. I think your mother and wife could find work at our alehouse. They're certainly trained how to spread their legs, from the size of your family." Alex's eyes crinkled at the corners as he chuckled. "Mayhap Kenzie will become my leman. Even with only one good arm, we both know my cock is bigger."

Caitlyn and Kenzie gasped in unison. Caitlyn patted Kenzie's foot. "You know he would never do either of those things."

"I ken."

Caitlyn wasn't certain whether Kenzie believed her, since Alex sounded convincing even to her. She covered her mouth to stifle her moan when Sully's fist plowed into Alex's eye. From the force, Alex's opposite cheek hit the wooden frame. Caitlyn feared his eye swelling shut within minutes. She prayed he could see well enough to make his escape with her.

"You can hit me, but you have denied none of it. Your land burned, your keep gone, and your woman under me. You've said naught to prove me wrong." Alex continued to antagonize Sully. When the latter attempted to throw another punch, Alex jerked to the side. He slammed the side of his head against the small circular opening around his neck, but it angled him perfectly to sink his teeth into Sully's wrist. He clamped closed until he tasted blood, which he spat on Sully's face. His laughter echoed in the bailey.

"The only woman getting fucked soon will be little Caitlyn Kennedy. They made her kind to be plowed. She was bred from a whore to be a whore. Tell me: how rough does she like it?" Sully took control of the goading, but Alex's dark mien was his only response until Sully erred and leaned forward to whisper in Alex's ear. Getting too close, Sully was unprepared for Alex to grab his hair and yank him forward. His face collided with the wood.

"Speak of my wife like that again, and I will push a stick up your arse and fuck you until *you* know what it is to be a whore." For good measure, Alex pulled Sully back and slammed him into the frame once more. Dazed and bleeding, Sully stumbled away from Alex.

Alone once more, Alex sagged against the stocks.

His arm throbbed and ached with shooting pains radiating to his fingers. It had been pure fury that gave him strength. Whether or not his life was forfeit, Sully endangered Caitlyn, and for that the man was destined to receive whatever vengeance Alex could reap.

Caitlyn wanted to rush forward and free Alex the moment Sully entered the keep. She wanted to pull his head against her chest and cradle him in her arms, protecting him from the rest of the world. While his undeniable strength still mesmerized her, she'd trembled, waiting for Sully to drive his dirk or his sword into Alex.

"He can't kill him." Kenzie widened the gap between the door and the frame. "I think he's realizing the danger he's placing us all in. He might ransom Alex or hold him prisoner, but your mon will live."

For now. Caitlyn nodded, but internally disagreed with Kenzie's assessment. She wouldn't put it past Sully to be in the keep gathering more weapons to stick into various parts of Alex. Her husband played a dangerous game, and it did not convince her he would win.

"Stay here. I will go inside and make my way around until I can re-enter the bailey." Kenzie didn't wait for Caitlyn's response. She pushed the door wide enough for her swollen belly to pass through before it shut, leaving Caitlyn in the dark once more. She closed her eyes, pulling forth childhood memories. She recalled the day she met Alex, when he arrived with his father. She remembered how he'd stood bravely three days later when the Armstrongs rode out. It had been Caitlyn who found Alex tucked away in a storage building, crying from homesickness and fear. She'd given him what was left of a half-gnawed apple and invited him to go swimming with Cairren and her.

Caitlyn recalled the time the trio attempted to hide from an irate Collette, who bellowed at them in a mixture of French and English as she searched for them. They were running through the kitchens playing chase when Alex's elbow pushed a bowl too close to the edge, and Caitlyn's shoulder knocked it to the floor. The crockery shattered, and half of the night's pottage landed on the floor. Following her younger sister, Cairren slid through the scalding mess, grabbing the table. Her momentum pulled the table with her, upending it. That sent loaves of bread into the air. The children braved the dungeon, thinking it was the last place Collette would search, but it was the first place she went. She threatened to lock them away, forget where she placed the key, and let them starve, since no one else would eat that night. None of her threats were true, but eight-year-old Alex and Cairren and six-year-old Caitlyn were certain Collette meant every word.

Alone in the tunnel, waiting on tenterhooks, Caitlyn continued to reminisce about events throughout the years Alex lived and trained with the Kennedys. She didn't really remember a time before she and Alex were friends. He was as much a part of her life as she was her own. He'd said something similar during his last visit to Dunure before Caitlyn left for court.

"I don't know a life without you, Caity. You're as much a part of me as the air I breathe and the bones that carry me."

A noise beside the door had Caitlyn holding her breath. When she realized someone was about to open the portal, she slipped along the wall. She prayed the floral fragrance from the soap she used that morning didn't give her away.

"I swear I heard something down here when I passed by on the wall," a Scott guard insisted.

"Who's going to be down here? It's likely the

breeze moved the handle," another man's voice countered.

"But we can't tell. I should get a torch."

"What you should get is your arse back to your post."

Caitlyn assumed the huff and grumble came from the first man. She waited for the sound of the door closing, but it didn't come.

"Who are you? I ken you're a woman because I can smell you." The second man's voice was far too close for Caitlyn's comfort. She pulled the dirk from her waist and the one in her pocket, positioning them in her hands as Alex taught her. She'd thought him ridiculous when he insisted she and Cairren learn how to wield them in the dark. She'd argued that she would never roam passageways alone, and she would never wander far from a campsite fire. Now she wondered if Alex had the gift of second sight.

Caitlyn held her breath and held her ground. She'd thought her heart was beating rapidly earlier, but now it rang in her ears and pulsed in her throat. She felt her jaw clench, but she couldn't ease the tightness. Her palms threatened to let the dirk handles slide from them. She couldn't afford to get herself lost in the tunnel, nor could she let this person chase her back out the other end. She heard metal scrape against the stone wall before a spark lit against the wall. In the flash that it illuminated the dark corridor, she had a moment to comprehend the warrior's sword was moving toward her with force.

The guard's cackle echoed in the passageway, but it was a grunt of pain a moment later. Caitlyn ducked and came up under the man's arm, driving one dirk into his belly, and the other into his armpit. The sword clattered to the ground as Caitlyn yanked the blade free from his armpit. She twisted and shoved the other, trying to lever it upward. Terrified that she hadn't done enough when a hand wrapped around her throat, she thrust her free dirk wildly. Blood spurted across her arm from the artery that erupted. The man crumbled to the ground with a gurgle.

Tentatively, Caitlyn reached down to find the man's chest. When she felt no movement, she did her best to wipe her blades clean against the dead warrior's tunic. She grimaced but used her foot to inch him toward the wall and out of the way. She rushed back to the door and prayed no one came in search of the now-dead guard.

Alex watched Kenzie slip from the keep through a door he assumed led to the kitchens. She carried a covered dish she held above her protruding belly. She walked with surety as she approached Alex. He narrowed his eyes and surveyed the surrounding area. He spotted only the men standing watch on the battlements, and they faced away.

"I've brought ye food." Kenzie's gaze darted around in case anyone watched before she uncovered the dish to show Alex a dirk beneath a thin layer of apricots and chicken. Keeping her voice low and barely moving her lips, she explained. "I canna get yer sword, but Henry will. He's likely to kill Sully before any of ye do. Ma husband has nay coin to pay him. Henry willna fight for ye, but he will return what's yers since he owes nay loyalty to Sully."

She held food up to Alex, but he shook his head, not trusting the woman despite her outward kindness. He swept his gaze over the bailey and up to the walls, but no one paid them attention. But Alex was aware that didn't mean no one watched.

"I'm going to unlock ye and return to the keep.

Ye must wait at least ten minutes before ye try to move. I need people to notice me in the keep. Caitlyn will come help ye lift off the bar and guide ye to the tunnel. I'll be there to guide ye back out. Innes and David are waiting for ye both."

"Caitlyn's here?" Alex strained to peer past the ends of the wood restraints. His head only had so much space to move, but he craned his neck. "Why are you helping me? And why bring Caitlyn in here if you're supposedly freeing me?"

"I dinna trust ma husband nae to harm me or our children to force yer clan and allies to leave ye to him. I will do aught to protect ma children. I dinna wish to risk this bairn's life, but I have three other weans who depend on me. Caitlyn is less likely to be noticed. People will think she's soft-hearted when it seems like she brings ye water. Once she lifts the bar, ye canna dally. Ye must run for the tunnel. I'm going to step closer to make it look like I'm handing ye food. I'm going to slide this dirk into yer belt." Kenzie moved slowly, both to reassure Alex that she didn't plan to stab him and to keep her movements from drawing attention. Once she secured the knife and opened the lock, she backed away then spun on her heels. She wasted no time returning to the keep.

Alex closed his eyes, his heart pounding with fear for Caitlyn. He couldn't believe Innes accompanied her and allowed her inside the walls. He had no trouble believing Caitlyn did something so daring and reckless, but he'd believed Innes had more sense. He would never have agreed to trade Caitlyn's safety for his life. He let his head hang as his heartbeat rang in his ears.

"Do you care for some water?"

Alex jerked upward and slammed the top of his head into the stocks, unprepared for Caitlyn's lilting voice or the water ladle pressed to his cracked lips.

He hadn't had nearly enough to drink over the past few days.

"Caitlyn, once we are away from here, you and I shall have a long talk."

"If you say so." Caitlyn glanced around, but they still seemed to be of no interest to anyone. "I'm going to lift this from you. Can you get out?"

"Aye. Free my right side first, I can hold up the bar if you can move my other arm." Alex bore the weight of the heavy hinged piece of wood once his hand was free. He pulled his head back, and Caitlyn lifted down his arm. Without thinking, she wrapped her hand around his left-hand fingers and turned toward the wall and the hidden opening. Alex winced from the pain that shot through his numb limb. Pins and needles made it feel like it was on fire. He ducked his head and entered the secret passageway behind Caitlyn. As the door shut, they heard a voice call out that Alex escaped. "Now what?"

"Ye remain silent and follow me." Kenzie materialized from farther in the tunnel.

"Be careful," Caitlyn whispered to Alex. "There's a body near here. I had to."

Kenzie reached out a hand to Caitlyn, who grasped Alex's right hand. The trio trudged through the narrow, low tunnel. Alex banged his head several times, seeing stars in the darkness, but he continued to follow Caitlyn. He wished to draw the dirk Kenzie gave him, but it meant letting go of Caitlyn. He feared getting separated, and he didn't want to break the contact that assured him his wife was alive and well. Kenzie came to an abrupt stop, catching Caitlyn between her and Alex, who was unprepared. "Let me check if we are alone, and I will signal Laird Kennedy and his mon."

Kenzie eased the silent door open, looking in all directions, including overhead to the hillock's overhang. Satisfied no one lay in wait, she slipped out and gestured to Innes and David, who dashed toward her. As they arrived, Caitlyn and Alex emerged from the tunnel.

"Go and do nae look back. Do nae come back." Kenzie waited for no one to respond, pulling the tunnel door shut.

Alex glanced at Caitlyn, who watched him. The party of four took off into the meadow grass, but the movement alerted the guards, who raised the alarm. They heard the postern gate burst open. Alex checked back over his shoulder, dismayed to find at least a half-dozen men pursuing them. When he glanced at Caitlyn, she had her skirts gathered to her knees, but even with them unobstructed, her legs could never outpace the Scott warriors. He twisted and wrapped his arm around her waist, hauling her over his shoulder. He hissed, "Faster."

Alex pushed himself to run as fast as he could, desperate to get Caitlyn away from the encroaching danger. Even with her weight bearing down on him, he moved past Innes and David, who ran with swords drawn. As Alex passed them, the two warriors closed ranks behind Alex and Caitlyn, protecting Alex's back and Caitlyn's head. As they approached the camp, Innes released an ear-piercing whistle. They burst into the area as men from four clans rose and drew swords, scrambling to prepare for attack.

When Alex spotted Tavin and Brice, he hurtled toward his father and brother. Innes was right behind him. Without a word, he lowered Caitlyn to the ground, and the men surrounded her. Her tiny stature compared to the mountainous men made her invisible. Alex drew the dirk from his waist while Innes, Brice, and Tavin stood with their swords raised. Alex raised his arm, ready to launch the knife when a voice approached.

"You need this." Henry and a handful of the gallowglasses emerged from the trees. No one had heard them hiding there. He returned Alex's sword before he and his men melted back into the shadows. Alex lost sight of him immediately and prayed his trust wasn't misplaced when he believed Henry wouldn't attack from the rear.

"What is going on?" Abraham demanded from the tree trunk to which Brice had bound him. "Who was that?"

"Your son's acquaintance." Alex glared at Abraham, even though he doubted the man could make out his expression. "He hired gallowglasses to capture me, but he wanted the satisfaction of killing me himself. Mayhap he should have, had he paid instead of expecting their services for free."

"Gallowglasses," Abraham spluttered. "That bitch."

Caitlyn tried to press between Alex and Brice, but the brothers were immoveable. She wanted to hurl insults at him, but Alex was faster.

"Blaming a woman for your son's pathetic behavior? You trusted your wean to run your keep and now you have four clans at your door." Alex snorted. "And I find you tied to a blummin' tree! You're hiding behind her skirts!"

"It's her fault," the laird insisted.

"Nay. Your son hired her brother, who got himself killed at the end of my sword."

"You?" Abraham guffawed, but he screeched when Alex launched his dirk toward him and embedded it in the trunk beside the trembling laird's head.

"That is how your men wound up injured in Stirling." Alex thrust his sword forward, bringing the tip beneath the laird's nose for a moment before step-

290

ping back into the protective circle around Caitlyn. "And that is how the gallowglass died."

The sound of men crashing through branches and running feet stomping toward them interrupted Alex's taunts. The camp kept their cook fires few and barely smoldering, so Sully and his arriving men came barreling toward them only to knock into one another as those at the front realized the size of the force they faced. There were nearly two hundred men amassed in the trees.

"Can you imagine how I would react if my sons made the foolhardy choice to endanger our entire clan?" Tavin stepped forward, and Alex, Brice, and Innes closed the circle around Caitlyn. "But then again, they could never be so foolish as to antagonize a clan that's allied with nearly everyone along the border. They wouldn't capture the heir to a clan that's already beaten your shiting-yourself-arses every time they crossed swords. And my sons most definitely do not defy the king when his son is their bluidy neighbor."

"Sullivan Scott, you have but one choice to make: die for your crimes here or face my father for them." Robert Bruce stepped forward. "My father placed me at the Hermitage to oversee Liddesdale and the border. You encroached on my land when you met the Armstrongs and Elliots at a spot I know they did not choose. You defied the royal decree to desist. Now you will face the consequences." Robert turned toward Abraham. "And so shall you."

"Me? I'll banish him for what he's done, but it wasn't my fault."

Stunned faces turned from Sully and Robert to Abraham, shocked that he cast off his son rather than take responsibility. Alex shook his head and rolled his eyes. "You raised the mon, and he's your tánaiste. Banish him if you want, but that won't remove the blame from your shoulders. Had you not picked a fight you couldn't win, your son wouldn't think he had a reasonable chance in hell of making my clan back down. This is as much your fault as his."

Sully reached behind him as Caitlyn strained to see. He grabbed hold of something and yanked. Caitlyn screamed when she spied his hand fisted in Kenzie's hair as he dragged her forward. The very thing she feared was coming true. The woman had sacrificed her life to free Alex. "She freed you. Now you will watch her die for her treachery."

Caitlyn acted without thought and later realized how foolish she'd been, but she squeezed beneath Brice and her father's bent arms and sprinted across the camp to where Laird Scott sat. Angling herself to reach the much larger man, but keeping her body protected by the tree, she pressed her blade to his throat and drew blood.

"You hired a mon to capture my husband," Caitlyn's voice filled the night air, her only accompaniment the odd crackle from a fire. "That mon underestimated Alex and died for it. You underestimate Alex repeatedly. Do not make the mistake of underestimating me. I will kill your father before your eyes." Caitlyn pressed firmer against the laird's throat, not at all certain she could go through with it. "Release your wife to my father, and I won't be the one to end his life. Underestimate me and don't comply, and you will be laird long enough to shite yourself, because you are not leaving here alive."

"Bloodthirsty little whore. No wonder you favor your little brown bitch." Sully sneered at Alex as he thrust Kenzie forward, using her as a shield, as he tried to back away from the Kennedy and Armstrong warriors who took umbrage with his insults to Caitlyn. He didn't notice Brice slip Alex a knife.

292

"I warn you now, say another vulgar thing aboot my wife, and I will face King Robert with your head dangling from my hand." Alex's calm voice contrasted with the tenuous situation, making many shiver. The Armstrongs and Elliots recognized the Alex who dragged Brice from the battlefield with one arm barely attached. The Kennedys old enough to remember Alex as a lad recognized they were witnessing the determined man that boy grew into after proving himself over and over against the experienced warriors. "Release your wife as Lady Caitlyn said."

"She's my wife."

"And my cousin." Henry emerged from the woods a second time. "She bore you only daughters. She will return to the Hebrides since you are already a dead mon. I will not take Alex's right to kill you, but I will cause you great pain first. Let go of Kenzie and let her walk to my side."

"Worthless cu—" Sully howled with pain as a dagger embedded in his thigh and vibrated. Without thinking, he released Kenzie to pull the knife from his leg. She bolted toward Innes, who pushed her into the circle he, Brice, and Alex still formed. Henry stepped forward and reached out his hand to Kenzie. When she took it, the men moved aside. Like the wraiths they'd both been, Henry and Kenzie disappeared silently.

"Caity." Alex nodded to Caitlyn, who lowered her knife but didn't move.

"Aren't your kind supposed to be more obedient?" Sully sneered. "Or is that only when you're on your back?"

"Her kind?" Innes's low growl shifted attention to him. "Like the gallowglass, I won't take Alex's right to kill you, but speak another word aboot my lass, and I will rip each fingernail off before I cut off each

293

finger. Then I will pry your teeth from your gums with my dirk. Once you have no teeth in the way, I will cut out your tongue and wipe my arse with it, then stick it back in your mouth to swallow. Only then will my son kill you."

"Kennedy—" Abraham started.

"That gallowglass wasn't the only mercenary in your midst. Mayhap your wean never heard the story of how I met my wife, but you have. The auld Laird Mackay and I were as close as brothers when we sold our sword arm to whoever paid in France. Things that should stay in my past will come to haunt you if you even shift your eyes in my daughter's direction again."

Innes spared a glance at Abraham when he began, but he directed all his attention to Sully as he issued his final warning. Alex and Caitlyn exchanged a look when they heard Innes claim Alex as his son with no qualifier attached. Everyone heard the indelible bond that formed between the Kennedys and the Armstrongs. Tavin stepped before Abraham but held out his empty hand to Caitlyn.

"Everyone else is having such fun describing how they wish to torture your son. But I haven't forgotten aboot you. You stole from my clan and caused a battle that nearly took both my sons."

"Aye and left one worthless." Abraham screamed as a blade pierced the muscle below his shoulder. He tried to reach back, but his tethered arms didn't allow it. Caitlyn pulled the blade out and wiped it on the man's doublet.

"You insult my daughter," Tavin continued as though Caitlyn hadn't stabbed a man. "You hold no value in family, but mine is everything to me. No one threatens my children, by blood or by marriage. I grow tired of this standoff." Tavin lifted his gaze to Caitlyn. "I do not harbor any reservation that you wouldn't kill to protect Alex. But no mon here wants that on your conscience."

Caitlyn had told no one about the guard in the tunnel, and she intended to save that part of the story until a much better time. She knew the men in her life would have an apoplexy. Tavin pressed the tip of his sword to Abraham's chest. The two lairds locked gazes as Alex called Caitlyn away. She didn't hesitate this time. She stepped into his embrace, then moved into the circle. Tavin pressed until the tip punctured his nemesis's chest.

"Give me a fair reason to let you live." Tavin waited, but Abraham said nothing to him, instead directing his comment to Sully.

"Too bad she never bore you a son. Now our family line ends."

"Do you admit before all who are here that you provoked the Armstrongs?" Robert Bruce spoke after keeping silent for several minutes. "Do you take responsibility for your son and your men's actions against Alexander Armstrong?"

"He's still worthless whether I'm dead or alive." Abraham sneered at Alex, but his expression froze as he turned his gaze down to the sword protruding from deep within his chest. His eyes rose to Tavin's as the latter moved aside and pulled his blade free, causing a geyser of blood to erupt. Laird Scott was dead before his next breath.

TWENTY-FOUR

The camp grew still as everyone looked first at Laird Scott's slumped body, then at Tavin, who wiped his sword's blade across the dead man's shoulder. Tavin turned to his sons, nodding at Alex before darting his gaze to Brice. No one knew what to do next, but slowly all eyes shifted to Robert Bruce. Not only was he the king's son, he was also the Baron of Liddesdale, which made it unequivocal that he could be Tavin's judge and juror in his father's stead. Robert stepped to stand beside Tavin, placing himself between the laird and his nemesis's son.

"Laird Armstrong, you have had your justice for your son's abduction and confinement. The auld laird is dead and so too this feud will be." Robert turned toward Sully. "You shall have no say because you will accompany me to Stirling, where I will report your nefarious deeds to the king. I am certain he will lend an ear as I recount what I've seen. You'll do well to pack lightly."

Sully's face had blanched when his father died before him, but now it grew mottled as anger bled from every pore. He lunged toward Alex, moving behind Robert's back. It was Robert's blade that slipped horizontally beneath Sully's chin, the blade